Praise f

"... an impressive debut and a promising start to a smart new mystery series." — Kirkus Reviews

"If you've ever wondered what Stephanie Plum would be like with a little experience in life under her belt, Nanci Rathbun has the answer. ... Her heroine is flawed and complex, her plot perfectly constructed to bring out all of the facets she's created. For mystery lovers, or fans of romantic suspense, Nanci Rathbun is one to watch." — Shelf Awareness, October 8, 2013

Praise for *CASH KILLS*

PI Angelina Bonaparte "reminded me at times of Parker's Spenser in her detecting, her sense of humor, and her flamboyant sartorial style. ... *Cash Kills* is a first-rate mystery that combines police procedural with private detection and it features a compelling lead character and a marvelous cast. It's entertaining, fast-paced and suspenseful, and is highly recommended." — Reviewed By Jack Magnus for *Readers' Favorite*

"To find justice in the midst of lies and cover-ups, Angie must face her own fear of trusting another. Readers will relate to her humor, vulnerability and dedication to the truth." - IBPA Benjamin Franklin Silver Honoree for digital ebook excellence — September 2014

Praise for *HONOR KILLS*

"I found *Honor Kills* an extremely satisfying read. It ticks all the boxes of a good detective mystery, and the lead character Angie is extremely easy to empathize with. It's not often you come across a middle-aged PI hero, who is also female. The plot was intricate and full of twists and turns as befits such a mystery story. Having read *Honor Kills*, I am motivated to read the other books in Rathbun's series, which is probably as high a praise as a reviewer can give an author. – 5* Review by Grant Leishman for *Readers' Favorite*

"Nanci Rathbun takes the time to explore why her characters doggedly pursue their objectives; and this too makes *Honor Kills* a superior read in a genre that too often focuses on the 'whodunnit' over the 'why pursue this inquiry' question. The result is another spirited Angelina Bonaparte mystery that requires no special familiarity with predecessors in the series in order to prove satisfying to newcomers and prior fans alike." – Reviewed by Diane Donovan for *Midwest Book Review*, April 2018

Honor Kills

Angelina Bonaparte Mysteries #3

Nanci Rathbun

Published by Dark Chocolate Press LLC
http://darkchocolatepress.com

FIRST EDITION
ISBN: 978-1-9867634-3-1 (Print)
ISBN: 978-0-9987557-5-5 (Digital E-book)
Library of Congress Control Number: 2018901555
Rathbun, Nancianne.
Honor Kills / Nanci Rathbun
FICTION: Mystery/Suspense

Cover design by Nathaniel Dasco
http://BookCoverMall.com

Formatting by Polgarus Studio
http://www.polgarusstudio.com

Author photo by Michele Rene Chillook, Dubuque, Iowa

Published by Dark Chocolate Press LLC
http://darkchocolatepress.com

Dedication

This book is dedicated to my sister Barb, who has stood by me my whole life and who is the best beta reader ever. Thanks for reading my books, over and over, as I revise and publish. You make me look much better than I would without you.

Acknowledgements

I wish to thank my critique partners at the NoCo Writers Group in Loveland, Colorado, for their encouragement, support and eagle eyes as the manuscript progressed. Any remaining mistakes are mine.

Chapter 1

Which death is preferable to every other? The unexpected.

— Julius Caesar

I parked on the street and sat for a few moments in the dark of a cold Milwaukee January night. How do you tell a woman whose husband abandoned her and their children fifty-eight months earlier that you found his obituary online? Would Marcy Wagner be relieved? I didn't think so.

When she hired me to locate him, after the Greenfield Police Department found no evidence of foul play and closed the missing persons case, I did all that any private investigator would do to find him—interviews at the middle school where he taught and with the neighbors and the police investigators, as well as repetitive online searches for credit reports, DMV and court records, and even fishing and hunting license applications. No one had anything but praise for Hank Wagner. They described him as solid, reliable, good with the kids, and particularly strong in helping those with math deficits. He was a late and only child whose parents were deceased, with no other blood relatives, so that avenue was a dead end.

Last year, I considered luring Trekkie Hank into the open with an ad for the rare Mego Star Trek Phaser Battle Game. I consulted Larry

Phillips, owner of AAAA Auctioneers, for guidance on how to market the item, although I didn't actually possess one, but I didn't follow through with it. The logistical nightmares, and the possibility of being sued by a fanatic Trekkie, made me rethink that strategy. But at our initial meeting, Larry mentioned that he needed help at the store, which was, frankly, a disorganized mess. His wife, who was also his assistant, had walked out on him. Marcy needed work, so it seemed a natural fit. She'd been there ever since.

Although Marcy told me Hank was a good husband and loving father and his colleagues described him as reliable and well-liked by both staff and students, I considered him a weasel. How else can a man who cleaned out the family's bank accounts and left his wife with few resources to raise their three young children be viewed? But after monthly contact with Marcy—I ran searches for Hank every month and usually only charged her for one out of three—I had a fairly good reading on her. The news would hit her hard.

The cold seeped into the car. I gathered my briefcase and purse and stepped out. Greenfield was a lower- to middle-class suburb of under forty thousand on the southwest edges of Milwaukee, heavily populated by people who wanted to escape the urban school system. The bungalow-style house fit the neighborhood.

Marcy came to the door, looking cheerful. "Come in, Angie." She took my coat and we settled on a plump-cushioned sofa in the small living room. Kids' toys and books were scattered around. An older CRT-style TV sat on a small corner table. "Excuse the mess," Marcy said. "Henry had a science project to finish for school tomorrow and it was getting late, so I didn't make him pick up. And Marjorie, well, she's good at getting out of stuff. She was only a year old when Hank left. I suppose I'm too easy on her. As for poor Susie, she gets the typical middle child leftovers. I try to give her individual attention, but time gets away from me." She pushed overly-long bangs back from her forehead. "Before you tell me why you're here, would you like some decaf?" She gestured to a carafe and cups on the coffee table.

When the pouring was done, I set my cup down and removed Hank's death certificate and obituary from my briefcase. "I'm afraid I wasn't entirely honest with you earlier. I didn't want to tell you this over the phone." I took her hand in mine. "My new intern, Bobbie Russell, ran the usual searches for Hank today. I'm sorry, Marcy. Hank died a couple of weeks ago, on December 29th, in a Stevens Point nursing home."

The color leached from her face and, as she started to tremble, I took her cup and placed it on the table. She stared at me and whispered, "He's dead? Hank is dead? How?"

I handed her the death certificate.

Original Certificate of Death, Henry James Wagner, Male, Pronounced Dead December 29, 2016 3:15 AM, Age 42, DOA-From Nur. Hm., Hospital or Nursing Home-Padua Manor, Marital Status-Never Married
Manner of Death-Natural, Immediate Cause-Liver Failure, Cirrhosis
Funeral Service Licensee-Figgs Funeral Home

"Liver failure," I said.

Marcy's eyes went wide. "Hank didn't drink or smoke. He was only forty-two. How would he get cirrhosis? And why didn't he call me? I would have helped him, even after what he did. He didn't have to die alone." She began to cry, softly at first, then louder and harder. I put my arms around her and held her until she quieted and then handed her a tissue from my purse.

With a gulp, she sat back, wiped her eyes and blew her nose. Then she took a slow sip from her coffee cup. It had to be lukewarm by now, but it seemed to steady her. "I always thought he'd come back, Angie. That, one day, he'd get in touch and come home and tell me why he left. That he'd ask to be part of the family again. That I'd let him." Her eyes held so much sadness, so much want. "He was a good husband, a good father, a good man. I never understood how he could walk out the way he did, in the middle of the day, before his classes were even over. That wasn't Hank, that wasn't the kind of man he was." She took a ragged breath. "Now I'll never know. Unless … was there a letter?"

"I don't know." I took a deep breath and pointed to the marital status on the paper she held. "The death certificate lists him as 'Never Married.' I'll call the nursing home and funeral director tomorrow morning."

At that, she straightened and her head snapped up. "Never married?" She gazed back to the death certificate. When she spoke, her words were low and mournful. "So he abandoned us even in death. He didn't want us, even then."

I didn't have a response to that. "Can I call someone to come and stay with you?"

"My mom hates Hank for what he did. She'll do the 'good riddance' routine. I don't want to hear that right now. You can't live with a man, love a man, for twelve years and not feel grief when he dies." She paused and then said, "I'll call my older sister. She'll come over." Marcy stopped twisting the tissue. "And what do I tell the kids? We should probably have a funeral, for their sakes. Where is his … body?"

"I'll find out." Even though she knew how to contact me, I gave her a card. People get scattered during a time of shock. I assured her that I would be available any time she needed to talk and headed back to my car.

My high-rise condo was empty when I arrived home. Wukowski and I don't live together, but we gave each other keys in November, right after we finally got around to saying the L-word to each other. Although we didn't see each other every night, tonight I missed having him greet me with a kiss.

After my marriage of twenty-five years ended, I dated sporadically, but never settled into a stable relationship until I met homicide detective Wenceslas Tadeusz Wukowski. Ven-chess-louse Ta-doosh. Polish names are quite common in Milwaukee, but not the Christmas carol king! Small wonder he goes by Ted. We started out as adversaries on a prior case. By the time we admitted our attraction for each other, I'd gotten used to calling him by his last name. When I told him I didn't sleep with men unless I knew their real names, he 'fessed up. His mom, the MPD's HR people and I might be the only ones who knew the truth.

In his capacity as a Milwaukee homicide detective, Wukowski deals with violent death on a regular basis and has an almost irrational fear about women in danger. His sister was attacked and killed while in her teens—hence his mother's dread of strangers—and his partner, Liz White, was savagely murdered during a drug investigation some years ago. He and I reached a tenuous balance concerning my PI work. I don't take cases that might involve violence—none of them had, before I met Wukowski—and he respects my right to act according to my principles. Since my work generally centers on employee background checks, spouses wanting to know if their partners are unfaithful, and locating missing people when the police have given up, it isn't much of a problem.

As I headed for the bedroom to shuck my work clothes, I got a text from him: *Don't expect me tonight.* I texted him back: *Be careful out there.* It was a standard line we both said to each other. I hadn't seen much of him since Thanksgiving Day, when Wukowski was called away to investigate a body on the lakefront bike path. Since then, two other bodies were found in areas used by joggers and bikers. The *Journal Sentinel* christened it the Bike Path Murders. I promised him that I'd use the treadmill in the condo gym until the killer was found.

I brewed a cup of herbal tea and settled on the sofa, watching the lights twinkle on Lake Drive, seeing the occasional steady beam from the breakwater's edge. My ex was a cheater. Wukowski's wife left him because she couldn't handle the stress of his job and his mother's agoraphobic reliance on him. Marcy's husband simply disappeared. My intern Bobbie recently confessed that he was worried about his partner's fidelity. Examples of good marriages—even good relationships—were few and far between, in my experience. As for Wukowski and me, it was early days. Was this a strong and steady kind of love, or one that twinkled in and out of existence like the lights along the lake shore? Time would tell. I headed for my bed and a chapter or two of the latest Louise Penny mystery.

Chapter 2

No one can be happy who has been thrust outside the pale of truth. And there are two ways that one can be removed from this realm: by lying, or by being lied to. — Seneca

The next morning, after exercising, I enjoyed the benefits of my multiple-head steam shower, followed by routine moisturizing—creams for my face, body, décolletage, hands and feet—before wrapping myself in a soft terry robe and padding into the walk-in closet. With no scheduled face-to-face client meetings, I decided on a casual business look: an angora boat-neck sweater in teal, with tobacco brown wool slacks and a deep brown leather blazer. Underneath, however, was another story. I'm a bit of a lingerie fanatic, which Wukowski loves. I chose a soft-cup ivory demi bra with dark blue lace and matching thong, hoping that my guy would be with me tonight to discover the sexy present underneath the somewhat staid wrappings.

As I dressed, gelled my hair and did my makeup, my mind wandered to the Wagner case. What compelled a family man and dependable teacher to simply bolt? Marcy needed answers. Someday, her kids would, too. I wasn't ready to close the file yet.

My east side office on Prospect is in an older building close to my condo. The sign on the door reads AB Investigations, with Neh

Accountants underneath. AB stands for Angelina Bonaparte. Neh Accountants is a one-woman firm run by my friend, Susan Neh. We met when we both worked for Jake Waterman, she as a forensic accountant and me as an apprentice investigator. When we each decided to go out on our own, it made sense to share office space and reduce expenses. Expenses weren't an issue now, with both of us well-established. Still, with my intern, Bobbie Russell, joining the business, I might have to search for new quarters. It's pretty cramped in our one-office, one-conference room space.

Juggling briefcase, purse and Starbucks coffee, I unlocked the office door and disarmed the security system. After divesting myself of coat, hat and gloves, I fussed at the mirror a bit with my hair. I stand five foot three, so the wall mirror on the back of the coat closet door was set fairly low. A white-haired woman, fit and stylish, looked back at me. I ran my fingers through my hair to work out the hat-flattened areas and settled at my desk. My first call was to the funeral home listed in Hank Wagner's obituary.

"Figgs Funeral Home. Julie Ann speaking."

The voice was perky, with a girlish lilt, definitely not the sonorous tones I expected to hear. "Good morning. I'm calling about Henry James Wagner. The obituary listed Figgs. I was shocked to learn of his death. I wonder if you could give me some further information."

"If you'll wait one moment … ah, um … I'm afraid I can't provide information over the phone on that matter. Mr. William Figgs handled those arrangements. Can I have him return your call?"

Why the obvious reluctance to talk about Hank Wagner? I left my number and turned to a pending report for a local insurance company, who hired me to determine if their employee's claim of job-related carpal tunnel syndrome was valid. The woman apparently filed for some type of disability every year in December and returned to her family home in Door County to recuperate. This year, there would be no payout for Ms. I'll-be-home-for-Christmas. It took three weeks, since I wanted to enjoy my own holidays with my family and Wukowski, but I nailed her. I had video of four hours of non-stop needles clacking on Christmas Eve day as she and three other women settled in for a marathon "finish your gifts" knitting session at a little yarn shop in Fish Creek. If she could manage that, she could manage data entry for her employer.

I printed the report, proofread it, ran the invoice program that Susan developed for me, and stuffed the papers and a flash drive containing the video into the envelope. Cases like these were the bread-and-butter of my solo practice.

Bobbie strolled in around nine. He had a loose-limbed walk that exuded self-confidence and sexuality and, combined with his twenty-something Rock Hudson good looks, he turned heads wherever he went. Too bad for us women that he batted for the other team.

In the two months since I took him on at AB Investigations, he proved his determination and ability many times over. Bobbie and I were friends before he joined the firm. I worried that, if he didn't work out, it would impact our relationship. But he took a lot of the routine work off my shoulders, and brought in new clients from his partner Steve's fashion world and from his own contacts in the gay community. I was glad I could depend on him, although supervising an intern had its share of headaches. Bobbie was a dynamo with a real love for the work. He sometimes needed to be reined in.

"Morning, Angie," he said, as he hung up his outerwear. "How'd it go with Marcy?"

"Tough one. She still loves the jerk."

"Ange," he protested, "that's harsh. Not to mention speaking ill of the dead."

He had me there. Yes, I have issues, but who in my position wouldn't? Mr. Bozo, my ex (no, I don't call him that in front of our grown children or their kids), cheated on me twice, before I wised up and tossed him out. My business, as much as I loved it, exposed me to unfaithful spouses, lying employees, and grown children trying to rob their own parents, among other assorted assaults on decency. It wasn't a recipe to promote trust.

"I suppose you're right," I said, "but it really gripes me that he walked out on Marcy and the kids, and took all their funds, to boot."

Bobbie settled in the guest chair at the side of my desk. "So what's on the agenda today?"

"I called the funeral home to get some details about Hank Wagner's remains." The office phone rang. "Excuse me, Bobbie. This might be them. AB Investigations," I said into the phone. "Angelina Bonaparte speaking." Boe-nah-par-tay. Being Sicilian-American, I give it the true pronunciation, not the Gallicized version that the Little Corsican used to gain acceptance into French society.

A deep male voice said, "Ms. Bonaparte? This is William Figgs of Figgs Funeral Home and Crematory. Julie Ann told me that you called concerning Mr. Henry Wagner. May I ask how you are related to the deceased?"

I put the call on speaker for Bobbie and handed him a steno book and pen. "I'm a private investigator. Mrs. Wagner hired me to find her husband after he disappeared. That was almost six years ago. I didn't expect to find him dead."

At that, he gave a little huff. "No, indeed."

"Mrs. Wagner is very distraught. They lost contact when Hank left

Milwaukee. I thought if she knew about his last days, it might console her. And their children."

"Oh, my, I'm so sorry to hear that he left a family. The facility where he died, Padua Manor, didn't inform us of that." He paused. "They often call us when the deceased has no relatives or means of burial. Figgs has a long tradition of compassionate care for those who are unable to pay." That sounded like a PR line. "I hope his wife won't be upset with the arrangements. It was done with the best intentions. I assure you, this was entirely Mr. Wagner's fault for not informing the facility about his family."

Their reluctance to provide information earlier made sense now. It was a CYA strategy.

Mr. Figgs continued. "But then, nothing about this death has been normal."

Bobbie and I shared a glance. "How so?" I asked.

He took a deep breath. "Perhaps you should call his attorney. Frank Jamieson handled some of the post-funeral arrangements, including the obituary. After the cremation." His voice held tones of exasperation. "Frank told me that his client gave him detailed instructions about the timing of the events."

"Can you give me a phone number for the attorney's office? I'm sure Mrs. Wagner will want to contact him."

"Certainly." He read it off.

I asked where Hank's cremains were located, in case his wife wanted them interred in a family plot.

"I'm sorry to be unable to give her that solace," he said. "When we donate our services for indigents, we don't include private burial. Or an obituary." Again, he sounded exasperated. "There is a lovely chapel at Eternal Rest cemetery here in Stevens Point, and it includes a communal columbarium. Mr. Wagner's cremains are there. I hope she'll understand."

"I'm sure she'll be happy to know of your kindness," I said. "May I call you if there are any other concerns?" He gave me his private number.

After disconnecting, I brought up the death notice on my computer and read it once more. "This is very strange, Bobbie. Hank Wagner's been in hiding for years, and I mean deep. My initial search for him was as thorough as I could make it. He's the only locate I ever failed to find. And then he arranges for an obituary? Papers don't run them for free."

"Ange, you're making too much of this. Maybe there was insurance money and Hank set it up so Marcy would have something for the kids. Not everyone is a scammer, girlfriend."

Even taking that into consideration, the announcement of Hank's death was unnatural. "If he wanted to convey information or money to Marcy," I said, "this was a strange way to do it. What are the odds she'd find out from an obit in a Stevens Point paper? Why wouldn't he leave a letter to be delivered to her upon his demise? The attorney would see to that. 'Something is rotten in the state of Denmark.'"

"Is that one of your librarian quotes?"

I had a master's in library science, but realized after the divorce that the part of the job I loved was research. It served me in good stead as a PI. "*Hamlet*," I told him.

Bobbie waved it off and his eyes sparkled. "Let's detect," he said, with glee in his voice.

"I need to let Marcy know about this and get her to sign a release of information form for the lawyer." *Would it be hurtful or helpful for her to hear this?* I called her and explained about the obit. "I spoke with the funeral home director. They don't usually run an obituary for an indigent person. They told me that Hank arranged for it before his death, by leaving funds with a local attorney."

"Do you think that was his way of letting me know? So I wouldn't keep wondering and waiting?"

"Could be," I said. "It makes a strange kind of sense. I'll call the lawyer next, but he may insist on a personal statement from you, authorizing me to act on your behalf. If I email it to you, can you print and sign it, then scan it and email it back to me?"

"Sure," she said. "I'm at Quad-A. I needed to let Larry know that I would have to take time off." Her voice cracked. "I told the kids this morning. That was really hard. Please, Angie, find out what happened."

"I'll do everything I can," I told her.

Then Larry's twangy voice came on the line. "Don't sweat the expenses, Angie. I'm good for them."

After some shuffling and mumbling, I heard Marcy say, "I insist. It'll be an advance against my wages."

Once I got the signed form, I called Attorney Jamieson. His secretary told me he was in court for the morning, but she would see he got the message when he returned to the office. I explained that I would fax them a form authorizing him to speak with me on behalf of a client, and we hung up.

While Bobbie ran some pending background checks, I tended to paperwork. Getting invoices out in a timely manner and keeping good records are essential for a small business to succeed. Not to mention, Susan gives me a break on her accounting services, because I provide her with detailed and accurate data for income and expenses. She shudders at clients who come in with shoeboxes stuffed with receipts, but the extra billable hours needed to straighten out the mess mean she smiles all the way to the bank.

About eleven, the office phone rang. "This is Attorney Frank Jamieson. I understand you represent Mrs. Henry Wagner, Ms. Bonaparte."

Kudos to his secretary for giving him the correct pronunciation, and to him for using it. "That's right. Mr. Wagner abandoned his wife and children almost six years ago. I've been trying to locate him since then. My assistant came across the obituary yesterday. Naturally, Mrs. Wagner is distraught and wants to understand the circumstances of her husband's life since he walked out on the family. Did he leave a letter or message for her, Mr. Jamieson?"

"Call me Frank. No, I'm afraid not. I didn't even realize he was married. This is quite disturbing."

"What were the circumstances of your business transactions with him?"

"Very odd, Ms. Bonaparte. Very odd."

My skin began to prickle. "How so?"

"Would it be a huge imposition for you to drive up here? I prefer to talk in person."

"It's possible, but I hate to bill my client for work that could be accomplished on the phone. Give me some idea of why the drive is necessary."

"I do some pro bono work from time to time for folks at the local shelter who get into legal hassles. In November, I went to court on behalf of a woman named Doris, who was charged with vagrancy. Basically, it was harassment. She wasn't causing any trouble, nor was she a public nuisance, but some good citizen didn't like the look of her on the street in front of their store. Apparently, she talked me up at the shelter.

"After that, Mr. Wagner tracked me down at my favorite coffee shop and asked for legal help. He gave me his real name, but told me he went by Jim Beltran. When I asked why, he just shrugged and told me it wasn't illegal to use a pseudonym as long as there was no intent to defraud. So he knew a little about the law. Then he said he was dying and wanted to specifically arrange for an obituary after his funeral, not before. He was quite adamant about that. He told me he had advanced liver failure and didn't know if he'd make it to New Year's." Jamieson paused. "I thought it odd, because he looked healthy. His skin color and eyes were fine and his belly wasn't distended."

"You appear to be familiar with the symptoms," I said.

"Yeah, my dad was an unrepentant alcoholic." He sighed. "Anyway, Wagner refused to come into the office—he had the obituary wording written on lined notepaper—so I drafted a contract by hand and took a small payment then and there. He said the nursing home would call me when he died, but they'd use the Beltran ID. I ran the obit when Padua Manor notified me of his death. It's been bothering me ever since. Something doesn't add up, Ms. Bonaparte, but I'm not an investigator and I don't have time to dig any deeper. Maybe you do."

"Call me Angie. And to tell you the truth, this case has been vexing me, too, since the day Marcy came into my office and hired me to find her husband, fifty-eight months ago. Nobody simply disappears off the grid and then reappears in an obit." I glanced at my watch. "It's a two and a half hour drive from Milwaukee to Stevens Point. Can we meet this afternoon?"

"How about I buy you supper? Say, five-thirty? There's a great burger joint not far from the UWSP campus—Marvin's. Garlic cheeseburgers and Frank's fries. It's a cholesterol crash, but worth it."

"Sounds good."

He gave me directions and we hung up.

Since I would be making the trip anyway, I called for an

appointment at the nursing home where Hank died.

"Padua Manor. This is Mrs. Rogers." The voice was sweet, almost cloying.

"Good afternoon. My name is Angelina Bonaparte. I represent Mrs. Henry Wagner. Her husband, whom you may know as James Beltran—"

She interrupted me. "You'll need to contact our attorney." The sweetness turned sour as she rattled off the name.

"Mrs. Wagner isn't planning a lawsuit. She just wants to know about her husband's last days."

"That is confidential information, Ms. Bonaparte. Call our lawyer." With a click, the call ended.

Even given the unusual circumstance of a resident with a false name, that was an overreaction! My devious mind mulled over ways to gather information from them.

I walked over to Bobbie's temporary work space in one corner of our conference room. "Bobbie, the nursing home where Hank Wagner died shut me down when I said I wanted an appointment to talk with them. I need to get in there and look around. I'd like you to call and ask to tour the place. I'll be in Stevens Point tonight and tomorrow."

He grinned. "Can I go? I can pose as your husband."

That was mind-boggling! Bobbie was almost thirty years my junior. "Afraid not," I told him. "Marcy has a limited budget. While I appreciate all you do on an intern's stipend, I don't think it's fair to have you pay for a room and meals out of your own pocket."

"Oh, well, I have a kick-ass lesson with Bram tomorrow anyway. I hate to miss that, so it's for the best."

"What kind of lesson?"

"Krav Maga, self-defense with some offensive moves. The Israelis teach it to their military personnel." He shook his head. "Bram is one scary guy, even with a bum knee."

"I'll have to call him. I can use a refresher. He might have some moves that are effective for a smaller woman."

"I can almost guarantee it, Ange."

"Okay. Back to the Wagner case. Mrs. Rogers, who identified herself as the administrator, might recognize my voice when we meet, if she hears it twice today. So tell her you're my brother and that I'm leaving the area tomorrow and want to make arrangements for our dying uncle. Let's see what she says."

"What name should we use?"

"My mother's maiden name was Carson. We'll be Ann and Bill Carson. She can't connect us to that."

He moved to pick up the office phone, but I stopped him. "There's something hinky about this whole setup. I don't want to use a phone that might be traced."

"I have just the thing." He opened a small lockbox that was tucked under the conference table and removed a cellphone. "From Spider Mulcahey. Bram told me to disassemble it and put it back together again, so I'd know how to switch out the SIM card and locate the battery. It's prepaid, a burner phone."

Late last year, Spider and Bram, former Special Ops guys, helped us on the Johnson case. I nodded. "Go ahead. On speaker, please." I pointed to the number in my notes.

"Padua Manor. Mrs. Rogers speaking. How may I help you?" She was back to sweet.

"Mrs. Rogers, I'm in such a bind," Bobbie said. "My uncle Jake is in a bad way. He lives on the family farm, near Stevens Point. My sister Ann is with him now, at the doctor's office. They just recommended hospice care."

"Oh, my, that is very hard to hear, Mr. ...?"

"Carson. Bill Carson."

"Well, Mr. Carson, we'd be happy to assist the family. Would you like to come in for a tour?"

"That's just it." Bobbie's voice rose a bit, as if in suppressed panic. "I'm hundreds of miles away and Ann has to get back to her job in two days. A big client presentation, and she's the agency lead. Can you possibly see her tomorrow, say ..." he looked at me.

"Ten," I mouthed.

"Ten o'clock?" he asked her.

"I think so. Let me check." We heard papers rustle and the sound of quiet moaning as a door opened and closed. "Yes, that would be fine, Mr. Carson. Will your uncle be with her?"

I shook my head.

"I'm not sure he's up to it, Mrs. Rogers," Bobbie said. "My sister has his power of attorney, though, both legal and medical. We hope to finalize things and get Uncle Jake situated quickly."

"That's probably for the best. Your uncle's most likely not in a state to make good decisions. We can help you with that. Tell your sister I look forward to meeting her." The call ended.

"Did you notice how she offered to help the family, to make things easier for us, but asked nothing about Uncle Jake?" I asked Bobbie.

"Yeah. Makes you wonder who the primary focus is on, doesn't it?"

"It does, indeed."

I gave Bobbie my itinerary for the next day and headed for home, after dropping the office mail at the local post office. My condo was a treat to myself after my divorce, along with my black cherry Miata convertible. I caught some sideways looks when I sold the family house and the Buick Park Avenue, but those weren't the real me. I didn't regret the years I was married—after all, I had two great kids and three wonderful grandchildren—but when the time came to break away, I realized just how much of myself was submerged in the identity of wife and mother. The real me wore sexy underwear, lived in a classy condo and drove a great little roadster, except in the winter.

Wukowski convinced me that the Miata convertible was impractical for winter driving, so I had a short-term lease on an AWD Mazda CX-5. I had to admit that it handled better in snow and slush than my post-divorce car fling.

Once home, I fired up my laptop, using an Ethernet connection. Wireless is notoriously easy to tap into. Anticipating a high-fat supper with Jamieson, I pulled yogurt and fruit from the fridge and prepared a cut of hot tea. After booking a reservation at a little B&B near the campus, I settled at the kitchen peninsula and ran a background check on Attorney Jamieson.

He was the older son of parents from the Stevens Point area, single, with a bachelor's in public administration from American University in D.C. and a J.D from Marquette University in Milwaukee. After law school, he clerked for a well-respected federal court judge in Chicago, then returned to Stevens Point and opened a solo practice. His web page listed family law (legal separation, divorce, custody), wills and probate, and small business law as specialties. That struck me as odd. I would have imagined, with his educational background, that he was set on a career in politics, or perhaps aiming toward a federal or state court appointment.

I also ran searches for James Beltran and Jim Beltran. The surname, I learned, was Spanish in origin. Many of the hits were for Filipino men. None connected to Hank Wagner.

Lastly, I checked into the Padua Manor facility where Hank died. It was small—only thirty-five beds—and locally owned and operated. It had several violations listed on the Wisconsin Department of Health Services website. Since the records were only made public in 2012, it was a pretty good bet there were earlier violations, too.

After my meal, I loaded my few dishes into the dishwasher and went to my bedroom to pack an overnight bag. The clothes I selected this morning were a bit too casual for a meeting with an attorney, even one who offered to buy me supper at a diner. A woman in my profession, and one who is a bit older, needs to dress for the respect she wants. I chose a very dark plum wool jersey dress, with long sleeves and a high boat neckline. Because the material was stretchy and my light bra and panties might show through, I replaced them with a black charmeuse set, whose smooth cup bra and thong panties would be invisible under the dress. A discreet silver necklace and earrings, dark thigh-high stockings and two-inch black heels completed the look. Then I refreshed my makeup and headed north on US 41.

Ordinarily, I would stop at Shreiner's in Fond du Lac for a pecan roll, but that would defeat the restraint I showed at lunch. Instead, I bought coffee at a Starbucks there, used the facilities and drove on.

Stevens Point is situated along the Wisconsin River, almost at the center of the state. It's a small city of nearly twenty-seven thousand, with an additional ten thousand students at UWSP, a campus that is recognized for its natural resources program.

I parked and entered Marvin's, located at the edge of the UW campus. Scanning the tables, I saw a sprinkling of students, persons wearing suits and several families enjoying a meal out. A nondescript man rose from a booth and approached me. I recognized him from the head shot on his website. "Ms. Bonaparte?" he said. "I'm Frank Jamieson." We shook hands and he politely directed me to the booth.

As we walked, I took a few seconds to mentally assess him. Jamieson stood about five-ten and weighed around one-seventy, with brown hair and brown eyes. He wore an off-the-rack navy blue suit, between Hugo Boss and JC Penney quality, with a classic fit that was slightly looser in the chest than was currently stylish. I recalled from my background check that he was thirty-five years old and unmarried. His features were regular and his expression benign. Statistically, he was the epitome of average for American males.

"Thanks for meeting me, Ms. Bonaparte."

"I thought we agreed to be Frank and Angie," I said, careful not to show any sign of flirtatiousness. He struck me as a man who would run from that.

"We did ... Angie. How was your drive?"

"No problems. I listened to an audiobook along the way, Neil Gaiman's *The Ocean at the End of the Lane*, a fascinating story about childhood memories and the many faces we all wear. I didn't even notice the time."

"I confess, I don't read much fiction."

"Let me guess. Political memoirs and legal reviews."

His laugh changed the topography of his face, from mildly pleasant to interesting, with prominent dimples on each side of his mouth and rather wickedly upturned eyebrows. Very attractive, until his expression settled into its usual lines. "You got me pegged, Angie."

"I did a little research on you before I left Milwaukee," I confessed.

"Very wise."

A waitress stopped at the edge of the booth, with order pad in hand. "Trust me?" Frank asked. I nodded, and he said, "Two garlic cheeseburgers with garlic fries." He asked for an iced tea and I followed suit. Then he settled back in the booth. "To the business at hand. It was not a pleasant experience for me to contact Figgs with the information that their indigent client, Jim Beltran, was really Hank Wagner. William Figgs was quite put out when he learned that there was enough money to cover an obituary. And of course, there was the hassle of getting the death certificate changed."

So that explained Figgs' exasperation on the phone. "I ran some preliminary checks on Jim and James Beltran," I told Frank. "There aren't many people with that name in the country—under a hundred. None of them matched Hank Wagner."

His eyes narrowed at that. "Most men who leave their families are quite careless. He seems to have been very thorough in covering his tracks."

"If it weren't for the obituary, I don't think I would have found him. Very aggravating and frustrating, Frank, to search month after month for someone and never get a single hint of where he might be or what he might be doing, and to know that his family is going through financial hardship because of his actions. That's why I kept looking for him, long after my client's funds ran out. I didn't want him to get away with it." I opened my briefcase and handed him a copy of the marriage certificate.

He shook his head while reading it. "I wish I'd done a search myself, when he first came to me. I might have found his family. They could have had a last chance to connect."

And wouldn't that have made Marcy's life easier, I thought. Then I took a mental step back. It wasn't reasonable to expect an attorney to go to that length to confirm a client's marital status.

Jamieson handed me a document on 8 ½ x 17 paper. "A copy of the will for your client," he said.

He sat in silence while I perused the two pages. Outside of the standard legalese, there was one pertinent paragraph of bequests. All Hank's personal belongings in Stevens Point (did he have assets elsewhere?) would go to a local shelter, including an older car, but not the contents of the car. How odd!

I asked Frank for his take on it, but he simply shrugged. Then the waitress put our plates down in front of us. Frank smiled his creased-dimple smile. "You're gonna like this, Angie." We tucked in.

Being Sicilian-American, I have a love affair with basil, oregano, cumin, sage and garlic. Marvin's cheeseburger on a hoagie bun did not disappoint. It was meaty, juicy, and flavored well with garlic salt. The fries were also garlic-laden and delicious. I didn't finish the half-pound burger, but I enjoyed the effort. Frank managed to down all of his. We pushed back our plates, ordered coffee and waited for the busser to clear the table.

When no one was nearby to overhear us, I said, "I plan to dig into Hank Wagner's life here in Stevens Point. His wife wants to know about his last days and, if possible, to understand why he left her and their children. I'd like to talk to some of the other, uh, clients at the shelter. Can you introduce me to Doris?"

"I can, but don't be surprised if she doesn't have much to say. Folks there are suspicious of outsiders."

I sighed. "Well, I can try. Would you take me over there tomorrow? Maybe in the afternoon? I have an appointment at Padua Manor at ten tomorrow morning.

"How about noon at my office? We'll walk from there." He gave an indelicate snort. "As for Padua Manor, don't accept any food or drink while you're there, and wear something that can be sterilized."

"Really?" Several of the violations in my earlier research were for unsanitary food preparation and failure to follow practices to reduce risk of infection. There were also violations for mishandling patient medications. It sounded like an unsavory place. "It's that bad?" I asked.

"It has a rep. The residents are mostly on government assistance, without family to be sure they get decent care. There've been three cases of suspicious death in the last eight years, but not enough evidence to bring charges." He shook his head.

"But they're a licensed hospice?"

"Just in the past few months, from what I understand." He leaned over the table and spoke in a low voice. "It's easier to get pain medication prescribed for someone in hospice care. Makes me wonder if that was a motivation for their deciding to set some beds aside for hospice."

That thought brought me up short. If Dante was right about hell having circles of punishment, I hoped those who preyed on the helpless were in one of the hotter areas.

Chapter 3

A beautiful lady is an accident of nature. A beautiful old lady is a work of art.

— Louis Nizer

The B&B was small and cozy—chintzy, in the literal meaning of the word. I unpacked, took a long hot bath, brushed and flossed and gargled to get the taste of garlic out of my mouth, and settled into bed. My call to Wukowski went to voice mail. I told him I was in the Point trying to locate a deadbeat dad and that I expected to be back in Milwaukee tomorrow. I asked if he would be free that night—meaning, how about some steamin' hot sex?

Absolutely, moja droga! was his reply. Moy-ah drow-ga. Polish for "my dear." It seemed we were on the same page.

I watched a PBS documentary without really paying attention. When I turned out the light, bits and pieces of the Gaiman audiobook, about a young boy whose father was a mythical monster, kept popping into my head. My father was no monster, but he had a life apart from what I knew. He ran a fruit and vegetable business, but he also held sway in the local Mafia, from which he was now "retired." I knew no details of his hidden life, even though I chose to use it at times for protection. Only a fool would threaten Pasquale Bonaparte's daughter! I dreamed of the many-headed Hydra and woke to the smell of coffee, bacon and blueberry muffins. Breakfast was served.

I donned a navy business suit and plain white blouse for the nursing home visit. Downstairs, I enjoyed the muffins and coffee, along with fruit, but skipped the bacon, eggs and waffles. There was still a slight taste of garlic on my tongue. I hoped I didn't smell of it and longed for my steam shower. Garlic is one spice that can be sweated out.

I asked the young couple who ran the B&B to hold my room until one o'clock. I wanted to return after my visit to Padua Manor and change clothes before I went to the shelter. My professional look might put off the residents.

At nine-thirty, I headed for Padua Manor, circled the block to get a feel for the neighborhood and parked in their back lot, which was punctuated by potholes and crackled blacktop. The building was one-story, L-shaped, with a patio in the shelter of the L at the back of the building. Dilapidated plastic chairs sat in a straight row along the short wall. A woman in scrubs stood smoking at the entry.

"Good morning," I said. "I'm here to see Mrs. Rogers."

"Ya hafta go around the front and ring the bell for entry." She made no eye contact.

I carefully walked the uneven concrete path to the front of the building and depressed the bell for admittance.

A stout, motherly woman opened the door. "Ms. Carson?" she asked. I nodded. "Please to come in," she said, moving aside for me.

The entry hall evoked feelings of wretchedness, with its musty smell of urine, disinfectant and oatmeal combined. As Mrs. Rogers escorted me to her office, I walked past vacant-eyed women parked in wheelchairs in the hallway and heard a man's moans from a room with a closed door. Mrs. Rogers ignored the sounds, walked to a door and slapped a card to a reader. With a click, the door unlocked.

Her office was a complete contradiction of the rest of the facility: clean, tidy, with citrus overtones that emanated from an infuser plugged into an outlet. She indicated a chair for me and then sat behind her desk. "I understand that you need placement for your uncle."

I nodded. "Uncle Jake lives near here, on the family farm. My brother and I are his only living relatives." I spoke in clipped tones, intended to convey my need to hurry up and place the old coot. "He's been dealing with liver failure and the drugs aren't working. He can't live alone anymore, even with the day help I hired. It's time for hospice care. Bill saw on your website that you provide that?" I let the question hang there.

"Well, we do in certain cases. Some hospice patients need palliative care, like IVs and feeding tubes. We don't have the skilled nursing staff for that."

"Oh, Uncle won't need more than medication to keep him comfortable." I paused and she waited. "Mrs. Rogers, I am a busy woman. I live in Los Angeles. I need to find appropriate care for my uncle and get back to my job as soon as possible. People rely on me." I hated the way I sounded, like a woman too wrapped up in herself to give a damn about a dying relative.

"Well, now, of course you do, Ms. Carson. And that's why we're here, to help those who need assistance and to relieve their relatives of caretaking." She extracted a manila file folder from her desk and handed it to me. "Here are the papers you'll need to sign. Let me get you a cup of coffee while you read them over."

Her belief that I would make an immediate decision astounded me. Then I reflected on Frank's words, that most of the residents here were without family and reliant on government assistance. For them, it would be a matter of taking any offer on the table.

"Before I do that, I'll need to take a tour of the facility." I rose to my five-five stature (in heels).

Mrs. Rogers swiveled toward me. "Well, my, of course you will. What was I thinking?"

The next twenty minutes were agonizing as I toured the dining room, a two-person bedroom, the physical therapy room and the chapel—a closet with a Bible and standing cross on a table. Permeating the whole place was an atmosphere of life without hope, of being parked in a hallway in a wheelchair, waiting. "Because I could not stop for death, he kindly stopped for me," wrote Emily Dickinson. The residents here were waiting for Death's carriage to stop and invite them for a ride.

All but one. At a table in the common room, a woman sat working a jigsaw puzzle. Her white hair was coifed and tinged slightly blue, and her dress, though out-of-style, was clean and pressed. She held herself with dignity and looked me in the eye as we passed. When Mrs. Rogers moved down the hallway, she shook her head at me and mouthed, "No." Then she pressed her forefinger to her lips.

I acknowledged her message with a nod and continued after my guide, noting the bathroom on my right. As we entered the office again, I said, "May I please use your restroom?" I gave a sheepish smile. "Too much morning coffee."

"Of course," Mrs. Rogers replied. "It's to your left as you go back down the hall."

I went into the unisex lavatory, wrote my cellphone number on my business card, counted to ten, and peeked out. Mrs. Rogers' door was just closing. She'd watched to see where I went.

I tiptoed down the hall to the common room and approached the lady with the blue hair. "Here's my card. Would you call me? Please? I need your help."

"I will, dear. Now hurry back, so Mrs. Mean doesn't see you." She shooed me away with one hand as she tucked my card into the bodice of her dress.

I returned to the office, picked up the papers and extended my hand to Mrs. Mean … uh, Rogers. "Thank you for your time. I'll look these over and get back to you later today. I have one other place to visit this afternoon."

For a second, Mrs. Rogers' eyes slitted and the corners of her mouth turned down. Then she resumed a placid smile. "I'm sure your uncle would be very happy here. And our charges are the most reasonable of any in the area. Don't wait to decide. We fill up fast. And we currently have only one bed open."

I assured her that I would not be dilatory and escaped into the morning sunshine, taking in great gulps of cold fresh air and congratulating myself on being years—decades—and a loving family away from that world.

I had an hour before I needed to meet Frank Jamieson. Back at the B&B, I changed into casual clothes for the shelter visit. I wanted to look approachable to the residents there. Black dress jeans, a plain sweater in deep green and black half-boots with a two-inch cowboy heel.

My host, Devon, offered me tea in the parlor. I retrieved my book from my briefcase—I never go anywhere without reading material—and settled down while he brewed Earl Grey. As he approached with a lovely china cup and saucer, my cellphone played Billy Joel's "The Stranger."

"Hello," I said.

"This is Augusta Simmons, from Padua Manor. The lady you gave the card to."

I sat up. "Augusta, thanks so much for calling me. Are you in a place where we can talk without your being overheard?"

"Why, yes, I'm in the park down the street."

I was a little startled by that. I assumed that the Padua Manor residents were not allowed out by themselves. But … what if they weren't? Had she somehow gotten out without permission?

"So you're not restricted to the facility?" I used a gentle tone, hoping not to upset her.

"Many are, but not me, dear. I'm the sane one and I can still walk. Oh, and I have some money, so they let me have my little treats. I told them I wanted to go to the drugstore for some mints."

"Why don't I drive over and meet you?"

"Wait." I heard her take a deep breath. "What's this about?"

I debated telling her the truth, but decided that I'd done enough lying for one day. I used Hank's assumed name, though, because that's how Augusta would know him. "It's about a man named Jim Beltran. He died at Padua Manor on December twenty-ninth. He was estranged from his wife. She wants to know more about his last days, but Mrs. Rogers refused to talk to me about him. I'm afraid I told her an untruth this morning, posing as a woman who wants care for her elderly uncle."

"So this isn't related to payment for Myrna?"

"Myrna?"

"My sister. She's a resident at the home. She has dementia."

"No, this has nothing to do with her or you, personally. I only want to talk to someone who was there when Jim died."

"Well, then, I think I can help you."

It was a five minute drive, but she was a much older woman and the thermometer at the B&B showed thirty-six degrees this morning. I helped her into the car and checked her surreptitiously for signs of hypothermia. Bundled up in a red wool coat, with red knit scarf, hat and mittens, she resembled a cardinal wearing black snow boots. "Red suits you," I said, pulling away from the curb.

"I love a pop of color, don't you?"

"Indeed I do. Would you like to go somewhere for a cup of coffee or tea? Or would you be in trouble for being gone too long?"

"Oh, no, they don't pay any attention to me, as long as I show up for supper. I'll just tell them I ran into a friend and we grabbed a bite to eat."

She suggested a family restaurant on the outskirts of the city. Once we settled into a booth, she leaned toward me and said, "Now, dear, I must forbid you to put anyone in that damnable place."

Her tone was so sweet and her face so unperturbed that my jaw dropped at the mild expletive. It felt as if Tweety Bird's granny swore at me. "Augusta!" I waggled my finger at her.

She smiled. "There's still some pepper in the old girl." Then her face became solemn. "Ms. Bonaparte—"

I interrupted to give her the correct pronunciation and said, "But call me Angie."

"Angie, Padua Manor is a horrible place. It's understaffed and the staff they have don't care. They're lazy and some are even mean. Like Mrs. Rogers."

"She abuses the residents?"

"Not so that you can file a complaint. She skates just this side of the laws and regulations. But she never does anything nice or helpful. It's always about stretching out a dollar with her, at the expense of decent food or regular baths or even such things as changing a diaper. Mean old bat!"

"Why are you living there, then? Surely you have other options."

"*I* do … but my sister, Myrna, doesn't. Her husband died and left her piled high with debts. She's on Medicaid, like most of them, so there are very few options for care. I can't abandon her, so I stay, and I pay sometimes for little treats and better care for her, and I watch out for her to make sure they don't neglect her. She has dementia, but she still knows me. They're happy to take my money and leave me be. I'm their only private pay resident, see, so they gouge me."

She's a saint, I thought, *to live in that place for the sake of her sister.* "Augusta, as I told you, I'm trying to find out what happened in late December to a friend's husband, Jim Beltran. He was in hospice care there. He had liver failure at a fairly young age, only forty-two. Did you know him?"

"Not to say, knew. But I saw him in his room from time to time. He looked pretty bad, all skin and bones, and yellow. I knew he wasn't long for this world."

"Was there anything unusual about his death?"

She pursed her lips in thought. "Nooo. But it was odd, the same night he died, Karl went missing."

"Karl?"

"Karl Jorgensen. A night attendant. Nice man. One of the few who took good care of us, at least as good as he could. He'd get an extra blanket or hold somebody's hand if they were sad or scared. He'd come in and talk with me sometimes." She chuckled. "Said he and I were the only ones in the place that still had our wits about us."

"And he disappeared?"

"Mm-hmm. Odd, isn't it? I knew Mr. Beltran had passed, because the funeral home sent the hearse for him and I saw the gurney in the hallway outside his door. Then their man wheeled it into the room, came out a few minutes later with the body all covered up and the paperwork lying on top, and Karl walked him to the door and waited until the hearse pulled away. When Karl saw me in the hallway, he came over and told me to go back to bed, sort of harsh-like. He never used that tone of voice before, in my hearing." A look of surprised hurt passed over her face. "Then he went back into the dead man's room. Never came out. Just disappeared."

I felt my eyebrows rise high on my forehead in amazement. "He just walked out, in the middle of the night, and left the residents on their own?"

She nodded. "I got back in bed, after he chastised me, and never realized. The morning crew was mighty put out that he abandoned his duties, and that he wasn't there to give his report. Mrs. Rogers was on her high horse about it, too. I heard her berating the poor charge nurse about staff responsibility. But really, what did she have to do with it?"

"How very odd," I said, wondering what the connection was to Jim-Hank, if any. "What did Karl look like?"

"Well, dear, he didn't look like a Karl. You'd expect a blond-haired, blue-eyed Scandinavian, with a name like that. But he had dark hair and a dark complexion, too. Stood maybe five-ten. He was stocky, but it was muscle, not fat. I saw him lift some of the heavy residents with ease, more than once."

"If you saw him on the street, what kind of work would you think he did?"

She thought for a moment. "Bartender. Because, first, he was good at managing multiple tasks; second, he looked like he could handle himself in a fight; and third, he had a way with people, calming them if they were upset, listening if they were sad, helping with things like a checkbook that wouldn't balance." She grimaced. "I never was good at arithmetic."

"Did you ever see him in street clothes?"

"Oh, my, I felt so sorry for him the one time I did that I tried to offer him money. He looked just like a hobo—I guess nowadays you'd say 'homeless person.' But he wouldn't take a penny, said he had nicer things, but there was no sense wearing them to walk to the Manor in the dead of night. He didn't want to get mugged. So I let it go. But I'm not sure I believed him."

"I don't suppose you have a picture of him?"

She shook her head. "No. Sorry, Angie ... but there would be one in the office. The staff all wear picture IDs." She leaned forward. "I could try to get in there for you and find it."

I was horrified. "No!" She jumped back a bit in the booth. I gentled my tone. "No, please don't do that, Augusta. It could be dangerous if you got caught. I may be able to get one through the state licensing bureau. Was he an LPN?"

She gave a genteel snort. "Mrs. Mean would never pay an LPN's salary at night. Karl was just an aide. Not even a CNA. He told me he was working on his certification, though."

Thirty-five souls, most ill or in stages of dementia, under the care of one unskilled person, all night. It was criminal, and I intended to file a complaint when I got back to Milwaukee. Meanwhile, I reassured Augusta that I would be able to get a picture of Karl through legal channels. "Please keep our meeting secret and act like you always do at the facility."

"Snooty and nosy, you mean?" she asked me.

"Who calls you that?"

"Mrs. Rogers." She smiled. "I'm glad she thinks badly of me, as bad as she is herself. Plus, she stays away from me."

"Let's keep it that way," I said. "By the way, how did you call me?"

"My cellphone, dear."

"Do you always have it with you?"

"Oh, yes, ever since an aide stole my last one and used it to run up charges. I never leave my cellphone out of my sight."

"Good. Let's program my number into it. But don't put my real name. Mrs. Rogers knows it. Use ... Terry. That's my aunt's name."

"Terry." She took her phone from her purse and set me up in her contacts list.

I chided myself for thinking that she wasn't competent to do it. Then I assured her that she could call me at any time, day or night. We left the restaurant and I drove her back to the park. I wanted to take her to the front door of Padua Manor, but didn't want anyone to see her in my car. Something was definitely off at the nursing home. I didn't want Augusta caught up in it.

Chapter 4

By doubting we are led to question, by questioning we arrive at the truth.
— Peter Abelard

Jamieson's office was a small storefront near the UWSP campus. When I arrived, he was sitting at the secretary's desk, with the phone to his ear. "Yes, Mr. Carrero, Friday at ten. Be sure to bring the contract with you. *Hasta la vista.*"

He hung up and approached me. "Angie, good to see you." He looked me up and down. "Good choice of clothing. Nice, but not fancy."

I smiled. "That was my intention."

"My secretary, Alice, is at lunch." He made a Vanna White sweep of his arm. "Welcome to the legal offices of Frank Jamieson."

The waiting area was clean, but spare, with wooden chairs lining one wall and a slightly scarred table holding copies of the *Wall Street Journal*, *Stevens Point Journal* and *Stevens Point City-Times*, as well as tattered issues of *Field and Stream*, *Wisconsin Sportsman* and the *Wisconsin Natural Resources* magazine. Apparently, Frank was a news junkie and outdoorsman.

He ushered me into his office, which was decorated with good-quality, but obviously well-used, furniture. Offering me a visitor's chair, he turned away and opened the door to a small closet. There, he hung up his suitcoat and tie, unfastened the top button of his dress shirt, and pulled on a tan shawl-collared sweater with a big wooden button at the joint of the collar. Very Fred Rogers, low key and non-threatening. Turning to me, he said, "It's about a ten-minute walk from here. Okay with you?"

"Of course. Uh ... maybe I should leave my purse here?" I hated feeling that the shelter clients might steal from me, but people who are down on their luck can be forced into choices they wouldn't otherwise make. The old dictum, "Better safe than sorry," sprang into my head and I barely managed to stop myself from speaking it.

Frank nodded to the coat closet. "Probably for the best."

I extracted my cellphone and put it into my coat pocket, and we headed out into a sunny, cold day.

As we walked, Frank gave me some background on A Place To Lay Your Head. "It's from Jesus' statement to the crowd in Matthew 8: 'Foxes have holes, and birds of the air have nests, but the Son of Man has nowhere to lay his head.' A local priest decided to open the church for overnight 'visitors,' he called them. Some of the parishioners complained, and he reminded them of Jesus and asked if they would refuse him a place to sleep. I guess the congregation took it to heart, because within a year, they purchased a rundown house, rehabbed it and opened the shelter. They have a women's side and a men's side, with Mrs. Ramirez, a regular gorgon, guarding the gate at night to be sure there's no crossover. Not so much to discourage sex as to protect the women."

"They don't accept families?" I knew that women with children were one of the fastest growing homeless populations.

"No, they're not set up for that. But they find places for them through other county services. It's not perfect, Angie, but it's a damn good effort."

"Sounds like it," I affirmed. From his low-key but passionate defense, I assumed that Frank was personally vested in the facility.

He continued. "The residents leave after breakfast, supposedly to look for work." He grimaced. "There's not much out there for them. They return for an evening meal, enforced prayer time, and community time before lights out."

"Enforced prayer time?"

"I know, it sounds draconian, but the staff says it helps keep the peace. And they rotate among various faith traditions—Catholic, Protestant and Jewish, but also Muslim, Hindi, New Age, pagan—if the practitioner will come, they're welcome." He laughed. "The folks at St. Mark's were a little taken back when Father Al first proposed it. But he wanted it to be a place where anyone would be welcomed, religious or not. And St. Mark's gets a lot of help and input from other local churches and some non-religious organizations."

Now that was an interesting concept! The Catholic church of my youth would never allow a non-Christian presence at a Catholic facility. "So where does Doris fit in?"

He grinned. "She's a pistol, as my old man would say. She doesn't talk about herself much, but, from her demeanor, I suspect she was raised a country girl."

"That's a long way from homeless," I observed. "Can't go much lower."

"Not so." His voice turned deep. "You can be a fugitive, a criminal, an addict, a pedophile, an abuser …" He let the litany trail off.

It brought me up short. *Am I so comfortable with my personal prosperity that I look down my nose at those who have less?* "I'm sorry, Frank, that was judgmental of me."

"It was," he agreed, but his voice was soft. "Most of us are." He stopped and gestured to a big old building across the street from where we stood. "Here it is," he said. "A Place To Lay Your Head."

The house was two stories high and symmetrical, like a much larger version of my papa's Foursquare in Bay View. The pediment above the oversized front door was supported by columns, and each side of the house boasted eight windows, four on each story. Once, it must have been a fine family home, with room for lots of children and servants. Its bones were still fine, but the obvious signs of wear and tear, even of neglect, were there: chipping paint on the siding, an upstairs window propped slightly open with a thick book, holes in the front door where a prominent knocker once hung. Still, she was a beautiful old lady, if slightly marked by wear. More to the point, she probably could house forty persons in all those rooms.

"Who's there in the daytime?" I asked Frank.

"Staff and cleaners, mostly. The residents are responsible for picking up their rooms, but some of them are paid a stipend to clean the bathrooms and hallways, and prepare the evening meal. And Doris. She's the *de facto* liaison, mother hen and sergeant major." His voice held admiration, amusement and a tinge of exasperation.

We approached the formidable front door and he rang the bell. From inside, we heard, "Hold yer horses." There was the sound of metal rubbing against metal, and light flashed from the peephole.

"Door viewer?" I asked Frank. He gave me a blank look. "You know, a peephole with a little sliding cover." He nodded. "Smart," I said, thinking back to the Johnson case, where my client Adriana was scared by a man using a reverse peephole viewer to look inside apartments in the building where I had secreted her for safety. Although this wasn't a safe house for abused women, I knew that many women in those situations ended up homeless. I was glad to see elementary safety precautions in effect here.

After the clicking of several locks and the screeching of an old-fashioned bolt, the door opened. "Frankie," shouted the woman who stood on the threshold. She rushed forward and enveloped Jamieson in a big bear hug, slapping him repeatedly across the back.

She dwarfed both of us, standing at least six-two and weighing in at around one-ninety. Overweight, but not fat. Her biceps bulged with each pat—pound?—across Frank's back. He turned his head sideways and grinned at me, then gently disengaged himself. Looking up—way up!—he said, "Doris, good to see you. You look well, as always."

"I'm jim-dandy, Frankie. Us farm girls, we never get sick." She stepped back a bit and turned to me. "Who's the lady?" There was a definite coolness to her tone.

"This is a friend and colleague. Angie Bonaparte, meet Doris Appleberg."

I held out my hand. She looked at it for a second, then wiped her own hand on the daisy-print apron she wore over jeans and a thermal pullover, and, with a fierce look on her face, took my hand. I recognized the battle that was to come and forced my hand as far into hers as possible, with the crotches of our thumbs meeting tightly, so that she couldn't get a good enough grip to squeeze hard.

She grinned. "You pass."

"Thank God. I wouldn't want to arm wrestle with you!"

Laughing, she said, "Most don't, after the first time." Looking back at Frank, she asked, "So, you want to come in?"

We followed her through the kitchen, where a young woman chopped onions and an older man tasted liquid from a huge pot. "Janelle, can ya bring us some coffee into the dining room?" Her speech was a curious mixture of meticulous pronunciation—she pronounced the "g" in "dining"—and colloquialisms, like "jim-dandy" and "ya."

The room held eight round tables, each large enough to seat ten. Doris led the way to the one farthest from the kitchen pass-through and we sat, clumped together. Janelle brought a tray with carafe, cups, sugar, creamer, teaspoons and napkins, and walked away without a word. Doris called, "Thanks, hon," to her and poured us each a cup. Taking a slurp, she said, "So, what's up?"

"You remember Jim Beltran, Doris? The guy who went into hospice care in December at Padua Manor?"

"Yeah, I remember him. I was surprised he passed so fast. He didn't look all that sick, to me."

"Well, Angie here is trying to find out about him. Seems he had a wife and kids, but he lost contact with them. They want to know about his life after he left the family."

She didn't say anything immediately, just took another swallow of coffee and stared down into the cup. When she looked back up, it was to face me with guarded features, her mouth thinned into a line. "Why?" The single word lay there in the silence.

I took a sip of coffee, using the moment to organize my response. "He walked away from them, Doris," I said. "Now he's dead. They want to understand why he abandoned them."

"No good trying to understand why someone does something," she told me. Her tone was flat, unemotional. "Ya just gotta move on. It's better that way."

I thought for a moment. I wanted to acknowledge the pain that her words exposed. "Sometimes that's true, but not always. He was a good husband and father, before he skipped out. They can't get over him doing that." I sighed. "It's an overused word, but they want closure.

And his wife wants to get any personal effects that he left, even if they're trivial and worthless. It's not about value, it's about having something that was his."

Her hand went halfway to her chest, then stopped and dropped back to her lap. I guessed that she wore a locket or had something precious tucked into her bra. She exhaled. "Most of us have addictions. Booze, drugs, stuff we battle every day. When Jim told me about the cirrhosis, I was surprised. Far as I know, he didn't go to meetings and he sure didn't have the beat-down look. Don't mean it wasn't a problem, though. Lots of folks put on a good front, until they finally fall apart. Maybe he didn't want to fall apart in front of his family."

"I can see that," I said. "But is it possible to never be over the line if you're really an alcoholic? He was the ideal family man—go to work, come home, have supper, play with the kids. There didn't seem to be time for him to drink."

She looked at me, a long hard look, then she turned to Frank. From the corner of my eye, I saw him give a slight nod. "The thing about Jim," she continued, "he was real quiet. Friendly, but he didn't open up about himself, ever. Like he had a secret he would take to his grave." She snorted. "Come to think of it, I guess he did."

With a glance away, she added. "He had a good heart, though. There's this homeless guy, Willie, that most of us tried to help. He wasn't interested. But Willie and Jim, they got along. I'd see Jim talking to him, out on the sidewalk where Willie would beg. Haven't seen the old wino for quite a while. Goes to show, doesn't it?" She slapped her palms on the table and rose. "Okay. I got a bag put away, stuff he left here when he went to the nursing home."

She led us into a back hallway and then a mud room, where tall metal lockers took up one wall, each with a heavy padlock. I surmised they wouldn't be compromised by an average set of metal snips.

"We store residents' stuff here for a year, if they leave it behind." She extracted a key from the large ring that was secured to her jeans with a chain. "Here's Jim's locker." Inside, there was a large olive drab duffel bag, the kind the Army issues. Doris grabbed the long strap and lifted it onto a work table. She took another, smaller key from her ring and opened the lock on the duffel. "There ya go," she said, stepping back.

Frank motioned for me to proceed, so I unzipped the bag. It was only half full. Doris and Frank watched as I emptied the contents of the duffel bag and examined the clothes—pockets, linings, seams, tags.

Doris interjected, "They've all been washed already."

"Just being thorough." I counted three flannel shirts, one pair of jeans, ten boxer shorts and ten sets of socks. No shoes. I looked at Doris. "Did he take other clothing to the hospice center?"

"Don't think so. He left without anybody seeing him." She grimaced. "I think he didn't want any hoo-haw, ya know?"

I nodded and turned back to the other contents of the bag: a can of shaving cream, a razor and some spare blades, a comb, toothbrush and toothpaste, and a container of deodorant. "Odd that he wouldn't want his toiletries," I said.

"They always give ya those little ones at the hospital or home," she told me with a shrug.

"They do, don't they?" I picked up his razor. "But this is a nice razor, not one of those disposable ones. And the replacement blades aren't cheap, either. Seems odd that he'd leave it here." I set it back on the table. "Doris, Jim's will specified that the shelter should get his belongings, except for the contents of his car. Can the center use them?"

"You betcha we can use the clothes. But not the other stuff. We can't give out used personal items."

I scooped the toiletries back into the duffel bag and zipped it closed. Maybe young Henry would want it someday. Turning back to Doris, I said, "Is it possible for us to look over the area where he slept?"

"Guess so, but I cleaned it out myself. All his stuff was in that bag." I stood silent for a few seconds and she sighed. "Follow me."

She marched back to the front of the house and up the commanding stairway, turning left at the top. Frank whispered to me, "I bow to the mistress of the silent pause." I grinned at him.

The men's wing housed seven bedrooms and a bathroom. Doris stopped outside the door of the farthest room, which faced the back of the house. "Here it is." She motioned us in and stood in the doorway.

Two beds and two lockers occupied the space. I looked around the room and the single closet and didn't see anything out of place. "I guess that's all, then, Doris. Thanks a lot for your help. Marcy will be disappointed, but I'm afraid that's nothing new to her."

"Yeah, well, there's one more thing I should oughta tell ya. Jim had this old beater car, a '79 Honda Civic. It's got over three hundred thousand on it, and it's a rust bucket, but it runs. He signed the title over to me the day he left here. 'Course, I had no clue it was his last day. He just wanted to have his affairs in order, he told me. He said the center could use it to get folks to and from work or shopping. It ain't much, but I wouldn't want ya to think I was hiding nothing. If his wife wants it, it's hers." She looked down at the ground.

What else is she holding back, I wondered. "I'm pretty sure Marcy will have no objections. I'll call her tonight, when she's home from work, and let you know for sure. Would you want to give me your number, or should I get in touch with Frank instead?"

She assessed me for a long count of three and said, "I guess you're okay. Come on back downstairs and I'll give you a card. If you get voice mail, it's not private, so just say it's Angie and let me know where to reach you."

I realized that my business cards were in my bag, back at Frank's office. "I'll do that," I said.

"Could I see the title, please?" Frank asked. "I want to be sure it's a legal transfer, Doris. For your sake."

"Hmph. Guess I know about a title transfer, Mr. Lawyer, but come on down to my office." She turned and clumped back downstairs and led us to a small side room off the dining room.

Frank leaned down and whispered to me, "I want to see what name he used on it."

"Good idea," I said.

Doris' office was a long, narrow room with swinging doors at one end. I suspected it had once been a butler's pantry. The old glass-fronted cupboards for china and glassware now held office supplies. At the end nearest the window, a kneehole desk boasted an older laptop. Doris sat down in front of it and unlocked a drawer intended to hold silver. Inside were stacks of file folders in slanted trays. She fingered through them and extracted a folder labeled 'Beltran.' "Here ya go." She handed the title to Frank.

He looked it over pretty closely. "I'd like to borrow this for a couple of days, Doris, and take it to the DMV to make sure the vehicle transfer is properly complete. That okay with you?"

"Yeah, I guess. Let me make a copy, though, for our records." She scanned the title using a small printer that sat on top of one of the lower cupboards and handed the original back to Frank. "Anything else I can help ya with?"

"Do you think we could look over the car, Doris?" I asked.

She sighed as she took a key from her key ring. "Thorough, ain't ya?"

I laughed. "Some people call me pita." She quirked a brow. "Pain In The Ass," I responded to her unasked question.

That got a deep belly laugh from her. "I got that," she said. "Car's in the back lot. You'll know it right away. It has more rust than metal. I'll be in the kitchen when you're done."

Frank and I went out the back door and down a set of wide wooden stairs to the Honda. It was indeed past its prime. I could see flashes of silver body, but not many. Frank wanted to help me, but I told him, "I'm used to looking for things that are out of place." I ducked into the front bench seat and examined the dash, the glove box and the floor. *Nothing.* With great distaste, I insinuated my hands into the juncture of seat back and bottom, longing for latex gloves. As expected, my nails came out gunky. A long soak in antiseptic would be needed ASAP. After repeating the process in the back seat and climbing into the trunk, I said to Frank, "We're barking up the wrong tree."

"I think you're right, Angie. Surely if Hank wanted something to be found, he'd make it easier."

As Frank started to lock the car, Doris exited the back door and came toward us, holding a plastic zip-lock baggie. "I almost forgot," she said. "Jim left this, too." She handed it to Frank.

"What is it?" I asked, as I sidled close to him.

"Fuses," Doris said. "Jim told me we'd need them, because they were always blowing. Funny, though, we ain't had to use them." She shrugged. "But I wanted ya to see them. I wanted to be sure nobody'd come back at me for not telling everything that Jim left."

"It's good to be careful, Doris," Frank said, "but please don't worry that we'd think you were hiding something." He put a hand on her big shoulder. "You're as honest as they come. I know that."

She sniffed. "Should hope so." Then she whacked Frank on the back. He lurched forward a bit, but managed to steady himself.

"We're almost done here, Doris. We just want to take a look under the hood."

Frank unlocked the car and I climbed into the front seat and popped the hood. He leaned into the open door. "The fuse box is under the dash. You check it out while I pretend to look at the engine.

I located the box and wrestled the cover off. Inside the box, wedged between two rows of fuses, was a piece of stiff paper. I eased it out, replaced the cover and exited the car. Once under the hood with Frank, out of sight of the kitchen windows, I examined the paper. It was long and narrow, thick like manila paper and perforated on one end. It reminded me of the tabs I used to slide into hanging file folders in the days before adhesive printer labels. Carefully printed in block letters was the sequence $x9Y#nOS7PybNCRekUW@S-Mail.com.

At last, a clue! "Marcy gave me his Gmail account when he first disappeared. It's still open, but it gets nothing except spam," I told Frank. "I've never heard of S-Mail, and there's no password. And what a strange login!"

Frank peered over my shoulder. "Very strange. Let's head back to my office and see if we can figure it out."

I tucked the paper into my pants pocket as Frank released the rod holding the hood open. It fell with a clang. "Careful," I told Frank. "It might disintegrate."

We returned the bag of fuses to Doris. I used the kitchen sink to wash and scrub my hands. Frank told her that he'd be back with the car title and shouldered the duffel bag.

Once at his office, he settled at his computer and searched for 'S-Mail.' "This is one very secure provider, Angie. They don't even store emails in their servers. Once it's opened, it's deleted. That's one way to be sure the NSA doesn't track you." He looked at me. "Of course, you'd either have to be a conspiracy freak or doing something illegal to need that level of security."

"What the heck was he hiding?"

Frank shook his head. "No way to know, but he knew what he was doing. If he hadn't come to me for the obit, I doubt anyone would ever connect Henry Wagner to Jim Beltran. The man certainly had layers."

"Too true." Spider Mulcahey could get access, if anyone could. "But I know someone top notch who might be able to peel the onion. I'll call him when I get home and ask him about S-Mail. If there's a way in, he'll know. For now, let me check with Marcy about the clothes and the car." I went to the closet, took out my purse and entered Marcy's number on my phone.

After four rings, she answered, sounding breathless. "Angie?"

"Hi, Marcy. I'm still in the Point." *How should I explain Hank's unbalanced insistence on secrecy? Better to skirt the issue, for now.* "I interviewed one of the residents at the shelter where Hank was staying. He left a few personal effects. Do you care if they keep Hank's clothes? They're nothing fancy, just flannel shirts, jeans, boxers and socks."

"No, of course I don't mind."

"Great. They'll go to good use. Second thing. Hank drove a rusted-out 1979 Honda Civic that he signed over to them, so they could help get people to work and back. It's got more than three hundred thousand miles on it."

"No objections there, either. Let them have it."

"I'm bringing back a duffel bag that held his stuff. I assume you won't want his personal toiletries."

"No." She sounded deflated.

"Uh, one odd thing. He had a pretty expensive razor. I thought it

was strange that he'd spend money on that when he lived at the shelter and drove a beater."

"Hank had very sensitive skin. His face would break out in little bumps if he didn't use the right razor." I heard a little catch in her voice. "He even used Nivea shave cream. I teased him that he was a softie, and he said 'only when it comes to my face.'"

Huh. There was no Nivea in the bag. "Okay. I wish there was more I could tell you. I'm heading home now, Marcy. I'll call you. Be patient. I'm not giving up."

Frank gestured at the tab. "Mind if I make a copy? It might be better to have one in a remote location."

"Good idea. But don't scan it to your computer. Print it instead. Computer files can be recovered, even after they've been deleted."

His eyebrows went up. "Okay, I'll just use the copy function and put it in my safe." He lifted the printer lid and turned back to me. "I have to say, this is the most excitement I've had in ages. Your job is pretty interesting."

"Most times, it's just sitting at a computer running traces or in a car keeping someone under observation. There's a lot of boredom, interspersed with flashes of excitement. It appeals to me because I love to solve puzzles."

"I have to think it appeals on a deeper level, Angie, or you wouldn't be such a bulldog about a runaway husband." He cocked his head to one side. "You're a crusader."

I felt a blush rising. "Somewhat. I hate lies. The truth is always preferable, no matter how painful."

We parted with promises to keep in touch. Outside, I slung the duffel bag into the back seat of the Mazda, retrieved my personal luggage from the B&B and headed for Milwaukee, Wukowski and, hopefully, smokin' hot sex.

Chapter 5

Make love when you can. It's good for you. — Kurt Vonnegut

It was almost seven when I got back to my east side condo. Leaving my overnight bag in the entry hall, I kicked off my shoes and settled on the couch with a glass of wine, wondering when Wukowski would arrive. The Lake Michigan shore was outlined by lights along Lake Drive, with the spectacular Burke Brise Soleil of the Milwaukee Art Museum in full sail. Some say it resembles a bird in flight. I see a submerging whale's tail.

My mind began to mull over the puzzling behavior of Hank Wagner in his last days. I sent a short text to Spider Mulcahey. He now ran a security business, but still did some work for the government. His Delafield farmhouse boasted a very high-tech and well-protected home office. *Spider, why would an average guy use S-Mail and how can I read one of his emails?*

The landline in the kitchen rang and, when I picked it up, Spider said, "Only conspiracy freaks and people with something to hide use S-Mail, Angie. And guys like me, on general principles. So who's the client and why do you need to access his S-Mail?"

I explained the background of the case and told him about the S-Mail address we found stuck in the fuse box of Hank's junker. "It will mean a lot to Marcy if he left a message for her."

"If he wanted her to know something, there are more straightforward ways to communicate."

"True. That's why I'd like to see it before she does."

"The thing about S-Mail is that once a message is read, it's deleted from their server, with no way to retrieve it. So you only get one shot at reading it."

"It can be printed, right?"

"Sure. But ask yourself, why was he hiding? It wasn't simply to avoid his responsibilities as a husband and father. This guy went to some lengths not to be found. And not many people even know about S-Mail. It smells like an attempt at deep cover to me."

"Maybe. But now that he's dead—"

He interrupted. "Are you positive he's dead?"

"I spoke to the funeral home director who took care of the cremation," I said.

"But how did he know it was Hank Wagner's body? Did the director know him before he died?"

"No. In fact, they cremated him under his assumed name."

"Angie, this guy was on the run, and it wasn't from his wife. Want me to do some digging?"

"I ran all the usual searches when Marcy first hired me, and every month thereafter. Nothing suspicious turned up."

"Send me what you have. I can go deeper than public records. As for the S-Mail, there's no way to access it without his password or a search warrant, and the warrant is only good until the message is opened. Is there any reason to get a judge to look at this?"

"I suppose not. A man's final email doesn't constitute a legal imperative."

"Let me see what I can do. Meanwhile, you keep looking for the password." I glanced up and saw Wukowski in the entry hall. "Will do," I told Spider. "Gotta go." I hung up.

"Hi, handsome," I said to Wukowski.

"Hey, Angie," he replied, his voice a monotone.

As I approached him, I saw the dark circles under his eyes and the slight slump of his normally squared-off shoulders—impressive shoulders, I might add. My man was down. I took his coat and hung it in the entry closet, while he removed his shoes and set them in the boot tray. Then I led him by the hand to the couch, turned on a table lamp, and sat beside him. "Tough day?" I asked.

"Another woman attacked. This time in Kosciuszko Park, in the wooded area behind the community center building."

The park was a south side recreation area, with a gymnasium, indoor swimming pool, tot lots and playgrounds. "That's terrible, Wukowski." I put my hand on his forearm. "Was she killed?"

"No. Raped and beaten senseless. She's in a coma, at Froedtert Hospital. The docs aren't sure if she'll make it. And if she does, there may be brain damage." He rested his head on the back cushion and closed his eyes. "She's only seventeen."

His weary response shocked me. The Wukowski I knew would be angry, determined, unstoppable. Then I recalled the story of his younger sister Celestyna, who was killed in her teens by a Hispanic gang seeking retaliation against a Polish gang. Small wonder this latest attack hit Wukowski so hard.

I went to the bar and poured a short glass of Sobieski, a kick-ass vodka he introduced me to a few months earlier. Placing it on the coffee table, I sat back down and loosened his tie. Pushing him forward a bit—I needed his cooperation, since he outweighs me by about eighty pounds—I removed his suitcoat and tugged him to lean back against me. With my hands massaging his shoulders, I quietly said, "There's a glass of vodka on the table."

He sighed and opened his eyes. "Thanks, *moja droga.*" After a swallow or two, he set the glass down and sighed. "This case is getting to me. Maybe I should head for home. I'm bad company tonight."

"Stay," I whispered.

We sat like that for perhaps half an hour. Somewhere in the interval, Wukowski's breathing changed and his head relaxed into my shoulder. I let him sleep, gently cradling him against me.

He woke with a start.

"Better?" I asked.

He didn't answer aloud, but put his arm around my back and maneuvered me into his lap. His teeth grazed my ear as he whispered, "Much better. You sure know how to improve my mood."

"There are even better ways, *caro,*" I assured him. Consolatory sex can be extremely effective!

Chapter 6

Everything we see hides another thing, we always want to see what is hidden by what we see. — René Magritte

The next morning, he grabbed a cup of coffee and left early for the homicide bullpen. I was pleased that the hangdog look and posture were gone and his chin was set in a determined way. *What would he have done a year ago*, I wondered, *before we met?*

Rick, the manager of the gym we used, once told me that after his partner Liz's death, Wukowski disconnected from everyday life and concentrated solely on finding her killers. He went through the motions of living, but his only real human interaction was with his new partner, Joe Ignowski. Even with Iggy, Wukowski held a reserve. Rick, Iggy, and Wukowski's mother were all happy that he was able to put some of the past behind him. So was I. I loved the guy and wanted the best for him.

The temps were predicted to be in the mid-twenties today. I showered and dressed for the office in tailored dove gray slacks, a soft brushed cotton mustard-colored shirt, and plaid wool challis shawl. Underneath, I wore a silvery silk charmeuse demi bra and high-cut briefs. Professional on the outside, sexy underneath. A perfect combo, to my mind!

Susan was hard at work when I reached the office with my Starbucks in hand. "Morning," I said.

"Angie, hi." She turned back to her computer.

That was unusual. Typically, she'd want to hear all about my trip and the latest case. *She must be on a deadline for a client*, I decided. I settled at my desk and booted up the server. Bobbie ambled in around ten o'clock. I don't quibble about his hours because he's only getting a small stipend in return for the work experience that will qualify him to sit for the Wisconsin licensing exam.

"Angie," he said as he hung up his coat, "how did things go in Stevens Point?"

"I got a lot of information, but all it did was confuse me. I'm hoping you can look at it with new eyes and maybe spot a pattern I missed."

"Could be," he said, with no attempt at modesty. We both knew he was good at reading people, a skill that comes in handy for a gay man in a straight world. "Shall we?" He gestured to the office meeting room.

I lugged in Hank's duffel bag and my briefcase and set them on the table. Then I went over the case notes with Bobbie. His running commentary made me smile. Mrs. Rogers was a "nasty battleaxe," Augusta was "a feisty old dear," and Frank Jamieson was "good-hearted, but naïve." When I described Doris and our interactions, he nodded and murmured, "Recovering addict. Cautious, but sharp. I bet she knows more than she said."

"I wouldn't be surprised. She trusts Frank, to a degree, but I think she'll always try to stay away from legal entanglements." I explained about finding the paper with the S-Mail login, and Spider's take on Hank's precautions. "Without the password, we're probably SOL."

"Hank wanted this to be found, Angie. But he wanted to be sure it was found by someone who would know what to do with it. Someone savvy."

I nodded.

"So it stands to reason that he left the password where it could be found, too."

"I guess we could impound the car and have it stripped," I said.

"No, I doubt he would use the same hiding place for both. Too simple." Bobbie picked up the duffel bag. "What about this?"

"I went through everything at the shelter. I left Hanks's clothes for them to use, but I was very careful to examine them thoroughly—seams, pockets, tags. All that's left are the toiletries he didn't take to the nursing home with him."

Bobbie donned latex gloves, opened the duffel bag, and spread the contents on the table before us. He pulled the bag inside-out, feeling and eyeballing every inch, but finding nothing except lint. Then he turned to the small pile of personal items. He shook the can of shaving cream and sprayed some onto his hand, smelling it and saying, "Yep." The stick of solid deodorant got the same sniff treatment. He squeezed all the toothpaste onto a paper napkin, then used one of the razor blade cartridges to cut the tube open. "In the movies, they hide contraband in toothpaste tubes. Not this one, though," he said.

Lastly, he picked up the razor and hefted it. "Feels right, but let's be thorough." He reached for his satchel, a cognac-colored leather piece that unzipped to lie flat. One side held a tablet computer, the other, tools in pockets. Bobbie extracted a multi-use gizmo and opened it. It had more gadgets than I could figure out, but one was a miniature set of pliers. Grasping the handle of the razor with the pliers, Bobbie squeezed until the handle broke. Then he peered inside and shook his head. "Empty. Too bad."

I was extremely impressed with Bobbie's shrewd examination of the duffel bag and contents. "That was very thorough," I told him. "I'm not sure I'd have gone to those lengths."

He sat, staring at the table. "There must be something we missed. He wouldn't give us the login without the password."

"Maybe it's in whatever he took to the nursing home," I said. "But he couldn't know they would retain his things, once he died."

Bobbie idly fingered the contents of Hank's bag. Flipping over the deodorant, he turned the small dial at the bottom. "It's hung up. And look at those scratches." He used a small blade on his utility knife to pry the solid deodorant out and peered inside. "What is that?" he muttered. With the tiny pliers, he reached inside the empty container and removed a small clear capsule, like something that would hold medication, less than two centimeters in length, with a white object inside. "Look at this, Angie!" His voice shook with excitement.

"Is there anything printed on the outside?" I asked.

After examination with a magnifying glass from his satchel, Bobbie shook his head.

"Try to open it without destroying the capsule," I told him.

Bobbie gently twisted and then pulled on it. His fingers, though slender, were too big to effectively grasp it. "I think I can cut around it without slicing into the contents," he said. When I nodded, he went to work. In a few seconds, a tightly rolled paper lay on the office table.

"Is it glued or taped?" I asked.

"Doesn't seem like it. Let's see if I can unroll it without damage." A tiny tweezer from his all-purpose utility tool got the process started. I carefully held the end of the small scroll as he pulled. It opened to about two inches, but it was only a quarter inch in width. We stared at the characters that were inked on it: 0/\/1'/u^^@|2c

Bobbie snapped a picture of the scroll while I carefully held it open. "It's strange," I said, "but at least it's not twenty characters long, like his login. It's certainly not something you could guess."

I considered using it to log in to S-Mail, but decided that doing it under Spider's supervision would be the wisest course of action, in case some other security measure was in place. I didn't want to take the chance of losing the message altogether.

Bobbie agreed, and placed the capsule and the paper in a plastic bag and then into his satchel. After I made a quick call to Spider at his Delafield farmhouse, Bobbie started to pack up for the trip.

"Bobbie," I said, "I'm very impressed with your insight and your level of preparedness today. I knew you took the internship seriously, but I had no idea how far you've come. Well done!"

He looked up and grinned. "Thanks, Angie. I'm learning from the best. Bram York seems ready to tackle anything!" His expression changed to a sober look. "And the best part is, he doesn't treat me differently because I'm gay. I wondered if that would happen, him being a former special ops macho-type guy."

"That's good to know," I told him. "As a woman, I had the same concern when I first met Bram and Spider, but they took me seriously and only pulled rank when their special expertise made it appropriate. I couldn't work closely with someone who was too close-minded to do less." I rubbed my hands together. "Let's go see what Spider can make of this."

Chapter 7

We dance round in a ring and suppose, but the secret sits in the middle and knows. — Robert Frost

The drive to Delafield from downtown Milwaukee took us along I-94, past the distinctive retractable dome of Miller Park, home of the Milwaukee Brewers baseball team, and on to the suburbs, exurbs and, eventually, the small towns and villages that would one day be swallowed up in the Madison-Milwaukee urban corridor.

"Angie, what are you going to tell Marcy?" Bobbie asked. "About the Beltran alias, I mean."

Tell the truth and shame the devil, Aunt Terry always said. "I made a personal oath when I started my business to adhere to a strict policy of openness with clients. They hire me, I tell them the facts. Then they learn to deal with them. She deserves to know, although it won't be an easy conversation. Not to mention, she might know something about Beltran. Where Hank came up with the name. What significance it might hold for him."

I turned into the long driveway of Spider's home. "People who disappear are often found because of things they've held onto from their past. Names, photos, even old IDs. That's one reason why I considered enticing Hank to come out of hiding with a rare Star Wars item for sale. He was such a fan, Marcy told me. In the end, though, I didn't want to be accused of fraudulently advertising something I didn't have. Reputation is everything in this business."

We approached a farmhouse with a huge six-bay garage and parked on the circular drive. Spider greeted us from the doorway and ushered us into the kitchen, a charming blend of glossy granite, stainless steel and dark wood. "Angie, Bobbie, this is my wife, Magdalena, and our son, Joey."

Magdalena's smile revealed a charming dimple on the right side of her face. She stood about five-five, and despite an advanced pregnancy, her bone structure indicated she was normally petite. Her long, dark-brown hair framed startlingly green eyes. "Welcome to our home. Please, come in." She turned back to Spider. "Len, *querido*, I have coffee prepared and some cookies."

Spider's legal name was Leonard Aloysius Mulcahey, a good Irish boy. He put his hands on her belly and said, "She's supposed to stay off her feet, but guests must be fed."

"Pfft. Baking cookies is nothing." Looking toward Bobbie and me, she said, "I know you are here to work, so I've placed things in the office."

Joey, a miniature Spider, with his spiky dark hair and moving eyebrows, jumped up from a Legos play table and approached us, clutching a Lego Batman. "My mommie's cookies aw the best. She uses weal sugah and buttah, 'cause you don't skimp on dessuht."

I smiled. Joey obviously had a little problem with his Rs. Hunkering down to his eye level, I said, "I agree, Joey. Dessert should definitely be made with all the real ingredients."

He nodded, suddenly a little shy. Returning to his Legos construction, he placed Batman in the Batmobile and vroom-vroomed it around the table.

"Thank you, Magdalena, for going to all that work," I told her. "It smells delicious." Bobbie nodded.

Spider hung our coats on a large wooden coat rack. "Let's head upstairs," he said.

At the end of a long hallway, he leaned down to look into a small rectangular box, mounted on the wall outside a door. "Iris scanner," he said. "Knows if you're alive, so pulling a *Demolition Man* won't work."

I shuddered, remembering the scene where Wesley Snipes escapes from a futuristic prison by gouging out the warden's eyeball and holding it up to a retinal scanner. The door opened and Spider ushered us into the windowless room.

'High tech' was not high tech enough to describe Spider's office. Electronic equipment was stacked on shelving on two sides of the room. Locked cabinets lined the other two sides. A large desk with a massive natural-plank top, sanded and finished to a glossy shine, dominated the middle of the room, with two smaller workstations flanking the desk and its tryptic of display screens.

We gravitated to cookies and coffee, placed on a small rolling stand near the door. Joey was right. Magda did make delicious cookies!

Spider pulled a couple of side chairs over for us and settled in the executive desk chair. "So let's look at this email," he said.

I showed him the phone image of the password.

"I guess he *did* love her," he said.

Huh? "How do you get that from this password?" I asked.

"It's Leet, Angie. Computer geek-speak, where you substitute symbols and numbers for letters. Like L-zero-V-three for 'love.' But this is a step up in complexity." He typed the password into an empty text file and then, symbol by symbol, showed us his interpretation:

<table>
<tr><td>0</td><td>O</td></tr>
<tr><td>/\/</td><td>N</td></tr>
<tr><td>1</td><td>L</td></tr>
<tr><td>’/</td><td>Y</td></tr>
<tr><td>u</td><td>YOU</td></tr>
<tr><td>^^</td><td>M</td></tr>
<tr><td>@</td><td>A</td></tr>
<tr><td>|2</td><td>R</td></tr>
<tr><td>c</td><td>CY</td></tr>
</table>

“‘Only you, Marcy,’” I read aloud. “You can look at that more than one way, Spider. ‘Only you,’ as in ‘you’re my only love,’ or ‘only you,’ as in ‘you’re the only one who should read this.’”

He rolled back in his office chair and grimaced. “I should have seen that. Jeez, is all this domesticity turning my nasty, suspicious brain to mush?”

Bobbie laughed. “Don’t worry about that, Spider. I took it the same way you did. Angie has a bit of a trust issue.” I raised an eyebrow and he hurried to add, “But that’s a good thing when it comes to the business.”

While we waited, Spider accessed S-Mail from a search engine called Duck Duck Go. “It doesn’t track your searches, so no one can find out where you’ve been online. Of course, it’s a little irritating to have to retype favorite sites, but that’s the price you pay.”

The S-Mail site resembled Gmail. Spider entered Hank’s supposed username and password and we held a collective breath until the inbox displayed. One message waited, with a Subject line of “For My Wife.”

Bobbie looked at me. “Do we open it?”

The email most likely contained Hank’s last words to Marcy. We couldn't intrude on that, I decided. "I think it has to be Marcy's call," I said. "Let's see what she has to say." I tapped her number in my cellphone and put it on speaker. When she answered, I told her that Bobbie and Spider were on the call because we needed their expertise to get to an email message that Hank left in a different system from his usual Gmail.

There was a long moment of silence before she asked, "Who is the message for?"

"The Subject line reads, 'For My Wife,'" I told her. "We don't know how personal it might be, or if it contains information you don't want to share."

When she spoke again, her voice was a bit subdued. "I'd like to read it myself first. Can you come over here, Angie? Just you?"

Spider pointed between himself and Bobbie, then typed, "Get her here, so I can use my equipment in case of a problem. And ask for something that would have his prints on it."

I felt my eyebrows rise at that. "I'm uneasy about doing this at your house," I told Marcy. "Hank used an ultra-secure email provider called S-Mail, and went to great efforts to hide the login and password. There might be another level of security involved when the message opens, one that I wouldn't be able to manage. Using S-Mail means that, once we read and close the message, it gets deleted. There's no second chance."

When she didn't respond, I said, "Could you drive out to my security expert's headquarters in Delafield? And bring something that would have Hank's fingerprints on it. Bobbie's here, too. He was instrumental in finding the hidden password." When she didn't answer right away, I offered, "What if we stay out of the room when you access the message? If you need us, we'll be on standby."

"Okay. That makes sense. But I want you with me at first, Angie."

"Then that's how we'll do it," I reassured her.

While we waited, we discussed strategy. If Hank's message was a simple good-bye, there was no reason for any of us to read it. If it seemed to contain levels of meaning, it would be up to me to convince Marcy to share it. As much as I wanted to respect her privacy, I also wanted to figure out what was running through Hank's mind when he set up this figurative scavenger hunt.

About thirty minutes passed before Magda ushered Marcy to the office door, where she stood for a moment, taking in the array of equipment. I walked over and gave her a hug, then gently propelled her into the room.

Spider stood and I made introductions. "For you," he said to Marcy with a flourish of his hand as he indicated his executive desk chair. "Bobbie and I will be outside the door." When she sat, he leaned over her shoulder and pointed. "Click here to open the message, then here to make a printed copy."

Marcy cast a sheepish look at the men. "I hope I'm not offending you by asking you to leave."

Bobbie spoke in a soothing tone. "Not at all. I wouldn't want to share a final message with others, either. Don't give it a thought."

The men exited and Marcy and I faced the monitor. I moved my chair back and said, "You read it first and tell me if you want me to look it over or not. But don't close it until we talk, okay?"

Marcy gulped and clicked on the message. After a count of ten that felt as if it dragged on forever, she said, in a small voice, "I want you to see it, Angie."

I edged the chair back around.

Marcy, you're reading this because of my death. I want you to know that I set up a life insurance policy before I left town. Call Rick Sturgis at his agency. There will be enough to take care of you and the kids until they're through college. If you decide to get involved with someone else or remarry, have a reliable investigator check out the man. You have no idea what is out there. I'm sorry, Marcy. I wanted the best for you and the kids. I wish things could have turned out differently. Hank

I read the email twice and then sat, silent, for a few seconds. Hank expressed contrition in the message, but he never expressed love. However, he had taken steps to secure the family's economic future. For some men, that *is* a way to say 'I love you.'

Marcy's eyes remained focused, unblinking, on the screen, her jaw muscles working and her hands clenching the arms of the desk chair, hard. I didn't see her chest move. She was unconsciously holding her breath.

"Are you okay?" I asked.

With a start, she turned away from the monitor and inhaled deeply. "I'm not sure." She gave a quick little shake of the head. "The message is so … impersonal. Not like the Hank I know. Knew. And I still don't understand why he walked away. He wasn't that kind of man, Angie. Something must have pushed him to leave, but what?" She closed her eyes.

I settled back into my chair. It was time to expose Jim Beltran. "Marcy, there's something else you need to know. Hank was living in Stevens Point under an alias, Jim Beltran. He even went to the nursing facility as Beltran. But he set up the obituary beforehand, and he told the attorney his real identity so that it would be published under his real name, Henry Wagner. Does the name Beltran have any special meaning? Or even Jim? Someone in Hank's earlier life?"

She drew in her eyebrows and a furrow appeared above her nose. "No. I've never heard of a Beltran. As for Jim …" She shook her head. "It's a common enough name, but not one that I recall Hank using in conversation." A moment of silence hung between us. "I don't get it, Angie. Why did he go to those extremes?"

"I'm not sure. I do know that on the night he died, an aide disappeared from the home. I have no idea if there's a connection between that and Hank's death."

She rose and walked away, then turned abruptly back. "I need to understand this. I need to be able to explain this to the kids. I can't live the rest of my life not knowing why he left and what he was doing while he was gone."

"I get that, Marcy."

"So I want to re-open the investigation. Not just routine searches and stuff. A real investigation that tracks backwards from where he died, back to me and the kids. I can't pay you until the insurance money comes in, though."

"No worries on that," I told her. "Hank's disappearance is my only failure to locate. It bothers me on that level, and because I want you to have closure. An overused word, I know, but it applies."

She wobbled a bit and sat back down. "Yeah. It applies, alright."

From the corner of my eye, I saw Bobbie and Spider waiting in silence outside the door. "Let's print three copies of the email," I said. "One for you, one for the insurance agent, and one for me."

She complied and the printer across the room started to hum. "Should I close it now?" she asked. Her trembling hand made the mouse wobble as it hovered over the Delete tab.

That's the last communication she'll ever have with her husband, I thought. *Small wonder if she's ambivalent about it.* "If you don't mind, I'd like Spider to run some algorithms to be sure there's nothing hidden in the message."

She nodded and I went to the door to tell them it was okay to come back in.

Spider and Bobbie took a minute to read the message. Bobbie whispered to me, "Cold, wasn't he?"

I nodded, while Spider's fingers flew. The message changed from English prose to what appeared to be a long set of programming statements, with words like 'headers' and 'encryption.' Spider scrolled up and down the document, selecting and highlighting from time to time, then turned to me. "No secrets here, Angie. It's just an email." He clicked the icon to print the screen of gobbledygook and another copy of the plain email. Retrieving the papers from the printer, he looked them over, nodded, and handed the copies Marcy printed to me. "Marcy," Spider said, "you understand that, once the message is closed, it's gone for good?"

"Yes," was her single-word response. Her chin rose in resolution and she reached past him. With one click, the message was gone forever. The moment of strength passed and her head sank slightly as she asked, "Should I notify them to terminate the account?"

I patted her shoulder and said, "Let's wait and see if there are any incoming messages from others who knew Hank through S-Mail, now that his obit was published."

Walking to the tray of Magda's goodies, Marcy poured a cup of coffee. After a long swallow, she said, "Thank you, all of you, for what you've done to help me discover what happened to Hank. And thank you, Angie, for telling the truth about what you learned in Stevens

Point. I needed to know. Should I come in and sign a new contract for your services?"

"No need. The case was never closed." I looked at Bobbie. "Marcy wants us to uncover what happened to Hank after leaving her and before he died."

He nodded. "Good for you," he told her.

"Hank's bequest will help me find out what he was hiding from me. Ironic, isn't it?" A tiny smile crossed her lips.

How heartening to see that she could find some sort of redemption in the situation. *She will get through this and come out stronger*, I thought.

Spider spoke. "It's probably symptomatic of my inner paranoia, but there are a lot of questions surrounding your husband's death, Mrs. Wagner. I'd feel better knowing that everything's buttoned up at your house. Why don't I come over in a couple days and put new locks on your doors? Maybe assess the windows and outside perimeter."

Marcy's eyes widened. "Is there a reason for me to worry about our safety? I could take the kids to my mother's."

Spider reassured her that his caution was based on his experience in the security business, not on any real concern. I knew that it also came from his years in special ops. A man doesn't survive that kind of duty without a strong inner sense of when something is off-kilter.

As Marcy searched her purse for car keys, she exclaimed, "Oh, I almost forgot," and brought out a baggie. "This is the Nivea shave cream Hank uses … uh, used. You know, for fingerprints?"

"Jeez," Spider muttered. "I forgot, too. I'll need to get a set of your prints, Marcy, for elimination purposes. It's all electronic. Takes just a few seconds."

After thank-yous from Marcy to each of us, I walked her to the door.

With a hug, I whispered, “I’ve gone through some rough patches, Marcy, and needed a shoulder to cry on or someone to rant to. You can call me anytime.” Her eyes glistened as she turned away. So did mine.

Chapter 8

Burglars know there's more than one way to skin a vault.

— James Chiles

We gathered around Spider's big desk. Bobbie looked at him. "*Are* you worried about her safety?"

"Not exactly worried. It's just ... there's something going on under the surface. Something that involved her husband. I want to be sure it doesn't spill over onto her or the kids. I didn't uncover much on him when I went digging. Birth certificate, school records, driver's license. He was so ... ordinary. Way too ordinary for what he did the past five years. There has to be something in his past to account for it, something that pushed him over the edge."

"Maybe he simply didn't want the responsibilities of a wife and family," I said. "It happens."

"Yeah," Spider replied, "but why the big hiding act? Did he make off with a ton of money?"

"No. Marcy told me he didn't touch his pension money. He absconded with a little over fifteen thousand from their checking and savings accounts, combined. It wasn't enough to incent him to skip out the way he did."

"And he sure wasn't living high in Stevens Point," Bobbie said.

"Although," I ruminated, "he didn't go into the shelter until eight months ago. He had money at the beginning, though it wasn't a lot. But even before the trail got cold, I couldn't locate him." I sighed. "Maybe he had a third identity."

"Could be," Spider said. "I'll run his prints through a couple of databases. Who knows?"

Bobbie grinned. "Hold on." He took the baggie with the capsule and tiny scroll from his satchel. "In case the crazy bastard wiped the razor before he ran out, this is the paper with the password." He laid the baggie on the desk. "It was rolled up and put into this capsule"—he indicated the clear capsule, almost invisible inside the plastic bag—"then hidden under a deodorant stick. Only reason I found it is that the wheel that rolls the stick up was stuck. I used gloves."

"Nice work," Spider told Bobbie, who preened a bit. Spider held the evidence bag up and gave a low whistle. "Curiouser and curiouser," he quoted.

"It does have the feel of Wonderland," I agreed. "One of the residents at the home where Hank worked—a mentally competent one, I might add—told me that the aide on duty went missing on the night Jim Beltran died."

"Angie, you didn't tell me that," Bobbie scolded.

I banged the heel of my hand on my forehead. "Sorry, Bobbie. I got so excited when you found the password that I overlooked it. However, the aide's disappearance may be unrelated to Hank's death."

Spider shook his head. "I don't trust coincidences. A man with a secret identity dies, another man disappears from the same place, on the same night. It's too fluky. What was the aide's name?"

"Karl with a 'K,' Jorgensen spelled 'sen.' Augusta, the resident who has her wits about her, said he didn't fit his Scandinavian name, though. He was dark-haired and dark-complected. About five-ten and muscular. Karl and she got along pretty well. He even helped her balance her checkbook."

Spider turned back to the keyboard. One of the three screens flashed and he said, "No Social Security records for a Karl Jorgensen in Wisconsin in the past ten years." His right eyebrow moved, but I wasn't sure if he quirked it, or if it was simply a sign of their perpetual motion. "Can you get me a set of Jorgensen's prints, Angie?" he asked. "Maybe from Augusta's checkbook? Of course, I'll need hers, too, for elimination purposes. And a photo would be helpful."

"I can get the prints, if you trust me with your gizmo and show me how to use it. But the picture?" I thought for a moment. "The staff at Padua Manor wears ID badges with pictures, but I'd never get past Mrs. Rogers, the administrator. The facility and her office are both locked."

"Push button or key?" Spider asked.

"Neither. They use card readers."

"Even better." Spider's lips rose in a diabolical smile. He opened one of the office's many steel cabinets and motioned us over. "Ever see a rare earth magnet?" He extended a silver disk in one palm and a silver box in the other hand. Bobbie and I both shook our heads. "Very powerful," Spider told us. "This baby is made from neodymium. It's less than four inches in circumference and under an inch thick, but it can hold four hundred pounds."

I waited, sure there was a reason for this lesson.

"The thing is," Spider continued, "card reader devices read the unique magnetic force embedded in a plastic card, identify the pattern and match it to a database entry, and then disengage the locking mechanism on the door. A strong enough magnetic force will scramble the reader and cause the lock's bolt to withdraw for a second or two." He grinned. "And you're in."

"You mean, *break in*?" It wasn't as if I'd never done it. Bobbie and I illegally entered his former place of business to get evidence to exonerate Tony Belloni, but that was a case of trespassing, since we had no intent to commit a crime once inside. Breaking into Padua Manor to steal information from a computer or paper file would expose us to a charge of felony burglary, if we were caught. I could lose my P.I. license, Bobbie would never get his, and Wukowski would explode in ice cold anger. Wrestling with the possibilities, I finally decided there were times when wrongdoing was the only way to set things right.

Spider placed the disk and box on the wooden floor and walked back to his desk. We followed like preschoolers on a field trip. "You have to be extremely careful with the magnet, though. It can badly pinch any part of your body that's between it and iron. And there are newer readers that aren't disrupted by external magnetic force. The good news for our nefarious purposes is that the manufacturer hasn't retrofitted the original readers with the newer design. How old is the facility?"

"Not new," I said. "And it's pretty ratty-looking. According to Augusta, they never spend an extra cent, so there's a good chance their readers are vulnerable."

"That's to our advantage," Spider told me. "If the magnet doesn't do the trick, I can create a box that will capture the code when the administrator puts her card up to the reader. Then I can make a duplicate card. But let's try the easy way first.

On a second huge monitor, he brought up several satellite images of Padua Manor. "What about surveillance cameras?" Spider asked as he zoomed in and out of various portions of the pictures, which didn't look like they came from Google Maps. *Probably some highly sensitive source*, I thought.

"None that I saw, and you can bet they wouldn't invest in high-tech hidden cameras." I tapped on my cellphone, planning my next move. "The moon will be a waxing crescent tonight, and the forecast is for mostly cloudy skies in Stevens Point. Perfect weather for a *sub rosa* investigation."

"A what?" Bobbie asked.

"Undercover," I told him as I scanned the ten-day forecast. "The weather will clear tomorrow and remain clear the rest of the week, and tonight's moon will cast the least light until next month. This is our best shot at getting into the facility unobserved. Looks like a trip is in order. A very late-night trip."

"I'm going," Bobbie said, his voice firm.

Images flitted past my mind: of Bobbie, dressed all in black and quivering with excitement at a rendezvous with an informant; of Bobbie, keeping a cool head when a madwoman with a gun confronted us while we rifled her office in search of evidence that would link her to a murder; of Bobbie, shielding me with his body as a ruthless killer pursued us down I-94. Bobbie was a good man to have at your side. I nodded to him. "It's smart to have backup."

"Wish I could be there, too," Spider said, "but—"

"Don't even think of it," I interrupted. "Your family needs you close at hand right now. We can pull this off."

"I know you can," he affirmed.

Bobbie and I both preened a bit at that. Then we all settled in to discuss strategy and logistics for nearly another hour. Spider seemed so sure we'd be able to get in that I began to picture the possibilities.

Before we left, Spider donned latex gloves and used baby wipes to clean the magnet of fingerprints, and then placed it in a soft leather pouch. The pouch then went into the box. "Steel provides a magnetic shield," Spider cautioned, "but it can leak. It's best not to get the magnet near anything electronic. Keep it in the car trunk, away from the engine, and don't put it near your computers or cellphones." He hefted the box in one hand and wiped it down, too. "I'll walk you out."

After saying good-bye to Magda, we quietly exited the farmhouse, so as not to disturb Joey's "quiet time"—a euphemism I remembered well for "I don't want to take a nap." Spider put the steel box into the trunk of my Honda, and told us to text him when we arrived at the Manor and again when we left. "I'll be awake, waiting," he said.

As we merged onto the freeway, Bobbie spoke. "It's scary, what that man can do."

I agreed.

Chapter 9

Shh. We're being stealth! — Adam Brody on *The O.C.*

I spent the afternoon in the office. Like Spider, I couldn't let go of the frustrating feeling that we'd only touched the surface and there was more to discover. I logged onto my desktop and, on a whim, sent an email to Hank's S-Mail account: *Henry Wagner, James Beltran—who are you and what made you run?*

Thinking he might have other email addresses, I sent messages via the usual players—Gmail, Yahoo, Hotmail, AOL, Thunderbird—to his bizarre login, but they were all undeliverable. Next, I tried lesser-known and high-security providers, but still no luck. Tomorrow, I'd have Bobbie check for permutations of James/Jim/Diego Beltran. Since there were under a hundred and fifty in the US, it would be much easier than searching for a name as common as Henry Wagner.

After supper, I tried to nap, but my puzzle-obsessed brain refused to shut down. At eleven, I picked Bobbie up. He was dressed as I requested, in dark colors, but not so alarming as to resemble a cat burglar about to pounce. I hoped I achieved that same effect in my black jeans and running shoes, with a navy pea coat over a dark maroon shirt. We reviewed our strategy as I drove.

"I'll leave the car in the apartment parking lot that Spider suggested.

From the satellite images, it appears we can cross from the back of that building onto the Padua Manor property."

"Right," Bobbie said as he scanned the street maps that Spider provided, using a pinpoint flashlight clasped in his teeth.

"It's okay to use the overhead light," I said with a small smile. Bobbie was in full undercover mode.

"We're close," he muttered. "We should keep our eyes accustomed to the dark." His index finger traced a path down the map. "We want to gain entry from the back door of the nursing home. It's in the lee of the L that the building forms, so we shouldn't be easily noticed."

I nodded. "And once inside, the administration office is to the left, in the short wing. The residents are all housed in the long wing. If we can avoid the person on night duty, it should be an easy in-and-out, like Spider said."

Bobbie folded the map and replaced it in the glove box. In case we were challenged, it wouldn't do to have it on us. "You're sure there will only be one aide there?"

"Pretty sure. Jorgensen was on duty alone the night Hank died."

"We could call Augusta to find out," he suggested.

"I thought about it," I told him, "but I don't want to involve her unless there's no other way. She and her sister, Myrna, are too vulnerable."

"Right." His voice was slightly tense.

With a quick glance at his face, I turned back to the road. Traffic along I-41 was almost nonexistent, now that we'd passed Waupaca. The dashboard clock read 1:48. Stevens Point was coming up fast.

We rolled up to a stoplight on the outskirts of town, with no one behind us, and I popped the trunk lid. "I think you should pull the battery pack out of the hatch now," I told him, "and then sit in the back. That way, there will be less noise and activity when we get to the lot."

"Good thinking." He leaped out and extracted the steel box, inside its grocery bag, and jumped into the back seat before the light turned green.

I sedately pulled away. "Go ahead and take it out, Bobbie," I said over my shoulder, "but use gloves. We don't want prints on the battery, in case we have to ditch it."

"Will do."

His terse responses fed my own tension, and I was keyed up already! Breaking and entering was well outside the scope of my usual work. I took a deep breath and slowly exhaled, then did it again. All these years later, Lamaze breathing still calmed me.

From a side street, we surveilled the apartment building. It was now after two a.m. and only a single light shone, from a third floor flat. I pulled into one of three empty visitor spots and cut the engine. Looking back, I asked, "Ready?"

Bobbie's high baritone was steady. "Ready." He slipped the neodymium disk into the pocket of his black parka, set the steel box inside the shopping bag and placed it on the rear floor. With a nod, he lifted his parka hood over his head and opened the door. No interior lights shone. We disabled them before leaving Milwaukee.

I pulled a too-large knit hat over my distinctive white, spiky hair, opened my own door and stepped out. Bobbie rounded the car and, arm in arm, like a couple returning home from a late night party, we ambled to the building and slipped into the darkness at the back.

A single bulb illuminated the steel door leading to the dumpster behind the building. The units on this side lay asleep in shadow. I nudged Bobbie's arm and he followed me to the unlit corner, where the apartment building grounds abutted the nursing home.

Padua Manor's parking area held a beat-up Chevy Silverado. I pointed and whispered, "One person on duty." Bobbie acknowledged with a nod.

The Manor's windows were black, save for one. The bluish-white flickering of a fluorescent tube escaped from between the slats of its partially closed blinds, casting alternating stripes on the patio. I spotted movement inside.

I sat back on my heels, glad that the slats angled slightly downward, allowing me to see into the room. A man wearing scrubs filled a coffee cup and walked over to a brown vinyl sofa. I tugged on Bobbie's arm and he joined me near the ground.

"We'll have to wait until he leaves the room." I spoke in low tones.

Bobbie's only response was "Crap" as he settled on the cold concrete.

The next ninety minutes were an eternity in the bitter January cold. The aide refilled his cup, he took a sandwich from the small fridge and ate it, he plugged coins into a vending machine and devoured a Snickers bar, he flung a magazine to the floor and settled on the couch again, covering his upper body with a coat. He tossed, he turned, he adjusted himself, but he never left the blasted room!

My mind wandered to Wukowski. How did he stand up under frigid surveillance conditions? Or did he have someone less senior take care of the routine work? I doubted it. He valued control far too much.

That led me to consider how Wukowski would view this venture. Of course, what we were about to do was illegal—if we ever got inside, that is. But was it wrong? By my standards, we were searching for the truth in a situation filled with lies. I saw no conflict with my own ethical code, as long as we did nothing to harm an innocent person.

Bobbie tapped my hand and motioned for me to follow him.

Staying in the shadows, we slipped to the other side of the apartment building. I started when Bobbie wrapped me in an embrace, but he leaned down and whispered, "We're lovers, remember?"

"We're going to be frozen popsicles if that guy doesn't move. When in blazes does he check the residents?"

"My guess," Bobbie said, "is right before the morning shift is due. We can't wait that long, Angie. Our only hope of getting inside is if he leaves the room. We need Augusta."

The finality of his tone penetrated my cold-induced stupor. "You're right," I told him. "Even if one of us creates a diversion, he might not hear it from the breakroom. It'll have to be Augusta." Within the shelter of Bobbie's parka, I pulled up her number in my Contacts list and placed the call.

She answered after three rings. "Terry?" Her voice wavered.

"That's right," I said, happy that she remembered to use my pseudonym. "Are you all right? It's awfully late for you to pick up so quickly."

"It's Myrna. She's having a bad night. I'm in her room. It calms her."

"Augusta, I need your help for a minute or two. No longer, I promise."

"I wouldn't want to leave the Manor. I'm in my nightclothes. Perhaps we can meet tomorrow."

"It isn't a meeting that I need tonight. Can you rouse the aide on duty and get him out of the break room? Maybe make him come down the hall to see if Myrna needs medication."

"She probably does, poor thing, but the doctor refuses to prescribe. Benadryl is all they give her, to make her sleepy. I can ask for that."

"Would you, please?"

"Of course. Can you tell me why?"

"Not now, but I will, I promise. As soon as I can. Meanwhile, the less you know, the less involved you'll be."

"You just leave it to me. I'll keep him down here for at least five minutes, more if I can."

"You're a dear. I'll call you tomorrow." *If I'm not in jail.*

We returned to our observation corner. Within seconds, Augusta steamed into the room, clad in an ankle-length, deep purple, quilted robe and matching quilted slippers. We watched as she stood, hands on hips, then finger pointing out the door, then hand tugging the man's sleeve as she bent down to chastise him.

Afraid for her safety—she was petite and fragile, one push would send her to the floor—I held my breath until he levered himself up and slowly moved to follow her. As they disappeared from view, Bobbie and I sprinted to the card reader on the outside wall. The battery was more than an inch away when we heard a satisfying click and the lock disengaged.

The hallway was empty. We quietly moved to Mrs. Rogers' office, where the magnet again worked its magic—or should it be physics?

As I eased her door shut, we heard a man's voice coming toward us. "Yeah, yeah, I know, but there's nothing else I can give her. She'll settle down in a bit. Just relax, ma'am."

After waiting several minutes in the warmth of the office to allow the aide to plop himself back on the couch, Bobbie took the pinpoint flashlight from his parka and slowly played it around the room. He paused at a filing cabinet and again at the computer on Mrs. Rogers' desk. Deciding that trying to break into a computer was beyond my skill and his, I shuffled over to the metal cabinet, careful not to trip or dislodge anything along the route.

To my relief, the push-in lock was disengaged. The top drawer glided open when I gently pulled. Bobbie held the flashlight, while I scanned the tabs that identified each folder. This one drawer was devoted to suppliers of such mundane things as paper and hygiene products.

The second drawer contained pharmaceutical folders.

The third held patient records. I searched for "James Beltran," but there was nothing.

In the bottom drawer were employee records, filed in alphabetical order by surname. I quickly located "Jorgensen" near the back, gave Bobbie a thumbs-up, and extracted the folder. To my chagrin, it was empty.

I methodically examined the contents of every file in the drawer, and even the bottom, hoping against hope that the paperwork might have accidentally slid between folders. No such luck! I replaced the Jorgensen file and closed the drawer.

Apparently, Mrs. Rogers felt impregnable within her card-protected room, because her desk, like the file cabinet, was unsecured. I opened drawers, finding the usual assortment of office supplies in the flat middle drawer, and administrative paperwork in three others, with a stash of candy in the last. There was no hint of Karl Jorgensen.

When my arm accidentally brushed against the computer mouse on the desktop, the monitor activated, asking for a password.

Bobbie reached past me and rifled through a rotary file of business cards, perched on top of the desk. "Bingo," he whispered as he showed me a card labeled 'Security.' Under a listing for Commercial Security Services, Bobbie's index finger pointed to the word 'Paduamanor1.' I typed it in and, when the display changed to Mrs. Rogers' desktop, we fist-bumped. *Was she slack or simply naïve?* Didn't matter. We had access!

I glanced at the time in the system tray: 4:32 A.M. From the breakroom, we heard beeping and the aide's low growling yawn. A door opened in the hallway. We froze.

A squeaky clatter, calling to mind a wonky supermarket cart, was followed by tinkling noises as small objects hit a surface. I took a notepaper from Mrs. Rogers' desk and wrote, "He's getting 5:00 meds ready." Bobbie read it and added, "That means he'll be down the other hall soon, to pass them out. Let's move."

The Documents folder contained a Personnel subfolder and, nestled under it, a folder titled "Jorgensen, Karl." It held three files: ID, Application, and 1-Month Eval.

Bobbie passed me a new note. "No time. Email them to yourself."

"Can't leave a trail," I wrote.

He held up a finger to indicate I should wait, took out his cellphone, and tapped in a message. In seconds, there was a small flash and he handed the phone to me.

Send to jabberwocky@hotmail.com read the response to Bobbie's query to Spider. I quickly complied.

Moving back up the tree to Documents, I navigated to the Patients folder and emailed 'Beltran, James' to Spider's odd Hotmail address.

Time to get outta Dodge, preferably without any gunfights. I closed the documents and folders. Surely the system would be back in a locked state by the time Mrs. Rogers came in. I didn't picture her as an early-to-work person. We waited, silent, in the darkened room. At last the cart squeaked its way to the residents' wing.

Bobbie eased the office door open and peeked out. With a thumbs-up from him, we exited the room and he gently closed the door, waiting to hear its soft click. We were outside in seconds. I held Bobbie back with one hand while I scanned the longer side of the building. Soft light escaped from the edges of a window. The aide was on his rounds and the rest of the rooms were dark. We speed-walked to the apartment building and the car.

While Bobbie secured the neodymium magnet in its steel box and set it in the hatch, I took the passenger seat and texted Augusta. Although she was tech-savvy, I didn't know if she would understand current text abbreviations, so I took care to make the message standard English: *Thanks for your help. All is well here. If there are any repercussions, contact me right away. Delete these texts and get a good rest. Terry will call you later today.*

Bobbie settled on the driver's side as I messaged Spider: *Leaving now.*

Within seconds, my cell vibrated and 'Spider' appeared on the display. "Angie here," I said. "I'm putting this on speaker."

"No problems?" Spider asked.

"Looked like the third shift aide was settled in the break room, right next door to the administrator's office, for the night. Augusta distracted him, or we'd never have gotten in."

"Good that you had her on your side." He cleared his throat. "Did you look at the docs you emailed to jabberwocky?"

"I didn't have time."

"Ordinarily, I would discourage using a cellphone communication to open sensitive data, but it's highly unlikely that anyone will pick up our conversation or your keystrokes on that stretch of highway. I think you'll want to see them ASAP, so I'm emailing them to you now. Magda's water just broke. We're on the way to drop Joey off at a neighbor's and then to the hospital. I have maybe five minutes."

"Spider, this can wait! I don't want you to take any chances with those babies or your wife."

"It's okay, Angie." Magda's lilting voice broke in. "You're on the car speaker, so Len's hands are free. Joey's asleep in back. I haven't even had a contraction yet."

"Well, okay, if you're sure. Hold on." I pulled my tablet out of my bag and logged on. "Got the email."

"Open ID first," Spider told me.

It was a photo for a picture ID. The face that stared back at me was Hank Wagner's. He wore scrubs. "What the heck!" I held the tablet up for Bobbie to see. We exchanged startled glances and Bobbie pulled over onto the shoulder.

"Exactly," Spider said. "Hank was Jim Beltran at the shelter. Then he got a job at the nursing home as Karl Jorgensen."

"But why?" I asked.

"I'll leave it to you to figure that out. We're at our neighbor's house."

"Let me know when the little ones arrive. I'll say a prayer for a safe delivery and healthy babies. In fact, I'll text Aunt Terry to start her prayer chain rolling."

"Oh, thank you, Angie," Magda interjected. "Len has mentioned her. Your aunt's prayers mean a lot to me."

"Later," Spider said and the call ended.

Bobbie voiced what I was thinking. "Hank was one devious guy. I wonder how many more identities he had."

"My head aches trying to keep track of the ones we already know about, Bobbie." The adrenaline rush letdown had kicked in and my head truly did ache. I felt exhausted and shaky. Rooting in the door pocket, I found a squashed granola bar inside a still-intact wrapper and took a few bites. When the wobbles receded, I turned back to the tablet and opened the file labeled "Application."

"He applied at Padua Manor in October and they hired him that week," I told Bobbie. "He worked there six days a week, until the day he disappeared. I just ran a quick search for the address on Jorgensen's application at Padua Manor. Fake, but the street name is close enough to a real location that he could claim he wrote it down wrong, if challenged."

"Like I said, he's a cagy one."

"Word!"

Bobbie snorted.

"Hey, my grandchildren keep me current! Especially the boys. Those two know way too much." A few keystrokes later, I said, "The phone number is in service. I'll have to check who it's registered to when I get to the office. Same with the email address, which is Hotmail, by the way. No ultra-secure S-Mail for Jorgensen."

"You can't run the query from the car?" Bobbie cast me a wry grin. "I'm kinda anxious to catch this guy."

"No, really?" I gently mocked. "I couldn't tell! As for running a check now, remember, it's a pay-by-query database. I never use my cell or wireless for anything that requires a credit card."

"Gotcha."

I gave the 1-Month Eval file a quick perusal. Karl got high marks for attendance and punctuality, but Mrs. Rogers noted that he "spent too much time with residents." That burned me! Most of them were old and isolated, and needed all the human contact they could get. I read the line aloud to Bobbie.

"Woman's a witch, and that's probably unfair to witches," he said.

The Beltran folder held intake records for a white male. I couldn't interpret all the medical jargon, but it was clear that he was an end-stage liver failure patient. His height corresponded to Hank Wagner's, but he weighed much less. That would be normal for a dying man, though. I pulled up the picture of Hank Wagner that resided on my tablet. He had blue eyes. Beltran's were listed as brown.

I closed the tablet and tucked it back into my satchel. Without further data, speculation was valueless. Leaning back, I closed my eyes.

After a glance my way, Bobbie suggested I relax and take a nap. I gladly complied, ruing the difference in stamina between twenty-something and fifty-something. Ah, well as Mr. Wordsworth said, "The wiser mind mourns less for what age takes away than what it leaves behind." With that, I slept.

Chapter 10

Rare is the human being, immature or mature, who has never felt an impulse to pretend he is someone or something else.

— George Pierce Baker

After promising to call the moment I heard from Spider, I dropped Bobbie at the Lake Drive estate where he rented a luxurious, if small, flat over the owners' multi-bay garage. My own condo welcomed me when I opened the door and stepped inside. I peeled out of the night's dark clothes, set the clock for two p.m., and slipped into bed and oblivion.

When the buzzer sounded, I reluctantly forced myself up. Any more sleep and I'd be awake the whole night. The single cup coffeemaker shouted for me from the kitchen even as my bed whispered, "Angie, come baaack." Coffee won out.

As I gulped down what I was sure would be the first cup of many that day, my cellphone played the opening bars of 'Secret Agent Man.' "Hi, Spider. What's the news?"

"Magdalena and babies are fine. Gabriela was born at 4:52 and weighs six pounds, eight ounces. Daniel arrived right after Gabriela, at 5:10 and weighs five pounds, eleven ounces. The babies only went to the NICU for an initial exam. They're healthy enough to room in with Magda. I am one happy, exhausted daddy!"

"That's wonderful! Do you need help with Joey?"

"Nah, his best preschool buddy's mom is keeping him for now. I'll go over there later, after I've rested up a little, and bring him to Waukesha Memorial to meet his new brother and sister." He chuckled. "Joey will be able to say Danny and Gabby, but Gabriela might be a little challenge."

I could hear it now: *Gab-wee-ella*. "What about help when Magda and the babies come home? Do you have relatives nearby?"

"Nope." His tone made it plain that the topic was off the table. "But we hired a baby nurse for the first two weeks. She'll be there during the day. I don't need much sleep, so I can pull night duty. Except for the actual feedings, of course. Magda is adamant that she can breastfeed two."

As promised, I alerted Bobbie to the happy news. On the drive to the office, I began to plan a shopping trip for baby things. With a singleton already in the family, they needed at least one more of everything. This would be fun!

I got to the office to find Bobbie at my desk, reviewing the files we pilfered from Padua Manor. He rose when I approached. "Susan has a client in the conference room," he told me. "Do you need some privacy? If so, I'll walk over to the coffee shop."

"No, don't go." *We three really need to rethink the office situation*, I thought, with a twinge of guilt at the idea of leaving Susan. After the usual handling of winter wear, I placed my briefcase on the desk and Bobbie settled in the side chair. "The task at hand," I said, "is to figure out where Jorgensen is now. You can use the laptop to run a reverse query on his phone and dig for information on the area he gave as an address. Quite often, a person on the run resorts to things that seem familiar. Not smart, but understandable. File whatever you find out on the shared drive."

While Bobbie handled the routine queries, I did a more thorough background check. Karl Jorgensen was a cipher, a non-entity. He had no Wisconsin driver's license, no voter registration, no income tax filing, no Stevens Point library card and was not listed in the Wisconsin Nurse Aide directory. Hiring an unlicensed person to provide care for the frail souls at Padua Manor had to be a violation of state regulations. I would definitely report Mrs. Rogers and the facility when this investigation ended!

When I glanced up, Bobbie handed me a couple of printouts. "No Eames Street, as you found out last night. Eames Court and Eames Road are in the city center, a couple miles from the U. Lots of student rentals there, so lots of transients, but not much crime. Perfect for a guy who wants to keep a low profile and not engage the police." He paused while I skimmed the data. When I looked up, he said, "The phone number is still registered to Karl Jorgensen." With a serious look, he asked, "Should we call it?"

I shook my head. "Based on the nursing home ID, Jorgensen and Wagner are the same person. If that's so, Hank's not dead and I don't want to alert him. He might go into deep cover again. And even though Hank hasn't done anything violent that we're aware of, there's still that body from the Manor. I doubt it was his, not with the way he orchestrated the obit and the private message to Marcy. So if he was indeed Jorgensen, the only aide on duty the night of the death, he had access to patient medication. Did he help speed up Beltran's departure from this life? And if he's starting to feel cornered, who knows how he'll react? No, we need to approach this from another angle."

"Obbo?" It was British slang for 'observation.' Bobbie was a fan of BBC mysteries.

I nodded. "That's probably a good move, but it will have to be you, Bobbie. Hank might recognize me."

"You've met?"

"Well, no, but … uh … he might have run a search on me." I sighed. Time to 'fess up. "After we read Hank's S-Mail message to Marcy, I decided to send emails to other ISPs, using the S-Mail ID. They were all undeliverable. But I was frustrated and sent a new message to Hank via S-Mail," I confessed, slightly ashamed of letting my emotions overcome common sense. "I guess my own experience with a cheating husband, combined with all the years I searched for Hank, got the better of me. I can usually set aside my personal feelings when I'm on a case."

"Don't beat yourself up for being human, Ange."

"I suppose. But let it be a lesson to you. Business and emotions don't mix well."

"I'll do my best to keep them apart," he told me. "So what did the message say?"

I opened it from my Sent Folder and let Bobbie read it. *Henry Wagner, James Beltran—who are you and what made you run?* "I sent it from contact@AB-Investigations.com. Once he had that, he could go to our website and find my bio. I deliberately chose to not include a head shot, but he could run a search and see news reports that contain a photo. The Belloni and Johnson cases brought a lot of unwanted publicity."

"That they did! I bet the truck stop video is still out there."

We were able to laugh, now. At the time, our lives hung in the balance as we raced to evade a murderous war criminal by scrambling into a load of huge pipes on the trailer of a semi making for I-94. Bobbie repeated his favorite line. "Good thing your assets weren't exposed when you made the leap, Angie."

"Well, you can see why I'm not the right person to run obbo."

"Right. But I'm not on the website or on the news, other than a poor surveillance camera picture of me helping you into the pipe. I can dress like a student and walk around the area, maybe talk to some of the locals and show the picture. What if I drive up there tomorrow? Maybe Spider can give me his digital fingerprint device and I can meet Augusta. Her checkbook statement should have Jorgensen's prints and I can get hers for elimination."

"Good idea. Let's call Augusta and I can introduce you on the phone."

"Sounds great," he replied. "Her help is what got us this far. I'd love to meet her."

I selected Augusta from my contacts and placed the call on speaker.

"Hello, my dear Terry," her sweet voice said. "I trust you're well after your little episode yesterday?"

What a great undercover agent she is! "I'm much better, Augusta. In fact, my young nephew, Bobbie Russell, is here and wants to say hello to you. I'm putting you on speakerphone."

"Ma'am, it's lovely to talk with you and I can't thank you enough for your helpfulness with my aunt," Bobbie said. "I was with her during the episode, and I can assure you that your prayerful intervention made all the difference."

Like Augusta, Bobbie was also darned good at disguising the real intent of this conversation!

"Augusta," I said, "I'm sorry I can't keep our meeting, but my doctor thinks it would be unwise for me to travel right away. However, Bobbie expressed interest in making a short hop up to Stevens Point and getting together with you. He knows everything that's happened and could fill you in."

"Oh, that would be just lovely, dear. How kind of you, Bobbie."

I could picture the twinkle in her eyes as she spoke.

"My pleasure, Augusta," he told her. "I'll be in the area tomorrow. Why don't we plan to meet for lunch? I'll call you when I arrive in town. Maybe I can even help you with that pesky bank statement that Aunt Terry told me about. You know, the one that your friend worked on with you?" She promised to find it and bring it along and we ended the call.

I turned to my partner in all but the legalities of getting licensed. I never anticipated how quickly Bobbie would integrate into this side of my life, but his grasp of the business grew daily and the revenues he generated by taking routine work off my hands could not be ignored. I would invite Bobbie to add his name to the letterhead and website, once he got his license. "Angelina Bonaparte, Senior Investigator" followed by "Bobbie Russell, Associate Investigator." It had a nice ring.

***

The conference room door opened and a tiny Asian woman preceded Susan into the outer office. Bobbie and I stood, out of respect for her age. "Angie, you remember Mrs. Ellingsworth?" Susan asked.

Susan filled me in on the Ellingsworth love life after I first met the lady. "If she owned a football team," Susan told me, "the second string would be on the field by now." I rounded the desk to extend my hand. "You look lovely, as usual." I recognized the Zac Posen sheath. It was one I lusted after for my own wardrobe. Over seventy *and* fashionable, a difficult combination to pull off.

"Ms. Bonaparte, I can say the same of you." The upper class British accent and twinkling almond eyes were a lethal combination. She turned to Bobbie, her gaze appreciative. "And this is?"

"My assistant, Bobbie Russell."

Bobbie slowly lowered his head to her extended hand and kissed it.

"Ahh, young man, I can see that you are trouble of the nicest kind," Mrs. Ellingsworth purred. "You must come to one of my at-homes. Soon."

"That would be a true pleasure, ma'am."

After her client left us, Susan turned to me and Bobbie, and laid the break-up mantra on us. "We need to talk."

Had I somehow offended her?

Chapter 11

For when two beings who are not friends are near each other there is no meeting, and when friends are far apart there is no separation.

— Simone Weil

I locked the outer door and the three of us settled in the conference room. Susan's eyebrows were drawn in and her mouth was slightly clenched, giving her a puckered chin. Something was stressing my friend and officemate. I asked, "Susan, are you feeling unwell?"

After a long inhalation, she said, "This is hard, Angie. I've decided to relocate my business. I'm getting a lot more clients and I need more space and privacy. I found a nice suite at a reasonable rent near St. Paul and Water. I didn't have time to talk it over with you before now. The owner is a family friend, so he's cutting me a deal." Her words came out in a rush, then she stopped and studied my face for a moment. "I'll really miss you." Her chin began to wobble.

I felt a moment of sadness for the end of our close association. Of course, we'd stay in touch, but it wouldn't be the same. Still, the regret was tempered with relief. "You know I'll miss you, too, Susan, but with Bobbie on board, I've been thinking that I need to start looking. Now I won't have to. The current premises will be fine for us, once you move. So it's all good."

Her brows and shoulders relaxed. “Thanks for understanding. I’ll pay my share until our current lease expires.”

“No need,” I said. “I want the space and you’re saving me the hassle of a move.”

Bobbie piped in. “I know you two are close and I hate to think that my presence is forcing you out, Susan.”

“No, this has more to do with timing and business expansion than with you being here, Bobbie. I decided to take on a part-time accountant to help with routine audits. I’ve been turning down work because my plate is too full. Seeing how you and Angie complement each other gave me the idea.”

We looked at floor plans on Susan’s tablet. Bobbie assured her that his partner Steve’s contacts could get her deals on office furnishings. Since Susan would take her desk and distinctive shoji-front storage units, I mentioned that we would need a second desk, too, something that would pick up on my sleeker modern style.

“I’ll have my *own* desk?” Bobbie asked, his voice a bit breathless. “You’re keeping me on?”

I lightly punched his arm. “For now,” I said with a smile. This wasn’t the right time to talk about his future at AB Investigations. “You still have to put in your time and get licensed.”

“I won’t let you down!” He reached to hug me, but stopped. “Is it unprofessional to hug your boss?”

“I think your boss approves,” I told him, “but not in front of a client.”

“Of course not,” he said as we hugged. Then I hugged Susan. Then she and Bobbie hugged. It was the most body contact the office ever witnessed, at least in my tenure.

Every new beginning comes from some other beginning’s end, Seneca wrote. His words captured the bittersweet moment.

Susan left to meet a client, and Bobbie and I returned to the outer office and our discussion of his upcoming trip. "When you see Augusta, make sure she and her sister Myrna are okay, and assess whether our nocturnal activities were noticed."

He nodded as he copied Augusta's contact information from my cellphone into his. "I will."

"Do you need some petty cash for gas and the meal?" I asked. "This might be an overnighter." I gave him the name of the B&B from my initial trip.

Holding up a debit card, he told me, "I'm good."

"Then don't forget to document your expenses for reimbursement." Bobbie wasn't fond of the paperwork aspects of the business, but I knew the necessity of keeping good records for the client and the IRS.

With a wave, he was gone, leaving me in the empty office. I wanted to get back to the condo in time to make a decent meal and enjoy some quality time with Wukowski. Our communication had degenerated since the advent of the Bike Trail killings. We were usually pretty good at talking about both the deep and the inconsequential. Maybe tonight would re-ignite that.

Chapter 12

Dancing is a perpendicular expression of a horizontal desire.
— George Bernard Shaw

It was dark when I got home. *We need comfort food*, I decided. I assembled a meatloaf and slid it and baking potatoes in the oven. When Wukowski arrived, I would start the veggies.

After pouring a glass of Charles & Charles rosé, I ran a bubble bath and settled in for a good soak. The citrusy aroma perked me up and the creamy lather soothed me. I sipped my wine, settled my head back on a towel, closed my eyes and fell into a semi-meditative state.

The sound of the front door closing pulled me back to the present. I decided to let Wukowski find me in the bubbles. *Hmm.* I rearranged a few with my hands and waited.

"Angie?"

"Back here."

He walked through the bedroom and stopped in the bathroom doorway. His usual erect posture had returned. I wasn't sure if anything else was erect, until he took off his suit coat and tossed it behind him. He was more careful with his shoulder holster and gun, setting them on the top shelf of the linen closet. I raised an eyebrow as he began to strip. "This isn't a two-person tub, Wukowski."

"We'll make do," he said.

We did.

***

The meatloaf was a bit crispy on top, but we enjoyed it anyway. After supper, with me in a nightgown and robe and Wukowski in flannel sleep pants and a t-shirt, we settled on the couch with small glasses of B&B over ice. I hated to break the mood, but it was better to bring the subject up now, while Wukowski was relaxed. "Any news on the latest victim?"

He tensed. "She's improving. They don't know yet when we'll be able to interview her." He tightened his arms around me. "We might have caught a small break. A hair. Just one. We don't know for sure if it's from the assailant, but we're proceeding as if it is."

"Can you get DNA from it?"

"No follicle, just the shaft, so the conventional means won't work. But the FBI labs are using something called mitochondrial DNA to give us answers. For now, we wait."

I snuggled closer. "I got some news today. Susan's vacating her share of the office." I explained the situation and added, "Bobbie can't wait to get his own desk."

Wukowski gave a gentle snort. "That guy's gonna need some reining in, Angie."

"I know. In fact, I do rein him in. But he surprises me."

A moment of silence hung in the air. Then he lifted me so that we were facing each other. "I have a great idea."

I nipped his ear lobe. "Really?"

"Not that," he said, with a little swat on my derrière. He rose and rifled through my CD collection, putting several in the changer and programming the selections. Jimmy Dorsey's "Helena Polka" began to play. He pulled me up from the couch and into a lively circle of the room.

Every Milwaukee wedding—even the Italian and Sicilian ones—features a polka set. I learned the vivacious dance as a young girl. Wukowski told me that his mother insisted that he take dance lessons in his early teens, because he was klutzy during his many growth spurts and she thought it would help his coordination. And, he said, the girls loved it.

I sure did. We didn't just hop from side to side—that's not a real polka! We moved forward and back together, did the sideways moves and twirled. From there, we swung into a cha-cha to "It's In His Kiss," which I always referred to by its subtitle, "The Shoop-Shoop Song." Then the selections slowed—"When a Man Loves a Woman," "Faithfully," "Lady in Red," and "In Your Eyes."

When Marvin Gaye's "Let's Get It On" started to play, Wukowski bent down and whispered, "Shall we?"

"Oh, yes," I said.

We danced down the hall to the bedroom.

Chapter 13

One good thing about Internet dating: you're guaranteed to click with whomever you meet. — Anonymous

Over coffee the next morning, Wukowski let me know that he would be tied up all weekend and wouldn't make it to the Sunday afternoon spaghetti Bolognese fest at Papa's. "Sorry, *moja droga*. Too much on my plate right now. No pun intended"

I mentally breathed a small sigh of relief. There was no denying the tension between Wukowski and Papa. Both were extremely polite, yet guarded, with each other. I put it down to father-lover tension.

After Wukowski left, I checked the weather report. Ten degrees above zero, with a wind chill of negative five. *Brrr.* I donned silk long johns and tank top over my silk charmeuse half-cup bra and panties. At some point, sexiness has to make way for practicality, but practicality should never be dull! A lightweight woolen houndstooth blazer in deep raspberry and black, paired with stretch-infused Italian wool black pants and a creamy shell, completed the look. I would tote my heels along, since the snowy landscape necessitated boots.

Thankful for a reserved parking space in an area of town where parking is ferociously contested, I arrived at the office and emptied the mailbox in the vestibule. It was the usual junk. My personal and professional mail goes to a rented box at a private service center, for the sake of both security and convenience. Jimmying a lobby box requires very little effort, and the service center can sign for items which might otherwise be left in the lobby.

I unlocked the door and disabled the alarm that Spider installed when we worked together on the Johnson case last year. After stripping off my winter outer garments and boots, I powered up the desktop computer and slipped into my heels.

How could I contact Karl Jorgensen without setting off his alarms? I had his presumed email address and phone number. I considered how Gmail automatically sent most unsolicited stuff to my Spam folder, where it accumulated until it aged enough to be deleted. I could set up a fake email ID and use it to send a message that looked like it was junk mail, which Karl would ignore or delete. If I didn't get an undeliverable response, I would assume it went through and that Karl's email account was still active.

Spider's warnings caused me to wonder if Hank/Karl might be savvy enough to trace an email to the server that sent it. Not wanting to risk it, I decided to use the downtown Marriott's business center. After printing an obnoxious email from my Spam folder, I suited up to go outside, and headed for the hotel. Prior to setting up my own shop, when I still worked for Jake Waterman, I caught a thieving hotel employee in the act and saved the manager's job. Glen was happy to grant me access.

First, I set up a Hotmail account for user RussianWomenOnline and created an email with the subject Date_ Russian _Women. The body of the email invited Karl to click a link and guarantee his dating happiness. In case he tried it, I included the link from my printed spam. With a press of the Send button, off it went into the ether.

I waited at the computer for ten minutes. No undeliverable message came back. Odds were that Karl's email was still in service.

After that, Glen and I shared a cup of coffee and some laughs over my undercover stint as a hotel maid. Someone was stealing from guest rooms and he suspected either room service or meal service. Once I understood the cleaning routine, I came in after midnight, attached small video cameras to the underside of each laundry cart and collected the data on a hidden laptop. It's amazing what an enterprising thief can hide under a bundle of dirty sheets and towels!

It occurred to me that Glen might also be able to assist me by making a phone call to Karl. If the hotel's number appeared on Karl's display, there was nothing to link to me. We went to the manager's office, where I coached Glen in what I needed him to say. He put his office phone on speaker and punched in the number, while I stood by with my cellphone's recording feature activated.

"Yes?" a male voice spoke.

"Hello," Glen said. "This is the manager of the downtown Milwaukee Marriott. I believe I may have a personal item of yours, a planner. I'm sorry to say it went through the laundry, so the phone number is not too clear, nor is the name. Is this Mr., uh, Jefferson?"

"No. I haven't been near Milwaukee or stayed at a Marriott, and my name isn't Jefferson." The voice was clear and clipped, with a no-nonsense tone.

"Well, please excuse the call. I'm sorry to have bothered you, Mr. …"

He let it hang there, while I hoped against hope that the person on the other end would answer 'Jorgensen.' Instead, we heard a click and the call disconnected. I stopped the recording.

"Does that help any, Angie?" Glen asked.

"I'm not sure. At least I have the voice. I'll play it for someone who knows Jorgensen." I extended my hand. "Thanks so much. I owe you one."

"Glad to help." He pumped my hand a couple of times. "Let me know the outcome, would you? I'm dying of curiosity."

As I headed to the parking ramp, Bobbie texted me that he was on the road to Stevens Point with the fingerprint device. Ordinarily, I would be concerned about his interrupting Spider's much-needed rest to pick it up, but Spider labeled himself as someone who needed little sleep.

The mundane realities of life needed attention. I returned to my condo to run the vacuum and do a load or two of laundry. As I worked, I pondered what seemed to be the frayed ends of this case.

A memory of Sister Mary Iranaeus, my sixth grade teacher, rose before me as I pushed the vacuum. Sister—or S'ter, as we would say—brought a beautiful tapestry to class one day and placed it on an easel. "What do you see?" she asked, and we detailed the lovely colors and images. Then she flipped it over. The back was a mass of threads and knots, the picture hard to discern. "Never forget that in this earthly life, we see the back, but the Master is weaving an exquisite world, which we will only view from heaven."

The Wagner case was like that, almost unrecognizable—but I had to believe there was a pattern that would emerge, that the picture would resolve and Marcy would, after five long years, finally get resolution.

My cleaner and friend, Lela (don't ever call her a cleaning lady!) had finally begun to get regular acting work, and regretfully resigned her weekly gig for me. I needed to find a replacement, but was reluctant to start the interview process while in the midst of this crazy case.

I attached the hose to the vacuum and bent down to attack the fuzz and dust under the bed. Perhaps we'd get lucky and Bobbie would discover Hank's whereabouts as Karl. Or maybe Spider would uncover the identity of the man who died at Padua Manor. The hum of the machine changed to a high-pitched whine. *So that's where Wukowski's missing black sock went!* I detached it from the hose, replaced the floor attachment with the small brush, and gave the baseboards some attention.

The man who died and was cremated as Jim Beltran entered hospice, which meant he had to be seen by a physician. So he was truly terminally ill and his death was natural, unless the attending physician conspired with Hank to kill him before his time. I doubted it. *How did Hank engineer getting another man into Padua Manor under Jim Beltran's name?*

The dryer buzzed and I left the bedroom to attend to the load. The satisfying snap, smooth, and fold routine soothed my mind. I carried the stack of linen to the closet and settled bath towels, hand towels and washcloths into their assigned places. Before I could close the door and turn away, Doris Appleberg's words rang in my head. *There's this homeless guy, Willie, that most of us tried to help. He wasn't interested. But Willie and Jim, they got along. I'd see Jim talking to him, out on the sidewalk where Willie would beg. Haven't seen the old wino for quite a while.*

That must be the answer! I walked into the kitchen, grabbed a paper and pen, and began to write. Hank arranged for Willie to get care and eventually die at Padua Manor as Jim Beltran. It benefited Willie, whose illness had progressed to the point where he could no longer live on the streets, and it helped Hank. With Willie's death as Jim Beltran, Hank's obituary would be published by Frank Jamieson. Anyone nosing around about Hank's death might come across the trail to Jim Beltran, as Bobbie and I did, and end the search once and for all. Hank would be free to live as Karl Jorgensen, or take on yet another new identity.

Which left Marcy in limbo, married to a man whose death was a fiction. She could not legally remarry or collect the insurance money she needed to raise their kids. Exposing his death as a lie might result in his dying in reality at the hands of whomever he ran from. And why did he run? Was Henry Wagner another persona? *Who was this man, really?* Until we had those answers, Marcy would be unable to live her own life without fear or constraint. That was simply unacceptable.

I pushed the vacuum into the closet. Cleaning could wait.

After interviewing Doris Appleberg at A Place To Lay Your Head, I'd transcribed the shelter information into my cellphone contacts. Doris was my link to both Jim Beltran and Willie. I tapped in the shelter number.

"A Place To Lay Your Head. Doris speaking."

Her voice was as formidable as her grip. I held the phone away from my ear. "Doris, this is Angie Bonaparte. Frank Jamieson introduced us on Monday and we talked a bit about Jim Beltran." As I spoke, I felt a small shock at the realization of all that had happened in the space of six days.

"I remember. How ya doing?"

"I've been fine. And you?"

"Just ducky." After a short silence, she said, "I guess this ain't a courtesy call. Did Jim's missus have an issue with our keeping the car?"

"Oh, no. She was happy that you could get some use out of it. But Jim's wife was touched by knowing that Jim was close to Willie. She'd like to do something to help him. When we talked, you mentioned that you hadn't seen Willie for some time. I'm curious if he might have surfaced again."

"That's nice of her. But sorry to say, I've not seen hide nor hair of the guy."

"Is there anyone else I could talk to about Willie? Another person who lives on the street?"

"Well, maybe Margie and Spike. Margie's always got an ear to the ground, and she useta buy Willie breakfast at Webb's now and then."

"Are she and Spike a couple?" Despite Bobbie's self-defense lessons with Bram, I didn't want to send him alone to find someone called Spike.

"Ya could say that." She snorted. "Spike's the dog, a pit bull who's a real sissy. Wouldn't hurt no one, but he looks mean and that helps keep Margie safe."

"Any ideas where I might find Margie and Spike?"

"They got a regular panhandling route. You up here today?"

"No, but my associate is. Do you think she'd talk to a man?"

"Long as he tips her. Tell him to mention my name." She gave me Margie's Saturday stops and times. "And wouldja let me know if ya find Willie? He looked pretty bad last time. Maybe he's in the hospital."

"Possibly. It's worth a shot. I'll call around."

"Tell Jim's missus not to give the old coot money. He'll just spend it on booze."

"Good advice."

"Don't think he's got anyone. I'd pay a visit if I knew where he was."

"I promise to call if I locate him. Thanks for your help." After I disconnected, I paused to reflect on the unusual community of the down-and-outers. Doris would be sad to learn that Willie was dead, as I suspected. To have someone sad when you die was more than many could say.

I texted Bobbie to call me when he could talk and finished vacuuming. Afterward, I brewed a cup of mint tea, which has the fortunate effect of being both soothing and invigorating. As I settled on the couch and surveyed Lake Michigan's steely blue waters from the bank of living room windows, my cellphone played the title song from *Cabaret*, Bobbie's favorite musical.

"Hi, Bobbie. How are things going?"

"Super, Angie. Well, mostly super. First, I met Augusta and Myrna. Myrna held a baby doll in her arms and just sat there, rocking and crooning to it. Pretty sad, especially when you contrast it with Augusta. Angie, I love that lady! What a hoot! She had on a peacock blue knit dress and four-inch leopard print heels. She's got it goin' on, for sure."

I smiled at the image. "So she's well? No one caught on to our dark-of-night break-in?"

"Augusta didn't think so. I met Mrs. Meanie—Rogers—when I got there. What a hatchet face! Then Augusta and I went to a local steakhouse for lunch. I got her prints and the paperwork that Karl handled. Hopefully, Spider can find a few minutes to run them for us."

"The family comes first. But knowing Spider, he'll start PDQ."

"Yeah, I bet he will." With an audible intake of breath, he said, "I've got news on the Jorgensen front, too. I canvassed some merchants in the area of Eames Court and Eames Road. The counterman at a local diner remembered Jorgensen. Said he was a regular, eight-thirty nearly every morning since October. Always got a twelve ounce Columbian with room for cream. Not half-and-half. He asked for the real stuff. He stopped coming in sometime in early January."

"Eight-thirty correlates with the end of his shift at the Manor." I opened the Application document. "He applied there in mid-October. So around that timeframe, I suspect he got lodgings somewhere nearby, but he kept his room at A Place To Lay Your Head. And that's why I wanted to talk with you."

"About his room at the shelter?"

"Indirectly." I paused to organize my thoughts. "I had a couple of breakthroughs today." First, I told Bobbie about my Marriott scam.

"So the phone number's in service and he answered?" Bobbie asked in an excited voice.

"I'm not certain it was Jorgensen, but a man answered. We'll keep that in our hip pocket for later. Here's the real reason I called. I may know who the dead man was."

"Who?" Bobbie tended to speak in short phrases when his tension level ratcheted.

"Well, there are times when I'm doing an ordinary task, like driving or showering, that I have an inspiration about something that's been roiling around in my head. This afternoon, as I cleaned the condo and did laundry, I got a sudden flashback to my interview with Doris at A Place To Lay Your Head. She mentioned that Jim was friendly with a homeless man, Willie, and that Willie was pretty bad off. She also told me that she hadn't seen Willie in weeks."

"Aha! So Willie is the guy who died as Jim Beltran at Padua Manor."

"There's no way to know for sure. I checked the patient files on Beltran that we smuggled out of the Manor. They didn't contain a picture or prints."

"Too bad."

"It is. However, I called Doris to ask if she'd seen Willie recently. I scammed her a bit, told her that Jim's wife wanted to do something to help Willie. No luck with a recent sighting, but when I wondered if anyone else on the street might help, she told me about Margie and Spike."

"Spike?" His voice was a mite hesitant.

"No worries. Margie's a panhandler and Spike is her dog—a pit bull who's, according to Doris, a sissy."

Bobbie laughed. "All bark and no bite?"

"Exactly! The interesting thing about Margie is that she has a regular route, based on the day of the week. So I'd like you to locate her and see what she can tell you about Willie and Jim. Show her Jorgensen's picture. Who knows? She might have spotted him on her rounds. Mention Doris Appleberg and have some cash ready. Margie takes tips." I gave Bobbie the Saturday afternoon itinerary. "Don't rush back unless you have plans."

"Not tonight. Steve's away on a buying trip." He paused. "Tomorrow morning, I'll also check listings for rooms for rent in the area of Eames."

"Good idea. Dress respectable, but on the edge of poverty. That's how Augusta described Jorgensen in street clothes."

"Okay. Should I call you after I talk to Margie?"

"Please do. I'll be waiting to hear what you find out." After that, I would contact Marcy and let her know about yet another of Hank's hidden identities.

With the call ended, I felt at loose ends. No Wukowski to cook for. No Wukowski to meet for drinks or a meal. No Wukowski to …

Get a grip! I chastised myself. I gathered cleaning products for the bathroom and set off down the hall.

Chapter 14

Whatever you want to do, do it now! There are only so many tomorrows.
— Pope Paul VI

My cleaning frenzy ended around seven. I checked the fridge. A grocery shopping trip went to the top of my to-do list. I called for delivery pizza, took a quick shower, and popped *Pride and Prejudice* into the DVD player. I owned the 2005 BBC miniseries with Colin Firth and the 1940 film with Lawrence Olivier, as well as *Lost in Austen, Death Comes to Pemberley* and *Bridget Jones's Diary*. Yes, I am a P&P devotee, but I draw the line at the film with zombies!

Tonight, I chose Greer Garson and Lawrence Olivier. Although the film is spoiled by a rewrite in which Elizabeth and Lady Catherine reconcile, the interactions between Garson and Olivier are so deliciously witty, Mr. Collins is so disgustingly servile and Lady Catherine de Bourgh is so atrociously snobby that I manage to overlook the "happy ending."

The pizza arrived. I put two slices on a plate, poured a glass of wine and pressed Play.

Just as Lizzie and Darcy's rapprochement seemed established at the Netherfield garden party (substituted in the film for the Netherfield ball), my cellphone played "Cabaret." I pressed Pause and answered.

"Bobbie, I hope you're not still working."

"Nope. I just got a room at the B&B. Nice place! And Devon is such a sweetie. He put a plate together for me when he found out I worked for you."

"Aw. Give him my regards."

"I gotta tell you, I don't think it was all about you!"

"Uh … okay. But I thought you and Steve were exclusive."

"We are, but it's fun to flirt, right?"

I smiled at that. "It is, indeed. So, did you connect with Margie and Spike?"

"Yep, in the parking lot of the Save-A-Lot grocery. She wouldn't talk to me unless I gave her fifty bucks to 'cover her losses' while she stepped away from her corner. I hope that's okay."

"Of course. It's part of the cost of doing business, albeit a little unconventional and a little high. I wouldn't think she'd make much outside a discount store."

"She explained a lot about the art of panhandling when we went to a local coffee shop. Seems people on the low end of the economic spectrum are more generous than well-off folks. Margie thinks it's because the 'riches,' as she termed it, were either uncomfortable around the 'poors,' or afraid of them."

"Makes sense," I had to acknowledge, remembering times when I looked away from a street beggar.

"The waitress knew Margie from some backdoor panhandling. She let Spike slide under the table. He really is a shy dog. He wouldn't even sniff my hand. Maybe he was abused before Margie adopted him. Anyway, we ordered sandwiches and coffee and talked a bit. Margie knew Willie for years. She said his last name was Parsons. About two years ago, Willie started having what she termed 'episodes.' He'd double over from abdominal pain and retch. Late last year, he started to vomit blood and he'd scratch his skin so hard, it bled. Margie tried to get him to go to an ER, but he refused."

"Poor man. That sounds terrible."

"Yeah." Bobbie cleared his throat. "So get this! In late December, just before Christmas, Willie told Margie to stop worrying about him. Said that all his troubles were over, that he had a nice place to spend his last days, with a clean bed, three squares and pills to help ease his pain and the 'itchies.' She never saw him again, and when she asked Jim, he told her the same."

I opened the Padua Manor patient record for Jim Beltran. End-stage Cholestatic Liver Disease was the diagnosis. The chart contained a notation for 'cholestyramine to relieve severe pruritis.' I quickly Googled pruritis. It was medicalese for itching. "That matches with the Jim Beltran records from the Manor, Bobbie. I don't know if we'll get any closer, unless we catch up with Hank/Jim/Karl and he's willing to talk."

"Maybe I'll get lucky when I look at rentals. Devon put me on to a couple of places. I'll search online tonight and check the Sunday paper tomorrow morning."

"Don't use your real name. And please be careful. If you sense any danger or even feel uncomfortable in your surroundings, leave! That's an order. And call me before you head back tomorrow. If I don't hear from you by, say, two o'clock, I'll call Devon and, if he hasn't heard from you, I'll call the police."

"I'll be in touch, I promise. And I'll be careful. And I'll pay attention to my gut. 'Night, Mom."

Before I could say more, the call ended. Damned whippersnapper! I finished my wine, poured another glass and resumed P&P.

Chapter 15

A happy family is but an earlier heaven. — George Bernard Shaw

Sunday dawned sunny and cold, too cold to run outdoors. It relieved me of the hated feeling of being constrained by someone else, namely the Bike Trail killer. I slipped into yoga pants and a t-shirt and headed for the building's gym and the elliptical.

A woman I frequently saw on the lakefront trail last summer was pounding the treadmill when I arrived. She gave me a little nod, then grimaced. "Exercising indoors is getting old, but I'm too chicken to run outside these days. I sure hope the cops catch that bastard soon."

"Me, too," I said, realizing how the killings impacted the whole community and especially women. I sent up a silent appeal for a quick resolution. After thirty minutes, I took the elevator back upstairs and checked my cellphone. Bobbie's text awaited me: *on the hunt*. I responded: *Watch out for bad guys*. Then I began preparations for the day.

Sunday Dinner at Papa's, which was always capitalized in my head, followed the same script each week. Aunt Terry went to Mass at eight, then returned home to ready the dining room and prepare *zabaglione*, a creamy custard which incorporates Marsala wine. A separate portion, without wine, would be prepared for my grandchildren, who attended with their parents.

Papa started the Bolognese sauce while Terry was at church. With the saucepan simmering, he would take a cup of coffee and the Sunday paper to his den and let the family commotion bubble around him until it was time to eat.

I aimed to arrive at eleven. Although Papa preferred to see a woman in a skirt or dress, I picked dark teal wool trousers and an eggshell sweater. The pants would accommodate playing on the floor with my grandchildren.

Terry greeted me at the back door with a hug and kiss. "*Mia cara nipote*, how are you?" She peeked around me. "No Wukowski today?"

I shook my head. "No, he's working all weekend. This case..." I let it trail off. Words came hard for such horror.

"*Povero*, to deal with such a thing." She crossed herself. "I pray they find the killer soon."

I nodded and headed for the den to say hello to Papa. I could barely see the top of his head behind the front section of the *Journal Sentinel*. "Papa ..." I stopped dead.

"MPD Incompetent?" read the headline. "3 Months with No Progress on Bike Trail Murders," the subhead asserted. My heart beat fast in indignation, knowing how many hours and resources the department was dedicating to the pursuit of the killer. *How dare they!*

"Angelina." A gentle hand settled on my forearm. "Are you all right? I called your name twice."

Papa stood at my side. I glared at him and he stepped back.

"*Piccola*," he said, "you're shaking. What is it?"

"This"—I grabbed the paper from the side table and smacked it, producing a satisfying crack—"this drivel! This bull! This poor excuse for journalism! That's what's wrong."

He perused the headline, placed a hand under my elbow and guided me to a chair. "Sit here for a minute. I'll be right back." He quickly returned with a cup of tea. "Tell me," he said.

"Wukowski's been working night and day to solve these awful crimes. Agonizing over each victim. Losing sleep." I raised the mug to my lips.

"Ah! I see. This *stronzino* reporter has insulted your sweetheart."

Papa never ever swore in front of ladies, so calling someone a 'little asshole' was a big deal. It somehow warmed my heart to know that he would defend Wukowski's honor that way.

He patted my hand. "So, Angelina, take some advice from your papa. Problems come and they go. The opinions of the world are like waves on Lake Michigan's shoreline." He tapped the paper that lay on the table. "'You can do nothing about what this person writes. But consider. *Le bugie hanno le gambe corte.* Lies have short legs. So wait, Angie. The truth will be revealed."

Papa's soothing, steady tone did more to settle me than his words. I closed my eyes and took a deep breath, centering myself. "I've been reacting like a mama bear, but Wukowski is no cub. Thank you, Papa." I rose and hugged him.

He resumed the recliner and nodded at the table. "Maybe you should leave the paper there."

I returned to the kitchen, where Aunt Terry gave me a quizzical look, but said nothing. As she chopped ingredients for a salad, I removed the Italian loaf from its wrapper and began to prepare garlic bread. The bread came from Sciortino's bakery and was *delizioso*, its outside crusty and its inside perfect to absorb the olive oil, butter, garlic and spices. *Mmm.* My mouth watered, just thinking about it.

My granddaughter bounded into the kitchen ahead of her parents, my daughter Emma and her husband John. I hunkered down to receive a hug from my namesake, nine-year old Angela, a ladylike bookworm with a good heart and an impish sense of humor. "*Nonna*, can I help?" she asked.

"Of course," I told her. "But first, go hug your *bisnonno*. He's in the den. And then wash your hands and come back. We'll find an apron and you and I will make garlic bread."

I shared hugs with Emma and John. He grabbed a cup of coffee and settled in the living room to watch whatever football game was on. The Packers weren't scheduled to start until three.

Emma glanced at the clock and uncorked the wine as the second wave came through the back door. David, my tall handsome son, and his wife Elaine preceded their twin eleven-year old boys, in an attempt to hold them back from exploding into the room. Making an end run around each parent, Patrick and Donald barreled over and hugged me. I noticed that their heads were now almost at my armpit. Too soon, they would be taller than I was. I hugged them hard, while they still wanted my hugs.

A jumbled chorus of *Nonna*s and requests and observations came to a halt, not because their parents shushed them, but because Angela entered the room with a stern, "Boys, stop talking over each other. It's rude." With a giggle, she took their hands and tugged. "Come see what *Bisnonno* has in the den!"

David looked at Aunt Terry. "What's he bought now?"

She shrugged. "Some sort of superpower twist-and-turn action figures. He watches Nickelodeon and the Disney channels to see what's popular." She smiled at Emma. "Of course, for Angela, he has a new book. The first of the Laura Ingalls Wilder Little House books."

"Oh, I loved those as a child," I said.

"I think that's why he bought it," Aunt Terry replied. "He remembered your joy."

I welled up a bit, but David came over and hugged me hello, so I recovered while my face was buried in his chest. Being short had some advantages, but not many.

Dinner proceeded as usual, with good food and good company and much love. While the men handled cleanup, I played some hotly fought games of Sorry! with the children. Then we all screamed ourselves hoarse, watching the Packers beat the Panthers and advance to the NFC playoff game. All was well with the world, my soul once again re-created, surrounded by my family at Papa's table.

Chapter 16

A baby is God's opinion that life should go on. — Carl Sandburg

Before heading for home, I decided to buy a few presents for the new Mulcahey babies at a local east-side boutique. Nine years had passed since Angela's birth and my last real shopping trip for newborns. So much had changed! I delighted in the cheeky humor of the infant clothes. Spider would get a chuckle out of the onesies adorned with computers. Magda would love the handmade caps to protect little ears from the Wisconsin cold. Yellow Submarine winter jammies also went into my basket, along with sleepers embroidered with 'Drinking Buddies.' For Magda, I chose a soft pashmina throw that would warm her feet during nighttime feedings. And for Spider, an irreverent but hilarious book titled *Go the F* to Sleep*.

Joey puzzled me for several minutes. Of course, I could buy him a shirt with "I'm the Big Brother" emblazoned on it. But I wanted something that would show I recognized him as a person and not just the twins' older sibling. A Batman night light gleamed from a display across the room and I recalled Joey's Legos table, with its miniature Caped Crusader. Perfect! The boutique enclosed my gifts in tissue paper and white boxes. I selected wrapping paper, paid, and left for home and a bout with tape and ribbons.

As I fashioned a black ribbon into a likeness of the Caped Crusader, the staccato notes of "Cabaret" sounded from my cellphone. "Bobbie," I breathed, "it's three o'clock. I got engrossed in shopping and wrapping for the Mulcaheys and didn't check on you. Is everything okay?"

"More than okay, Angie." His voice trembled slightly and he rushed on. "It took a while, but I tracked down Hank's other home in Stevens Point! He had a studio at a short-term place that caters mostly to people in transit."

"Had? He's not still there, then?" Disappointment seeped into my voice. I didn't want Bobbie to hear that, not after he'd done the near-impossible. "Of course, we expected him to be long gone. You did great, Bobbie. Tell me more."

"Well, I followed the leads that Devon gave me and also went the rounds of the listings in the Sunday paper. None of them panned out directly, so I went back to the diner where Hank used to get his morning coffee and ordered a late lunch." He cleared his throat. "The waitress started to flirt with me and I confess that I led her on a little."

Lots of women had that reaction to Bobbie. He came across as not macho, but not really gay. The term metrosexual fit him to a T. "Hope you let her down easy."

"Soft as dandelion down. But while we were chatting, I asked her about lodgings in the area. Told her I was new to town and starting a job at the U on Monday, but I needed a cheap place to stay while I looked for new digs. She sent me to a boarding house nearby. The landlady was quite indignant when I showed her Hank's picture. Seems he skipped out on December thirtieth, the day after Beltran's death at Padua Manor. Came in that morning, packed a bag and brushed by her on the way out the door, 'with barely more than a fare-thee-well.' Her words."

"Did he owe her?"

"Nope. He was paid up for the month. She was mostly upset that she was losing a good lodger. Said he never made a lot of noise and the rent was on time every month. He'd been there since October. That matches with his application and hire at the Manor, right?"

I checked my tablet. "That's right," I confirmed. "I wonder if he saw Willie going downhill back then and developed this elaborate plan to fake his own death."

"That's what I think, too. Guy was a real piece of work, wasn't he?"

"Quite the tactician, that's for sure." *Enough of one to enable Willie's death in order to meet his own plan's timeline, whatever that might be?* "They say a chess master can visualize five or more moves ahead. I'd put Hank in that league." I paused. "I'm thinking of *our* next moves, Bobbie. I'd bet money that Hank is no longer in Stevens Point. I just wish I could figure out where he'd go next."

"Somewhere obscure," Bobbie replied, "where he could blend in and disappear." With a sigh, he added, "I think this trail is cold. Should I head back to the city?"

"Might as well."

"I'll check with Spider about dropping off the fingerprint device with Karl's prints before I come into the office tomorrow, if that's okay with you."

"Of course. Take a couple of days off after that. You earned it. Another job well done, Bobbie!"

"Thanks, Ange. That means a lot to me. And I'm closing in on my hours to take the exam and get licensed, so I don't mind a bit."

"The time went by fast! We'll need to schedule a meeting to discuss your performance and the testing requirements. Not to worry, though, I know you're ready."

I would make him an offer of employment, contingent on passing the exam and being licensed, when we sat down together. I smiled at what would undoubtedly be an over-the-top reaction.

Chapter 17

False face must hide what the false heart doth know.

— William Shakespeare

Like Bobbie, I'd been putting in a lot of hours. I decided to take Monday morning off—one of the perks of owning your own business—and attend to grocery shopping. While I checked cupboards and fridge, preparing a list on my cellphone, its message indicator pinged. Spider's text read: *I ran the prints on Jorgensen. You'll want to see this ASAP.* It was addressed to both me and Bobbie.

Although I told Bobbie not to come into work today, I knew he'd want to be part of the discovery. In a few clicks, we arranged to meet Spider at the farmhouse at ten. Bobbie drove separately, since he had plans in Brookfield afterward.

The first words out of my mouth when Spider opened the door were, "Are they home?"

His eyebrows wiggled and he grinned. "Not 'til this afternoon. Meanwhile, with Joey in preschool this morning, I have a small window of time." He reached for the pile of wrapped presents I carried and placed them on the kitchen table. "We didn't expect that, Angie."

"Shopping for babies again was so much fun! I need younger friends so I can do it more often."

"Well, don't wait for more from me and Magda. Three's plenty, especially when they start coming in twos."

A tap on the door heralded Bobbie's entrance. "Hey, Daddy," he greeted Spider. "How's the family?"

"Everyone's doing great," he said. "But time's a-wasting. Come in and let's get started. I have an hour." He gestured to the stairs and we went up to the bunker he called an office.

Once we settled around the computer, Spider turned to us with a sheepish look on his face. "Normally, you'd have known this on Saturday at the latest, but with the babies coming, I kinda let things slide. Sorry."

"Spider, stop right now." I gave him my no-nonsense mom look. "Whatever you found out, it's not more important than being there for the births and taking care of your family afterward."

"Right, man," Bobbie agreed.

Spider gave a single nod, swung his chair to face the huge middle monitor and clicked on the desktop. Pictures of Hank Wagner and Karl Jorgensen opened, side by side. "Based on these, we surmised that Wagner and Jorgensen are the same person. But faces and pictures can be manipulated. Not fingerprints." He clicked on another icon and a thumbprint appeared under Hank's face. "This is from the Nivea shaving lotion bottle that Marcy provided." Then he clicked again. Under Karl Jorgensen's picture, another thumbprint was displayed. "This is from the checking account papers that Augusta gave Bobbie." Another click. "We don't have a photo of Beltran, but I got this partial print from the paper you found in the fuse box of his car." With a swipe, he superimposed the prints and turned to us. "They match, as you can see."

"So that confirms that Wagner, Beltran and Jorgensen are all the same man," Bobbie noted.

"Right." Spider grinned. "Now for the good part. You ready for another identity?"

Spider was enjoying the moment. I decided to play along. "At this point," I said, "you could tell me he's Pope Francis on a sabbatical from the Vatican, and I wouldn't be surprised."

With a glance my way, Bobbie waggled his right fingers in the classic 'gimme' gesture. "C'mon, man."

"Okay." Spider took a breath, turned back to the table, and opened a file on the second of his three monitors. A newspaper clipping appeared. "Read this." Spider handed Bobbie and me individual copies of the clipping, from the *Philadelphia Enquirer*, dated nineteen years ago. "PPD Calls Off Search for Mafia Accountant," read the headline.

> *Sources report that the police have called off their attempt to locate Tommaso Severson, reputed bookkeeper for the South Philly Mob. Severson's sister Letizia reported Severson missing four months ago. Rumor on the street is that Joseph "Skinny Joey" Merlino, reputed leader of the crime organization, has offered a $100,000 bounty for information leading to Severson's whereabouts.*
>
> *Severson is the son of a Sicilian mother, whose family has close ties to the mob, and a father who emigrated from Sweden and opened an apparently legitimate accountancy business.*

I looked up, puzzled. "Hank had something to do with this man?"

Spider clicked on a file and a very young Hank Wagner appeared on the screen. The head shot was quickly followed by a thumbprint. "This is from the FBI's database." He dragged the print over to the other monitor—don't ask me how that works!—and released it when it hovered over the superimposed prints of Wagner-Beltran-Jorgensen.

It was a perfect match.

Bobbie leaned forward and stared, then sucked in a fast breath and blurted, "What the hell!"

"Exactly," Spider said. "What the hell." He looked at me, waiting.

My brain shifted from astonishment to logic. I focused away and mused out loud. "So Severson ran from the Mob to Milwaukee, where he built a new life as Hank Wagner. Then, for reasons still unknown, he disappeared as Hank and resurfaced a few years later as Jim Beltran. That's when he masterminded his own death." A horrifying thought intruded. "He married Marcy ten years ago. He wasn't already married, was he?"

Spider shook his head. "That's one thing he didn't do to her."

"Thank God." Still, I felt slightly sickened at the thought of telling Marcy about her husband's past. With a jolt, I wondered, *Is the marriage valid if he used a false name on the license?* I needed to find out before I broke this news to Hank's supposed wife. I frowned. "If the marriage is legal, Marcy must decide whether to file for divorce or wait for Hank to contact her. And she can't claim the life insurance, with him still alive somewhere."

"Don't see why not," Bobbie said. "Unless we out him, who will know?"

"*I* will. I can't be a party to fraud, Bobbie, and you'd never get your license if it came out."

He wrinkled his nose. "Too bad. Marcy can use the money. But I get your point."

Focus on the case, not on Marcy. "Why did Tommaso run?" I asked Spider.

"There's a lot of conjecture about that." He pulled more papers from his desk and gave them to me and Bobbie. "Some of these publications speculated that he embezzled from the Mob and skipped out to avoid getting caught and executed. Others believed he couldn't stomach Merlino's tactics. Skinny Joey was young when he took over. He used violence to manage an unstable organization." He shrugged. "There was even a rumor that Tommaso went into the Witness Protection Program. I doubt it, since he never testified against the Family and there's nothing in the FBI database that leads me to that conclusion. So either Tommaso got scared and ran, or he got righteous and ran. One thing's for sure, he did a fine job of hiding."

I nodded. "He certainly did."

Spider shuffled his papers into a neat pile and checked his watch. "I need to leave in ten. Where do we go from here?"

The multi-layered ramifications of exposing Hank gave me pause. "Do we have to report this to the police or FBI?" I asked.

He thought about that for a moment, eyebrows working. "Severson's not wanted. I say no. But they sure would like to talk to him, Angie. What he knows can still bring down some major bad guys."

"If he can be found," Bobbie said, "and if he'll talk."

"The good thing is, Severson doesn't know anyone is still looking for Hank Wagner," Spider said.

Bobbie gave me a look. "Busted!"

Spider swiveled toward me and waited, one eyebrow up.

Feeling cornered, I admitted that I'd sent a new message to Hank via S-Mail, one that connected Hank and Beltran.

Spider's eyes rose to the ceiling as he thought about my dumb move. "Well, he hoped that someone would uncover the trail from Hank to Jim, or he wouldn't have hidden the S-Mail login and password as

Beltran. As far as he knows, we all think he died as Jim Beltran."

I slumped back into the booth, relief flooding over me. "So I didn't expose Marcy to danger?"

Spider shook his head. "Not from Hank, anyway. Seems as if he wanted to shield her and the kids, not place them in harm's way."

"I agree," Bobbie said. "After all, he set up this elaborate scam so they could get the insurance payout. That's not the action of a man with ill intent."

Spider muttered, "I really gotta check her house out, though." Then he turned to the computer and attempted to login to S-Mail as Hank. *That User ID and/or password doesn't match our records. Please try again.* "Looks like Hank closed his S-Mail account. No way to draw him out there."

"All is not lost," I said. "The phone number and Hotmail for Jorgensen are still in use." I filled him in on my Saturday Marriott activity. "Before I try to get in touch with him, I need to consult with a legal advisor. A Family legal advisor."

"Matthews?" Spider asked. He met Bart on the Johnson case.

"Right. I want to present a hypothetical to him, see if he thinks the Philly Mob is still after Tommaso, without using his name. See if it's safe for Hank to break cover."

"Angie," Bobbie interjected, "that could land you in hot water. The Milwaukee mob is nothing compared to Philly! How do you know Bart won't take it to someone who'll insist on the whole story in a, uh, unpalatable way?"

"I can be devious, Bobbie. Bart won't catch on." *Probably.* If he did, I would go to Papa.

That thought was slightly sickening. We hadn't talked about his role in the Family since I was a small girl.

My mind trailed back to little Angie, asking Papa why the kids at school teased her about her father being in a mob. Papa took her on his lap and asked her if she knew what that meant. When the child shook her head, he explained that the Mafia was an organization, like a union, that began in Sicily to protect those for whom there was no justice. With the odor of pipe tobacco wafting around her, he said that he joined when his papa took him to a meeting. He assured the little girl that there were both good and bad men in the union, that he tried to be a good man, and that he had sworn to a code of silence—*omerta*—on all their doings, so he would never discuss it with her again. Little Angie loved and trusted her Papa.

Grown-up Angie did, too. *Papa wouldn't let anything bad happen to me.*

"Spider, Bobbie," I said, "let me think this over." I pointed at Spider. "Meanwhile, you need to get going. Time to bring the babies home."

We hugged and headed out, Spider to his family, Bobbie to a shooting lesson with Bram, and me to put this new information into perspective and develop a plan of action. You don't go unprepared to a negotiation with a Mafia mouthpiece!

Chapter 18

Every question is a hypothetical question for everyone but the person who asks it. — Dan Savage

I drove back to the office and placed a call to Bart's office Gorgon, Bertha Conti. She answered the phone in her no-nonsense tone. "Law offices of Bartholomew Matthews."

"Good afternoon, Bertha. This is Angie Bonaparte. It's been a while. How have you been?"

"Fine, Mizzz Bonaparte." The honorific sounded like a curse word.

I once corrected her when she called me 'Mrs.' You didn't correct Bertha. She neither forgave nor forgot. *Move on, Angie.* "Good to hear that you're well. I'm calling to see if you can squeeze an hour out of Bart's schedule this week. I need to engage him as a consultant on an issue that requires his particular expertise. At his standard fee, of course." Paying Bart ensured that he would be constrained under the rules of attorney-client privilege to hold the matter confidential.

"Regarding?" she asked.

This would be tricky. I didn't want to tell Bertha much, but unless I made it sound worthwhile to Bart, she would stonewall me. "In the course of an investigation, I've come across some information that might benefit Bart's major client. I'm not free to discuss it, except with him, but I'm sure he will want to hear what I have to say."

After a moment's silence, she said, "Hold please." Frank Sinatra crooned *If I Didn't Care* while I waited. Then Bertha's raspy voice returned. "His calendar is very full, but I can slot you in at one this afternoon."

Was she playing me to see if I'd decline to rush? "I'll be there," I told her in my most cheerful voice, knowing it aggravated her. Then I gathered what I would need and headed into the cold.

Milwaukee's Third Ward, once the Little Italy of the city, has undergone gentrification since its early days. Art galleries, cafes, upscale restaurants, and clubs now dot the area that was populated in the 1880s by Italian immigrants, after the Irish moved up and out. Bart's offices were in one of the old original ironwork buildings on Plankinton Avenue. I parked and entered the building.

A Family consortium owned the property and assured that it had the best in both electronic and 24/7 human security. I entered the lobby, surprised to see Mighty Mary working days. Mary juggled engineering classes, weekend nights as a bouncer and her job here. She dwarfed the security desk and its bank of monitors. "Mary," I smiled, "how are things? You graduate this spring, right?"

"Yeah, and I can't wait to get a real job with normal hours, Angie. What with school during the day and working nights, along with studying and trying to keep a relationship afloat, I'm dying. I want a life! It's actually restful to staff the daytime desk during winter break."

"Hang in," I said. "A degree from MSOE will open a lot of doors."

"That's what I'm counting on. And they better be doors that lead to an office and buckets of money. Student loan repayment is looming." She shook her head before asking, "You going up to see Bart Matthews?" When I nodded, she stepped away from the desk and gave a Vanna White gesture. "My shelf is yours."

I folded and placed my outerwear there, to protect them from the fug that permeated the law offices. Both Bart and Bertha smoked several packs a day, despite laws prohibiting the practice indoors. He did pay for a spectacular ventilation system that spewed the foul air outside. I had to give him that. Even so, I would stink when I left and tried to minimize the cleaning bills by using Mary's shelf.

As I did so, Mary called upstairs. "Mrs. Conti, Ms. Bonaparte has arrived. Shall I send her up?" Bertha was always 'Mrs.'—and forget it at your peril! Mary put the phone in its cradle and gave a nod to the old marble stairs leading to Bart's second-floor office.

Bertha looked up when I opened the door. "Ms. Bonaparte," she brayed, lit cigarette in the ashtray next to her computer mouse. Her office uniform—white blouse, dark skirt, glasses on a chain around her neck—encased a tall, big-boned German woman of almost eighty. Her Sicilian husband died young in an internecine war. The Family stepped in to provide financial support and, eventually, the job with Bart. Bertha was as dedicated to the Family and the code of *omerta* as any soldier in its service.

"Afternoon, Bertha. Can I go in?" I nodded at Bart's shut door.

"One moment." She reached for a steno pad and pen and pressed a key on a mid-century intercom. "Ms. Bonaparte to see you," she told him.

"Send her in, please," his raspy voice directed.

When she followed behind me, I considered how to eject her without future ramifications. "Hi, Bart," I said. "Thanks for seeing me on short notice. This probably won't take a full hour, but I'm happy to pay for it. One thing, though. I'd like it to be off the record. No case notes." I studiously kept my gaze on Bart and away from Bertha.

He bent forward in his reinforced chair, all three-hundred plus pounds of him, and took a drag on his cigarette. "It's a bit unconventional, but we can handle it that way. I'll stop you if it seems problematic." He glanced at Bertha. "Bill it as legal consultation, no specifics. And we won't need notes unless I buzz for you."

With a scowl, Bertha marched to Bart's desk, where she hauled open his middle desk drawer. The sudden movement caused his heavy chair to roll back. Bart's mouth gaped open as she took a marker from the drawer and methodically blacked out the entry for my visit on his blotter. Then she exited and almost-slammed the door.

"Wow, that was intense," I said.

Bart looked at me. "Most unusual, but she can be overly zealous about her duties." He shrugged. "The Family owes her, and it's not easy to find someone who's willing to accept the nature of my clientele."

I settled in a chair across from Bart's desk, my feet not quite hitting the floor. "I'm in a bit of a quandary, Bart," I said. "First, I need to confirm that this falls under the aegis of attorney-client privilege."

He nodded.

"To be totally clear, nothing that I say here can get back to anyone in the Family."

He raised an eyebrow. "What you ask may signal a conflict of interest. I can't act as your legal representative if it will impact an existing client."

"I understand that, and I wouldn't put you in that position, except … Bart, you're unique in your area of practice. There's no one else I can go to. So let me present a hypothetical situation to you. No names, no identifying information. Just speculation."

"Go on."

I hesitated for a second, just long enough to assess how much I could trust Bart. When the Belloni case heated up to the level of personal threats against me, he urged me to step away, for safety's sake. And a few months later, when I investigated a Serbian attorney's involvement in the deaths of my client's parents, Bart connected me to Spider and Bram York—again, to preserve my safety. *But will he keep my confidence if revealing what I say would benefit a mob boss?* The alternative was to drop the case and let Marcy and her little family swing in the breeze. I had to take the chance.

"A person in another area of the country has a job within the Family that puts him—and I'll use the masculine pronoun, although the person might be female, because 'he or she' gets old—it puts him in a position to know privileged information. He decides one day to leave his position without notice. He takes nothing with him and causes no harm to the Family by his leaving. He disappears. For decades."

I stopped to assess Bart's interest. The cigarette lay unheeded in the ashtray, and he leaned back, arms resting on his belly and index fingers steepled under his chin, scrutinizing me closely.

Gotcha! "Here's what I want to know. Is it safe for him to stop running and hiding? Can he build a new life, a legit life, without worry that some wise guy might make him and decide to cash in on his dead body? Can you broker a deal with the other organization to that effect, and can you do it without exposing him?" I pushed back into my chair and waited.

The question hung in the room for some time. I stayed quiet, unmoving, while he considered.

"Whether it's safe or not depends on many factors—what he knew, who he knew, if the organization is still led by the same men, if any of them feel threatened by him or hold a grudge against him. It is too complex for me to know the answer, Angie. As for whether I would broker a deal, that answer is simple. No. To do so would be tantamount to making myself the repository of information that the other organization wants. That is not wise." His eyebrows lowered. "Not for me, and not for you, Angelina. Disassociate yourself from this person and do it immediately. Burn anything that links him to you. Establish *bona fides* that will make it appear impossible for you to have been where he was … or is. This could be a matter of grave and urgent danger. Do you understand?"

Bart's intensity shook me. "There are others, innocent others, involved," I said. "Persons who were part of his hidden life. If it became known that he had an association with them, they would be in danger?"

"I believe so, to the extent that I would advise them to make a new life somewhere far away from the person who began this charade."

"Charade? It's a nightmare, Bart! A man who has never revealed any part of what he knows from his time in the Family wants nothing more than to live simply and quietly. And you say he'll be hunted and hounded until the end of his days? And his family? That is unacceptable."

"I don't say it *is* so. I simply say it *may* be so, and counsel you to act as if it is, for safety's sake." He sighed and began to cough. After popping a lozenge into his mouth, he spoke in a hoarse, angry undertone, one I'd never heard from Bart. "I fear that your thirst for justice may outweigh your caution."

Then his eyes softened. "Angelina, I consider you a friend. I say these things to you as a friend. Walk away from this person, from this situation. Tell his family to do the same and to do it without hesitation." He extended his right hand. "He may be safe in his hiding place." Then his left hand came up. "Or he may not." He gestured toward me. "Will you tell him to take that chance? Or his family?"

My anger dissipated with Bart's sincerity. "I don't know," I breathed. "But there is a legal question that you might help with. He married under an assumed name and has children. Is the marriage legal?"

Bart swung toward his computer and began to type. "According to Wisconsin law, I believe so." He printed a page and began to read. "According to code 765.23, and I quote, 'No marriage hereafter contracted shall be void by reason of any informality or irregularity of form in the application for the marriage license or in the marriage license itself, if the marriage is in other respects lawful and is consummated with the full belief on the part of the persons so married, or either of them, that they have been lawfully joined in marriage.'"

He paused and peered at me over the top of the paper. "He could call himself Long John Silver, as long he and his wife intended to legally marry. Of course, she could claim it was fraud and seek an annulment. Even the Catholic Church considers the children of an annulled marriage to be legitimate." He handed the printout to me. "If she were my client, I would advise her to file for divorce, which is much quicker than the process for annulment, and then change her name and move away. As for the man—" he shrugged— "let him keep running."

"I'll talk to his wife," I said. With a grimace, I rose, retrieved my briefcase and extended my hand. Bart hesitated, and I could see that he wanted to say something more. "What is it?" I asked.

He heaved himself up and came around the desk. Putting his left hand gently on my shoulder, he said, "If you are determined to take this to the bitter end, it occurs to me that, while a lawyer would not be the one to negotiate in such a situation, a Family boss might." His eyes held mine. "Your papa might."

I froze, aware of Bart's eyes on me. My father's two separate lives, one as a fruit-and-vegetable seller and the other as Don Pasquale, met with a click, like handcuffs locking into place.

"I, uh, don't know if I can do that."

"I'm sure it would be uncomfortable."

Marcy's face, and the faces of her children, flitted across my mind. If she wanted this resolved, I really had no choice. My personal code stared me in the face. I'd use any means necessary to find out the truth. Any means. But I never thought that could include talking Mafia business with Papa.

As he steered me to the door, Bart said, "I will make no case notes." In the outer office, he told Bertha, "Ms. Bonaparte's fee for today is one hundred dollars."

Her penciled eyebrows rose. I knew it was considerably less than normal.

"Do you have cash, Angie?" he asked.

"I stopped at an ATM on the way here," I said, removing the cash from my purse.

"Then let us consider this consultation closed. Bertha, remove any notation in your calendar and phone log."

Her eyes flashed, but she turned to the computer and began to type.

I felt a bit wobbly as I descended the marble stairs to the lobby, and it wasn't from the depression caused by the many feet that trod them before me.

Chapter 19

Just walk out of your house and never go back.
You've just committed pseudocide. — James Altucher

AAAA Auctioneers was located about midway between my office and Bart's. I placed a call from my car, hoping to find Marcy there. "Quad A. Larry." The brusque greeting no longer surprised me. Larry ran a business on a shoestring and was perpetually in a rush.

"It's Angie Bonaparte, Larry. Can I speak to Marcy?"

"Yeah, sure. Hang on."

In a few seconds, her cheerful voice came on the line. I hated the thought of what my news would mean to her, but there was no way around it. She had to know. "Marcy, I have new information concerning Hank. Can we meet at my office today?"

"Can't you just tell me?"

"There's some physical evidence that I think you should see."

"Um, okay. What time?"

"Whenever you can get there."

"I'll leave now." After a brief hesitation, she said, "Is it bad?"

"It's ... unexpected. I'll be waiting for you."

I called Bobbie, told him about Bart Matthews' take on the situation, and asked him to sit in on the meeting with Marcy. "This will be a tough one," he said. "I'm on my way." Then I texted Susan, asking to reserve the conference room and letting her know the meeting would be difficult. She responded that she was at a client's office and would plan to stay away until tomorrow.

Marcy might be roaring angry or deeply sad at the news of what her husband had done. I didn't know if there would be tears, screams, silence, or some combination of all of them. Once there, I readied the conference room by placing two chairs next to the upholstered love seat, setting a box of tissues on the side table and heating water for tea. I put the myriad of papers that led to our uncovering Hank's real identity into order and made a set of copies for Marcy. Then I sat at my desk, centering myself for what would be one of the toughest things in my PI career.

Marcy arrived first and I ushered her into the conference room. "I have water boiling, if you'd like some tea." She nodded.

As I prepared a cup in the outer office, Bobbie popped inside. I nodded toward the conference room and said, "Hi, Bobbie. Marcy's already here. Would you like some tea, too?"

"No, thanks." He hung up his coat, squared his shoulders and walked over to greet Marcy.

I locked the outer door and entered the small room, setting Marcy's teacup on the table next to the love seat. Tension vibrated between the three of us. I picked up the paperwork and sat facing her.

"Bobbie and I did some undercover snooping at the nursing facility where Jim Beltran died. Remember I told you about the aide who disappeared that night?"

She nodded.

"His name is Karl Jorgensen." I handed her a copy of the ID picture. "I'll just flat out say it, Marcy. Jorgensen was another of Hank's aliases."

"What?" Her voice rose in shock. "How could he be Jim Beltran *and* Jorgensen?"

"He couldn't. We believe that Hank posed as Beltran at the shelter, then got work at the nursing home as Jorgensen. He had a friendly relationship with a homeless man, Willie Parsons, and eventually found a way to get Willie into the facility, posing as Beltran. Willie was truly sick from end stage liver failure. When he died, the nursing home notified Hank's lawyer of Beltran's death, per the admission papers. That started the process of getting the Henry Wagner obit published."

Marcy's face had a look of stunned incomprehension. I stopped talking and waited for her to process what I told her. After a long silence, she stammered, "S-s-so Hank's not dead?"

"That's right. We think he's still using the Jorgensen persona. He doesn't know we made the connection."

"Well, damn," she whispered.

"We're pretty astounded, too."

Setting my cellphone on the table, I told her about the Marriott scheme and said, "I'd like to play the recording to see if you recognize the voice. Do you think you can handle hearing it?"

She considered for less than a second before saying, "Yes. I need to know."

The voices of Glen and the man we assumed to be Karl Jorgensen were pretty clear, considering that Karl's came from a phone's speaker. "No. And I haven't been near Milwaukee or stayed at a Marriott, and my name isn't Jefferson," he said.

Marcy gave a slight intake of breath. "Play it again, please." After the second hearing, she nodded. "That's Hank alright. Did you notice how he said the word 'near'? 'Ni-ya.' I always kidded him about that, about how he said his r's, or didn't say them, in this case. He told me his mom had family in New England, and he learned it as a kid, but I always thought he sounded more like a guy from Jersey."

Or Philly, I thought.

Marcy's hand shook a bit as she gestured to the phone. "So he's alive. He's really alive." She used a tissue to wipe away the silent tears that ran down her cheeks.

I knew this was tearing her up inside, but I couldn't figure out a way to make what followed any easier. *Give me the words, please*, I silently prayed. "Marcy, there's something else." I gave her a copy of the newspaper article about Tommaso Severson.

Her hands began to shake as she discovered the reality of the man she married. "He was … Mafia?" Marcy whispered.

Bobbie leaned forward and put a steady hand on her upper back. "It appears he was connected, in his past," he said. "That explains all the subterfuge, the different identities, the fake obit. He wanted to disappear again."

"Did something happen with the mob to make him run from me and the kids?"

"It's possible," Bobbie said, "but only Hank can explain that, I'm afraid."

She sipped her tea and sat in silence for several minutes, looking through the paperwork. Finally, she nodded and turned to me. "So what now?"

I handed her the printout from Bart Matthews. "Using a fake name doesn't negate your marriage, but since it was instituted under fraudulent circumstances, you're within your rights to ask for an annulment. Or you could file for divorce, which will be simpler and quicker. That leaves you free to pursue another marriage down the road."

"I don't want another marriage," she keened. "I want Hank. Can you find him?"

You want Hank? The man who ran out on you? The guy with the secret life that he never shared with you? Bozo didn't even treat me that badly. However, human emotion stands outside of logic. I might not understand Marcy's feelings, but I had no right to judge them. "I don't know if I can locate him, Marcy. We have some leads, but a lot will depend on whether he decides to run again. He's quite good at disappearing."

"I want you to try," she said, her voice earnest. "At the very least, I want to talk to him, to have him tell me what happened and why he left. To have him tell me if he still loves me and the kids. Then I'll know what to do."

"Are you sure? The closer you get to Hank, the worse the consequences might be," I said.

"Such as?"

"The South Philly Mob is probably still very interested in silencing Tommaso Severson. As long as he's at large, he could take incriminating evidence or information to the government or the police. That makes anyone connected to him a means to flush him out of hiding."

Marcy gasped. "They'd hurt my kids?"

"We're not sure they know about the Hank Wagner identity. The fake obituary might've been his way to stop them searching for him, assuming they did know. Maybe he simply wanted to stop running. If we try to locate him, it might make matters worse."

"And if we just let it lie?" she asked.

"Then we're betting that they haven't uncovered his life with you, and that you and the kids are safe."

"That's not a bet I want to take, Angie." Her voice quavered.

"Nor would I. So the second alternative in this admittedly miserable situation is for you to file for divorce, take the kids and disappear. There are a couple of ways for that to happen. One, you relocate. You live normal, respectable, unremarkable lives someplace else. I'm no expert on how to do it, but I bet Spider is." I paused. "The hard part is cutting ties with everyone you know. Your family, your friends. It only takes one phone call home to find you, if anyone's looking. And that's a big if."

"I could never see my mom or my sister again?" Marcy's face crumpled. "My kids wouldn't grow up with their grandma or auntie? Or their cousins?" She covered her mouth and began to weep softly.

I offered her tissues as I rose to sit next to her. Bobbie's face reflected the misery in my own heart. "I'm sorry, Marcy," I said, rubbing little circles on her back. "I'm so sorry. There is another option. If I can find Hank, and if he agrees to provide the U.S. Marshals with information about his days in the South Philly Mob, Spider thinks there's a strong possibility they'd offer him the opportunity to disappear inside the Witness Protection Program. We could negotiate the same terms for you and the kids, whether you decided to go it alone or with Hank. But you would still have to cut ties with your current life."

After an interval, Marcy straightened up and blew her nose. "So either I stay and hope they don't know about me and never find out, or I invent a new life for myself and the children. And that new life could be with the help of the government, if Hank agrees to testify against his former boss."

I nodded.

"I can't do that to my family, Angie, or my kids. There's no other way?"

Anxiety crept into my chest, where it sat like a heavy weight. "One other, but it's very speculative and it might be dangerous." I took a measured breath. "Even though I've never been involved, I've known since I was little that my papa is connected to the Milwaukee Family and, via them, to the Chicago Outfit. You understand, I'm talking about the Mafia?"

Her eyes widened and she nodded.

"I would never do anything to betray you or Hank. The only ones who know about the link between Hank and Tommaso Severson are me, Bobbie, Spider, and now you. And we can keep it that way. But I have considered approaching my papa to see if he knows of a reason for Hank's sudden departure. Maybe Hank overreacted to something all those years ago and there's no real danger. And if there is, maybe Papa would broker a deal with the South Philly Mob to promise Hank future freedom in return for his continued silence."

Marcy stood and walked to the window. After a moment, she turned. "Would that put Hank in harm's way? Or us? I mean, would your father make them aware of what you tell him?"

"Not if I ask him to keep it to himself. But if there was an increased interest in Tommaso Severson when Hank disappeared, and if Papa makes the proposal, that means that others will be aware of Hank's current existence, although not necessarily his life after leaving the east coast. I wouldn't trust the word of the South Philly Mob, but I do trust Papa. They might see it as a reasonable compromise, which would allow you to continue with your life here and Hank to start over somewhere else. Or they might not, which would mean we'd be back to establishing a new identity for you and the kids."

"I'm so out of my depth here," Marcy said. "I can't make those decisions for Hank." She took the chair that I vacated earlier. Looking from me to Bobbie, she asked, "What would you do?"

I'd felt the protection that Papa's name and position offered me, as a child and an adult. I'd never been on the other side, worrying that Don Pasquale's people might harm me. *What would I do?* If someone threatened my children, and it was someone like the mob, whom I couldn't fight, I'd run like hell.

Before I could speak, Bobbie said, "Do you feel in imminent danger, Marcy?"

"Not really. But this is so unsettling. I don't know what's real and what isn't."

"I get that," he said. "As a gay man, I've felt unsafe, without knowing if there was any real danger. But it seems to me that if Hank thought all those years ago that the family was being targeted, he wouldn't have run and left you in harm's way. I think he ran to protect you from being involved."

She nodded. "But that still doesn't negate the possibility of danger."

"No, it doesn't." He sent me a look of commiseration. "What if we take a two-pronged approach? Angie will talk with her papa to see if there was or is any heightened interest in Tommaso, without his making any overtures to the east coast mob. Then she and I can attempt to set up a meet with Hank, to inform him of what we know and find out what he plans to do. Then we three get back together and share what we know. That lets both Hank and you make informed decisions. Do you agree, Angie?"

Maybe I'd been thinking too much like a mom and it took a more dispassionate person to see the bigger picture. Once again, I was impressed with Bobbie's insight. "That's an eminently reasonable plan. I also think we should take the cautionary step of having Spider set up personal security for you and the kids until we reconvene. He knows some good people. You probably won't even realize they're there."

"Bodyguards?" Marcy dropped her head into her hands. "I never thought when I married a teacher that I'd need bodyguards." With a sigh, she looked up. "With Hank alive, there's no insurance, but I'll find a way to pay the bill."

"We'll work it out," I told her.

After Marcy left the office, Bobbie called Spider, who promised to have a security team in place at the Wagner home later that day.

I retreated to my desk in the outer office. There was a very slight tremor in my index finger as I punched in the numbers for my family home.

Chapter 20

To a father growing old nothing is dearer than a daughter. — Euripedes

The home I grew up in represented security, love and safety to me. As I parked in the driveway, I realized this was the first time I dreaded coming home, the first time I felt unsure about how Papa would receive what I had to say. Squaring my shoulders, I entered the back door landing, removed my boots, and climbed the three steps up to the kitchen.

Papa sat at the table, a cup of coffee steaming in front of him. "*Piccola*," he said, rising to hug me. "Your Aunt Terry is not home this afternoon."

"I assumed she'd be on her hospital rounds, Papa." I removed my coat, hat and gloves and placed them on a chair. "I wanted to talk to you alone." Turning to the counter, I prepared a cup of coffee with Papa's new Christmas toy, a single cup brewer.

Papa waited for me to seat myself, then gave me a grave look. "So, *mia figlia*, is there a problem? Money? Or Wukowski? Surely not your health! Of course, I will help in any way I can."

Mia figlia. My daughter. Would our relationship be the same when this conversation ended? I mentally refocused. "No, Papa, it's nothing personal. Actually, it's business."

"Your agency is in trouble?"

"The agency is fine. Business is good enough for me to be able to offer Bobbie a job, once he passes his licensing examination." I set my cup on the table. "Papa, I need advice about a business matter that involves the, uh, Mafia."

With a huff, he leaned back. "That is not something I can talk about with you, Angelina."

"I'm not asking for information about actual deeds." I paused to align my thoughts, wanting to be careful about divulging identifying information. "I'd like your input on how an east coast Family interest might react to a situation that involves one of my clients."

"I see. Go on, then, but"—he shrugged—"I may not be able to help you with that."

"Understood. First, though, I have to ask for your confidence. This is a delicate situation and I can't take the chance that my client might be impacted if what I'm going to share got out."

He straightened a bit and I saw Don Pasquale emerge from Papa's face and bearing. "I will not divulge anything you tell me, unless keeping silence will harm the organization. Then I am bound by oath to act." He waited.

I mulled over the facts of Hank's situation and could find no real threat to the Family, although they might look at it otherwise. I decided to take the chance. *Surely Papa wouldn't betray me!* "My client is a woman with three young children. Her husband ran out on her several years ago. Recently, it came to my attention that he is in hiding from another branch of the organization, not because he violated their confidence, but because he chose to leave the business. For many years, he has kept silence—*omerta*. Is he in danger now, if he resumes a normal life? Can you find out if there is still interest in locating him?"

I held my breath, waiting to see if the Don or the papa would respond.

With palms together in prayer fashion, Papa tapped his index fingers against his lips, raised his eyes to the ceiling and thought. After some moments passed, he stood and fixed himself another cup of coffee. While it brewed and I squirmed in silence, he said, "Why did he leave the organization?"

"He wasn't a soldier." Papa's left eyebrow quirked at my use of the terminology. "He held a support role, I guess you could say, but the leadership was increasingly violent. That might have led to his decision. Regardless of his reasons, he disappeared and did nothing to put his former associates in difficulty with the police or others."

Returning to the table, Papa sipped from his cup. "Why do you wish to help him? Why not let him deal with his own issues?"

"He can't come out of hiding unless he knows one of two things—that the east coast group is not interested in him any longer, or that they are willing to strike a deal, granting him immunity for his continued silence."

"When a man joins the Family, it is for life, so the first option is impossible. As for the second, there can be no deal. He already gave his word. Keeping the code of *omerta* is the least that can be expected from him. He broke faith with the organization which he swore to defend." His gaze on me was cold. "I find little to admire in this man."

Over the course of the years in which I searched for Hank, I often felt the same way, for different reasons. For Marcy's sake, though, I needed to make Papa understand. "He started a new life, in a profession that most consider admirable. He married and became a father. No one, including his wife, knew about his former associations. He was loved and respected by many. Some might say that he did the honorable thing in leaving a life of disrepute behind."

Slapping his hands down on the wooden surface, Papa leaned toward me. "I have lived a lifetime in the Mafia. Is that what you think I am, Angelina? A man of disrepute?"

The question hung there as I struggled to phrase an honest, but respectful, answer. I knew that our relationship hung in the balance. "The papa I know, the man who raised me with love and supported me in every way that matters, is a man of honor. But there's another part of your life that is hidden from me. I don't know what that part of you is like." I looked down. "I don't want to know. I just want my papa."

"It is not to your papa that you appeal. It is to Don Pasquale." Never before had I heard such hardness in his words and his tones. "Can you acknowledge that?"

Could I, for Marcy's sake, and the sakes of her children? I raised my eyes. "It's a struggle, I admit, but yes. I acknowledge that it is Don Pasquale to whom I appeal."

"Then Angelina, I honestly see no way to help, other than to advise you to leave this matter to fate." He spread his hands. "All that my approach would accomplish is to heighten their awareness of the person you seek to protect."

"Hell," I muttered under my breath. I swallowed coffee as I struggled to swallow the reality of Henry Wagner's predicament. "I feared that might be so, Papa, but I felt compelled to ask. His wife will find this very hard to accept."

"She has built a new life without him?"

"Yes, from necessity. But she still cares for him, and she struggles to determine a path forward, now that she knows he is alive. She exists in a sort of limbo."

"No honorable man would put a woman in that position."

"You're right. It's angered me ever since I began to search for him."

I pushed my chair back and stood. "Maybe he could see no other way. Maybe he did it to protect his family. I don't know." I carried my cup to the sink and rinsed it, then placed it in the dishwasher. When I turned back, Papa—not Don Pasquale—waited.

"Angelina, *piccola*, I am still your papa." He opened his arms and I rushed into them.

"Nothing can change that, *papà mio*." Extreme relief rushed over me as I realized it was the truth.

Chapter 21

I beg of you… never assume an inner or an outer pose, never a disguise.
— Gustav Mahler

The tension of the day washed over me when I arrived home and locked the door behind me. I lay down on the couch and fell asleep, waking around eight o'clock to darkness and hunger. I still hadn't gotten to the grocery store, so carrot and celery sticks dipped in crunchy peanut butter, followed by a square of Ghirardelli dark chocolate with salted caramel, constituted my supper.

With a glass of sweet white wine at my side, I settled on the couch, opened my laptop and typed up the day's notes—and what a day it was! Hank's identity as Tommaso Severson, the painful talk with Marcy, followed by anxiety-provoking discussions with Bart and Papa.

According to the plan that Bobbie advanced, my next step was to contact Hank and find out if he would meet to discuss his family's future. How should I approach him so that he wouldn't simply duck and run? If Bobbie was right, he might respond to a threat to Marcy and the kids. I set up an email message to the Jorgensen address.

Karl, Jim, Hank, Tom—I am working for Marcy, not for your former east coast associates. I have no interest in exposing you. My only concern is to keep her and the kids safe. For that, I need

your help. Respond with a place and time. The matter is urgent.
Angelina Bonaparte

An hour later, the response hit my inbox.

Holy Hill grounds, 8:00 a.m. tomorrow. No negotiating on that. Park in the lot downhill from the Stations. Text me when you arrive. I'm sure you have my phone number. The Marriott was a good dodge. Be alone or I will disappear for good and the danger to my family will be on your head.

Despite his warning, I needed backup. The mantel clock that once belonged to my mother's family showed the time as almost nine-thirty. It didn't keep entirely accurate time, but close enough. Feeling guilty, I called Spider.

"Angie, what's up?" As always, he sounded alert.

"Spider, I just set up a meeting with Hank Wagner. Tomorrow morning, eight o'clock, at Holy Hill monastery in Hubertus. I'm sending you my email and his response."

After a minute or so, he said, "No way can you go there alone. I'm calling Bram after we hang up. We'll be undetectable, I promise."

"Good, because if we scare him off, I doubt we'll get another shot."

"Meet us at the farmhouse at five. Bram and I will take a northern approach and come in from the back of the grounds, which is a little over an hour, plus time to get into position. You'll take the usual route, which is only about thirty minutes. Once you get here, I'll set you up with a wire so we can hear the discussion. One sec." After some clicks, he said, "The online schedule says there's a six o'clock mass, so there will be people at the church early. I'm assuming that's not Hank's rendezvous point, but maybe we should station Bobbie in there, also wired, just in case. I'd contact Malone, but he's out of the country." Mad Man Malone was another former Special Ops whom Spider called on to protect us during the Johnson case.

"Bobbie will be thrilled," I said, "and he's a good man to have at your back. But Spider, what about Magdalena and the children?"

"No worries. The baby nurse will be here by six. Now you call Bobbie and let me get with Bram and work out our recon. Oh, and wear a coat with large buttons. I'll conceal the micro camera in one."

Next, I called Bobbie. As I expected, he was indeed thrilled. "A wire, like in *Prince of the City*?"

"I certainly hope not, Bobbie. They're miniaturized these days, and can transmit video as well as audio." We made arrangements to meet at my condo in the morning and rang off.

Time for some online homework. The Holy Hill National Shrine of Mary, Help of Christians, a Roman Catholic monastery, graces the peak of a deposit of retreating glacial gravel in Hubertus. Set within four hundred wooded acres, its twin spires are a landmark for miles. I remembered a field trip there when I was in grade school. The big basilica was majestic, but it was the small chapel which left a lasting impression. Pilgrims would go there to petition Mary for help. In the hall outside, a wall of discarded crutches testified to their healing. Little Angie believed the miracle stories the nuns told her. Big Angie wasn't so sure.

The grounds of the church were open to the public, and many came there to hike or picnic. In mid-winter, at that hour, it would probably be deserted. There were few online pictures to help orient me to the areas outside the church, so I would have to figure it out as it unfolded.

My weather app forecasted morning temps in the teens. I laid out thermal underwear and warm clothes and prepared for bed, sure that I wouldn't sleep a wink. When the alarm sounded at three-fifteen, I woke from vaguely disturbing dreams and groaned. Bobbie would arrive in thirty minutes for coffee and the drive to Delafield.

Being of small stature, I don't generally wear clothes with oversize prints or features, but I did have a black-and-white plaid wool pea coat with two-inch fabric buttons. It wasn't my warmest outerwear, but I hoped the other under-layers would suffice. When Bobbie buzzed, I wrestled into the coat and grabbed a bright red hat and scarf Aunt Terry knit for me, recalling how another of her scarves saved my life in the Johnson case. I might need the same good luck today, I reasoned, and the color would help Bram and Spider track me.

I did a double-take at the man at the elevator, who wore a black woolen overcoat, with a Homberg covering his graying hair. "What's up with the silver fox look?" I asked Bobbie as we headed for the garage.

"Not many men my age go to church, Angie, so I decided to be a little older."

"Very Richard Gere," I said, handing him an insulated coffee cup.

On the drive to Delafield, we talked strategy. "Hank will be extremely wary," I said. "I need to convince him that my only interest is in Marcy and the kids. If he thinks I might rat him out to Philly, he'll disappear and we'll never see him again."

"Let your natural compassion come across, Ange. Not just for his family, but for him, too. After all, if it's true that he went into hiding to protect them, he did a heroic thing, right?"

I pondered that for a few seconds. "I suppose ... but I can't help thinking about how much pain it caused. It won't be easy to look at him and not see Marcy struggling to raise the kids alone."

"I get that." Bobbie glanced away as he spoke. "But we all do things that aren't honorable, when we're pushed to the limit." His voice contained a memory that caused him pain.

Honor was a prime imperative for me. That might seem odd, coming from a woman whose job entailed spying on others and even breaking the law on occasion, but I only went to those lengths to establish the truth. Rationalization? I wasn't sure. "That's a good insight, Bobbie. I'll remind myself of that." Snow started to fall, and I concentrated on the roads.

At the farmhouse, Spider stood in an open bay of his huge garage/workspace, motioning us inside. "Hank might be savvy enough to notice if your car has more snow on it than a drive from Milwaukee would warrant," he said as we approached the door to the house. "C'mon in. Magda made cinnamon bun dough last night. They're almost ready to come out of the oven. We can add the icing once they cool."

Bram York stood at the rustic wooden kitchen table, a steaming carafe poised over ceramic mugs. "Coffee for everyone?" he asked.

We nodded affirmatively and began to divest ourselves of the winter gear. When the Homburg came off, Spider grinned. "Good look, Bobbie. Nice touch." Then he donned a hot mitt, took out a tray of delicious-smelling buns and carefully placed them on a waiting open wire rack to cool. We settled at the table, looking for all the world like a small group of friends who gathered for a very early breakfast.

Bram took the lead. "I ran recon last night, after Spider called me. Getting in after the brothers closed the gates for the night was no easy task. The land is full of physical barriers, mostly deep ravines cut by the glaciers. Add the trees and snow, and it could be a huge problem. No matter what Hank says, stay on the grounds proper, Angie, so we won't lose you. Don't go into the woods."

"Got it," I said.

"You carrying?" Spider asked me.

"My nine millimeter is in my purse. I can holster it under my coat, if you think it's necessary, but Hank's MO is to run, not to fight."

"You never know what you'll do when you're backed into a corner." Spider spoke in a matter-of-fact voice.

I was sure he'd been there and knew exactly what he would do. Me? I'd never had to raise my weapon, except on the practice range. "Okay, I'll have it with me when I leave the car."

Bram laid a hand-drawn map on the table and used his finger to trace a path. "There's a big iron gate that opens from the parking lot Hank specified onto a blacktopped walk. Along the walk are huge stone grottos, spaced irregularly. The walk diverges at one point, up a long set of stairs that lead to the church itself."

I pointed to the stone structures. "Those are the outside Stations of the Cross." My mind drifted back to grade school, as we "made" the stations on Good Friday, inside Gesu church. Each stop represented one of Jesus' moments on the way to his death. I would cry to see Mary hold out her arms to her suffering son, imagining a mother's pain at seeing her child in torment. In truth, it still moved me.

"Bram and I will be in the woods behind the Stations," Spider said. "One of us will be able to see you anywhere along that lower path. I contacted a local guy who's done some work for me. Name's Tiny Tim." He handed Bobbie and me a photo. "He's short, but strong as a bull. He'll cover the upper path. We'll all be wearing snow camo." He pointed to a mostly white snowsuit, with splotches of darker color in a pattern resembling tree branches. "Let's ice those cinnamon buns and then we'll get the wire set up, Angie. Although it's not really a wire. That's a holdover from pre-chip days."

The small transmitter fit easily in one of my coat buttons, its black lens blending into the fabric. After cautioning me to be careful while putting the coat on, Bram went outside and walked down the long driveway to the street to test the reception.

Once he and Spider agreed that all was as ready as possible, Spider turned to Bobbie. "You need to arrive in time for the Mass and then hang around inside the church, watching to see if anything looks suspicious. No need for a wire. You can just leave the worship service, go to the men's room and text my cell if you spot something that worries you. We don't want to raise Hank's alert level, so Angie can't arrive that early." He handed a set of keys to Bobbie. "These are for the green SUV in the garage. The plates are fake, so don't get pulled over. It's, um, disposable, so leave it if you need to."

Bobbie's eyes sparkled at that. Then he sobered. "What should I be looking for?"

"Someone who's obviously not there for the service. Someone who does a lot of watching. Since you'll be a watcher, too, be subtle. Don't turn your head much. Move your eyes instead. Take a place in the back of the church and use the opportunity that sitting, standing and kneeling during the Mass will give you to look the congregation over. I imagine most people will be regulars who know one another, so you'll need a cover story in case they approach you."

"Hmm." Bobbie's eyes rose as he thought. "I'm a recent widower. During her illness, my wife begged me to come here to pray for her soul when she died. Even though I'm not a believer, I thought it couldn't hurt."

"That'll work," said Bram. "But remember to look like you're in mourning."

We covered the various arrival times at Holy Hill once more, then Bram and Spider suited up in their camo and headed for the garage.

From the window, we saw them pull away in a huge Ford F650, towing two snowmobiles. "Looks like they'll come in from somewhere off-road," Bobbie observed.

Our drives would be under thirty minutes each on dry pavement, but the snow was still falling. He decided to leave at five-fifteen, to arrive for the six o'clock service. I wanted to get there by seven-thirty, so would need to head out around six forty-five.

Bobbie and I each had another cup of coffee and a cinnamon bun, then Bobbie used the facilities, hugged me, assumed his older man gear and headed out. The baby nurse arrived on the dot of six. After introductions, she grabbed a cup of coffee and a cinnamon bun and walked upstairs. I heard a door open, followed by the small sounds of the infants, but resisted the urge to invade Magda's bedroom as she breastfed.

Left alone in the farmhouse kitchen, I mentally rehearsed the discussion I planned to hold with Hank. *Don't let me screw this up, Lord,* I prayed.

Chapter 22

Assassin?...that sounds so exotic...I was just a murderer.
— Richard Kuklinski

The eastern horizon barely glowed with the precursor of dawn—technically, twilight, even though the term is usually only associated with the setting sun—as I drove north. Sunrise was at seven-twenty, but the morning clouds and falling snow would make the day a dark one. Thankfully, the roads weren't slick and the wipers were keeping up nicely with the windshield accumulation.

Per Hank's instructions, I pulled into the parking area that led to the outside Stations of the Cross. My cellphone showed it was 7:40. I didn't want to spook Hank, so I sat in the car until the digital display changed to 8:00 and texted Hank: *Here*

He replied: *Station 6*

Even though Spider assured me that he and his team would have me in their sights at all times, I sent him Hank's message and emerged from the car, shivering in the cold temperatures and biting wind. After locking my purse in the trunk, I pulled my knit hat down over my ears and raised my coat collar, then headed toward the tall stone arch that led to the path of the Stations. A sign warned that the walking paths were not maintained in the winter, but only two or three inches of snow lay on the ground. Too cold to melt underfoot from pressure, it squeaked under my boots.

No one was in sight as I ambled along, a devoted member of the faithful, stopping at each Station to bow my head and clasp my hands as an ardent litany ran through my mind: *Help me do the right thing; keep us safe.*

The path rose steadily uphill. When I arrived at the sixth Station, I bent over and put my hands on my knees, as if I needed to catch my breath after the steep climb. I surreptitiously swiveled my head. No Hank.

As I straightened up, there was a squeak-crunch and a brown-robed figure appeared from the steps leading up to the basilica. The peaked hood of the robe, pulled low over his forehead, hid his face. Except for the hands settled inside the wide sleeves of the robe, the walker called to mind the painting of St. Francis contemplating a skull.

At first, I took the walker for one of the Carmelite friars of the shrine, but then noticed that he wore snow boots. Discalced—shoeless or sandaled—Carmelites lived and worked at Holy Hill. *Were they allowed to wear boots?* I waited, my hand on the weapon in my outer pocket.

He stopped about six feet from me.

"Hank?" I would look a fool if this was really one of the brothers.

His head dipped. "Ms. Bonaparte." With a nod, he signaled me to walk in the direction opposite the parking lot entry.

The wide pathway allowed for several feet between us, enough to get off a shot if I needed to. "You've been hiding here since you left Stevens Point?" I asked.

"The brothers have a retreat house. I told them I was in a life crisis and seeking spiritual direction and guidance." The hood turned slightly toward me. "Not a lie, either. Now tell me why you're pursuing me."

Despite the softness of his tone, I heard him clearly in the cold stillness. "Marcy and your children need to determine the course their lives will take. A lot of that depends on you." I paused to consider how my actions seemed to him. "I realize that I coerced you into meeting me and that you have no reason to trust me. But for the last five years, I've been in touch with your wife and learned about your kids. I probably know them better than you do at this point. They're the reason I'm here."

Hank looked down and away. "That hurts." Then he turned back to me. "But I'm glad they have someone on their side."

"I'm not here to do you harm," I said, pulling my hand far enough from my coat pocket to show him the pistol grip. "If I wanted you dead, I could have shot you any place along this path and rolled your body down the ravine behind the Stations."

He slowly withdrew his right hand from the left sleeve of his robe. "Same here." The butt of a gun rested in his grip. "Colt M1911A1. A favorite of my former colleagues. I never owned one before I, shall I say, distanced myself from them. But I learned how to use it."

I had no wish to die here, holy or not. I looked out over the beautiful serenity of the Hill. *Spider and Bram are out there*, I told myself. *They've got your back.*

"Ever shot someone?" I asked Hank.

"Nope. You?"

I shook my head and took my empty hand from my coat pocket. "There's a bench up ahead. Can we sit and talk?"

The cold of the cement penetrated my clothes in seconds. Hank seemed to be wearing less than I did, but he showed no signs of being chilly. He removed his gun hand from the robe and pushed the hood back slightly, so that I could see his eyes. "Tell me about my kids." His voice held a pleading tone.

"Marjorie's in kindergarten now. Marcy calls her a little dynamo, always on the move. Susie's an artist." I smiled, remembering the watercolors on Marcy's fridge. "And young Henry appears to have the makings of a future scientist. Marcy's done well, Hank, raising them alone. It hasn't been easy."

"I'm sure." His words faded.

"Tell me how you came to be Henry Wagner."

It took a few breaths before he continued. "There was a guy I helped out of a jam, back when I was keeping the books for the Family. Dumb schmuck helped himself to money he was supposed to launder through his printing business. He needed the cash to finance an operation for his little girl, something experimental. No insurance. Would've been a dead man if I hadn't shuffled some funds around to cover him. He also used his business to make fake IDs and other documents for the mob. But he wasn't 'our friend,' he wasn't in the organization, you know?"

I nodded, recalling that an introduction as 'my friend Joe' meant that Joe was an outsider. 'Our friend Joe' identified Joe as someone in the Family.

Hank's face shifted subtly, with a look of both fear and torment passing over it. "After Merlino took over, everything changed. I had to get out. So I went to the guy. He owed me big time, so he made me new ID, even a teaching certificate from some school that burned down with all its records lost. And I made a new life for myself in Wisconsin. Got certified to teach. Met Marcy. Then the kids came along. It was perfect, Angie. All I ever wanted."

"So why the sudden disappearance, after all the years of normal life?"

"Damnedest thing. I left school on my lunch hour, to get a sandwich at a nearby deli. Every nightmare from the prior fourteen years stood at the counter. Two wise guys from the South Philly Mob. One of them was facing the window. I didn't know if he saw me, but I couldn't take the chance. A bus pulled up across the street and I got on it. I closed out the bank accounts, bought the insurance policy and a beater, and drove north."

He paused for a moment. "The car died in Eau Claire. I laid low there while it was in the shop. Once I stopped being so scared that every noise made me jump, I figured it was as good a place as any to hide. So I worked as a freelance bookkeeper for small businesses. Pizza joints, dry cleaners, that kinda thing. Nothing with criminal possibilities. No taverns, no places that sold lottery tickets."

"It sounds like an okay life," I said. "How'd you end up in Stevens Point?"

He took a ragged breath. "Thinking about it still makes me sweat. After a couple years, I figured it was past time to make a real life, so I worked out a plan for my death. Moved to the Point, spent a year there as Beltran, used the shelter as cover while I searched for a down-and-outer to die in my name."

"Willie," I said. "You didn't help him along, did you?"

"Nah, nevah!" His Philly origins surfaced in the outrage. "He had a good end, Angie. I didn't hasten it, honest." He sighed. "Thought I was real clever, but then you came along."

"What are the odds you were spotted, all those years ago?" I asked. "They might not know your Wagner identity." He'd wanted to know about his children. *Maybe he still cares.* I decided to push. "Marcy still loves you, Hank. She needs to get out of the limbo she's in, married to a ghost. She wants to talk to you. Maybe you two can work things out. You could join the Witness Protection Program and disappear for good. Marcy and the kids could be part of that package."

"No!" It was a quiet shout. "It's not worth the potential danger to Marcy and the kids. I know too much." He calmed and faced me. "I'd give my right hand for that, but it's just a pipe dream. You think I'da lived like I did for the last five years if I thought there was a chance? The government won't protect me unless I testify. I wouldn't make it to a courtroom alive. Either the Mob would get to me in person, or they'd use my family as a negotiation tool."

I placed my red-gloved hand on his brown sleeve. "Will you at least talk to her?" I pulled my cellphone from my pants pocket. "I'll place the call, so it won't be traced to you." I waited.

"Yeah," he said, "I'd like that, to at least tell her good-bye."

"Good." I pulled up my Contacts list.

From the woods, a sound like a tree branch breaking resounded. Our heads snapped up. When I looked back to Hank, a dark stain blossomed at the front of the brown monk's robe. He slowly fell forward onto the snowy path.

My mind took a second to realize that he'd been shot. "Spider, Bram," I shouted, "Hank's down. Gunshot to the chest." Fear screamed at me to run and hide, but I couldn't leave him there, alone, as his life leaked away. I pulled him into the lee of the grotto and knelt over him, pressing my red gloves to the spreading wetness on his robe. "Hank, stay with me. Help's on the way."

He stared at me for a moment and I leaned down to hear him say, "Love." Then his eyes rolled back.

"I'll tell them, Hank," I whispered. I pressed two fingers to his carotid and knew he was gone.

A buzzing sound from the woods refocused my attention as I crouched, far from both the steps to the church's upper grounds and the lot where my CRX was parked. "I know he did some bad things, God, but he was a good man at heart. Take him home," I prayed aloud. "And get me, Bram, Spider and Bobbie out of here safe."

Chapter 23

I'm not helpless. Although help may come, I'm my own rescuer.
— Melody Beattie

The stone grotto rose, sturdy and tall, behind me. I sprinted for its chest-high wrought iron fence and levered myself up and over, into the confines of the half-domed grotto and the face of a suffering Jesus being condemned to death. *Don't punch my ticket yet,* I prayed, climbing behind the statues, where I gazed on the back of Jesus' robe.

The buzzing sounded louder. I pulled the 9mm Sig Sauer from my pocket and unfastened the safety. "Spider, Bram, I sure hope you can hear me. Hank's dead. The shooter's somewhere in the woods to the east of the grottos. I'm hunkered down in Station 1, at the opposite end of the path from the parking lot." With the substantial rock surrounding me, I couldn't judge the direction of the now-louder sound. "I hope it's one of you guys coming in, and not the shooter," I said. "My gun is at the ready, so don't surprise me."

"It's Spider, Angie. Hold your fire." A body in white camouflage hung from the top of the grotto and dropped down into the snow. "You okay?" Spider asked as he extracted a rifle from a sling around his back.

"Thank God," I whispered. "Yeah, I'm okay. What the hell is going on here?"

"Looks like someone didn't want Hank to consider his choices. We can't worry about that now. Tiny Tim's got Bobbie. We're going to exfiltrate while Bram provides cover."

Exfiltrate? Must be Special Ops jargon.

"The sled's parked in the lee of the wall. I'll lever you up and over. Then I'll follow."

"You came in on a sled?" I struggled to process the data.

Spider crept to each of the side walls of the grotto, positioned the rifle, and darted his head out. "Snowmobile," he explained as he canvassed the area, then turned back and looked me over. "You'll need to ditch the red hat and gloves." He pushed back the hood of his thermal suit and pulled off a knit hat, colored to match the snow camouflage he wore. "Here," he said. "Not sure what to do about the gloves. I'll need to keep my hands warm enough to steer."

I reached inside my coat sleeves for the arms of the white thermal shirt I wore under a sweater. Spider yanked them down further and tied the end of each sleeve. If we got out of this alive, I swore to stop complaining about the problem of getting appropriately sized tops.

"Ready?" Spider asked.

No time to dither, I thought. "Let's do it."

Spider lifted his left shoulder and spoke into it. "Package is on the way, Bram." Then he slid the rifle back into its sheath and said, "Up you go."

My foot barely touched his cupped hands before I was hurtled over the stones and into the snow on the other side, where the sled idled.

A second later, Spider vaulted over, landed on his feet near me, and grabbed my hands to hoist me up and haul me to the snowmobile, using his body as cover. "Get on behind me and hold on tight," he shouted, pushing the rifle into a leather scabbard attached to the sled.

He gunned the motor and we tore off behind the Stations,

negotiating an uphill path around tree trunks and big rocks. It felt like a slalom course of speed bumps as my butt bounced up and down. I would be sore tomorrow—if there was a tomorrow.

"Heading down," he called out.

We dropped and bounced along, going airborne and then settling on land again, until we reached the bottom of the ravine. Between two walls of rock, the engine sounds reverberated around us and made me wish I were wearing earmuffs. I peeked around Spider's bulk. A tortuous path, riddled with large stones, lay before us, but Spider maneuvered with skill. Down here, the wind was negligible—a blessing, since my hands and feet were sending out pain signals.

I couldn't judge how long it took until the sled glided to a stop with the engine still idling. Spider turned his head to me. "Let's take a stretch while I assess the situation."

As I slowly levered myself up, the same funny little grunting noise my papa makes when he gets up from a chair escaped from my mouth. The ground rocked a bit under my boots.

With a ripping sound, Spider opened a Velcroed saddlebag. "Hand warmers." He pressed two small rectangles into my thermal-covered palms. "I didn't want you clutching them instead of me on that ride. More packages in there"—he pointed—"if you need some for your feet." The rifle came out of its scabbard and Spider moved to the end of the ravine's shelter, peering out and covering with the weapon, as he had in the grotto. I hadn't noticed the binoculars in their white case, until he put them to his eyes and surveyed the area.

From a pocket in his snowsuit, Spider extracted a cellphone. "Bram, we're at the boundary. Assessment?" After listening, he said, "Yeah, Angie's holding up fine. She's a tough little cookie." He grinned at me. "Okay, Cap, we're on the way."

The cellphone, binoculars and rifle went back into their various holding places. "Angie, the truck's parked about a mile away. We have to travel through the woods again, but it won't take long. Bram's confident the shooter's long gone, but he has the area under surveillance. Ready?"

This time, I wanted to say, *No, I'm not ready. I'm tired and sore and scared.* But I told myself to suck it up and get on the sled. Somewhere in the not-too-distant future, a bathroom and coffee awaited me.

***

Bram met us with the truck on Wisconsin Highway 67. I climbed up into the cab, with the help of Spider's automated Nerf bar and granny handle—his words, not mine—and huddled over the heater vent, waiting for the men to load the snowmobile for towing. While Spider drove north, Bram called Tiny Tim and put him on speaker.

"How're things on your side?" Bram asked.

"Ducky," came a tenor voice. "We headed out in my vehicle. Your passenger's car is still back there. Rendezvous as planned?"

"Affirmative."

We continued west and then south, heading for I-94. After about forty minutes, Bram turned onto a gravel road that led to an old collapsed barn near Johnson Creek. The doors of a Dodge Ram opened, and Bobbie and a small man jumped out. Bobbie ran over and enveloped me in a hug. "Girlfriend, you have got to stop making my heart cry for mercy," he said.

"Agreed," I mumbled into his chest.

Spider made introductions. "Angie, this is Tim Gunther. Tim, Angie Bonaparte. More proof that small can be damn tough."

Tiny Tim grinned and shook my hand. "Mighty glad to see you in one piece, ma'am."

His Texas twang rescued him from my ire at being called ma'am. "I'm mighty glad to be in one piece, Tim."

His arm around my shoulders, Bobbie steered me to Tim's truck. "We stopped up the road for coffee," he said, extracting two cardboard carriers, each holding four large McDonald's cups. "It's still too hot to drink."

"No such thing," I said, peeling back the plastic tab on the cover. Nevertheless, I used caution in taking the first sip.

Spider, Bram and Tim exchanged long glances. Bram spoke. "The body may not be discovered quickly, but we can't count on that. Was it out in the open?"

It? My mind knew that the lifeless shell next to the grotto was no longer Hank, but my heart protested. Still, it hurt me to refer to Hank's body that way. No time for sentiment now, though. We had to plan quickly. "He's lying in the lee of the station at the opposite end of the path from the parking lot."

Tim noted, "I didn't see any commotion from the immediate area, so possibly no one heard anything. Is the path clear down below?"

"Clear?"

Bobbie interrupted gently. "Is there blood on the path, Angie?"

"Some, I think. Once I hauled him to the edge of the grotto, I didn't look back. To be honest, he didn't bleed much."

"The continued snowfall could work in our favor then," said Tim. "I called a guy I know to drive my car out."

I drew in a sharp breath. "My CRX is still in the lower lot, with my purse locked in the trunk. Looks like I should expect a visit from the police."

"I decided it was better to leave it there, Angie." Bram's voice held a degree of foreboding. "Somebody knew where to find Hank, and it seemed to me that the only way that could be possible is if they were following your lead."

Oh, hell. My heart sank. "You think I had a tail."

"No, I think you have a hidden GPS device somewhere on the vehicle." He took a drink of coffee. "Unless there's a possibility of a leak. Who knew about the east coast connection?"

"Marcy, of course, but she just found out about it yesterday. She still loves the guy. I can't believe she'd share the information. But there's another possibility." I looked down into the depths of my coffee cup. "Or maybe two. I wanted to explore the option of reconciliation, to see if Hank could resume a normal life. So I paid a call on Bart Matthews, being careful to phrase the idea in strictly theoretical terms, with no details that would expose Hank. Bart's rather emphatic advice was to walk away as fast as I could, but he also suggested that if I found that impossible, maybe my dad would broker a meeting."

Tim gave a little start.

"My father has Family connections," I told him. "But he was unwilling. That's when I decided to contact Hank, to suggest the Witness Protection Program. He refused, saying that it couldn't guarantee his safety and might expose Marcy and the kids to danger." My hand shook slightly when I raised the cup. "Theoretically, Bart or my father could have taken the story to the South Philly Mob."

The idea sickened me, but I had to be realistic. Somehow, the word got out. Somebody knew about my connection to Hank and used it to get to him. I needed to close the circle, for the sake of Marcy and the kids.

Chapter 24

Three things cannot long be hidden: the sun, the moon, and the truth.
— Confucius

We agreed that the fewer of us involved with the police, the better. Tiny Tim and Bobbie left, while Bram and Spider plotted our next moves. We would drop Spider at the farmhouse, where Bram would pick up his own vehicle and then take me back to my condo. There, I would call the police, using shock as a reason for the delayed report. Not wanting my home invaded by cops, especially if one of them turned out to be Wukowski, I said, "Let's go to my office, Bram. I'll feel more in control there, and it will give me a chance to go through my files and remove anything I don't want the police to see."

"Your drive downtown will give me time to access any security cameras in the vicinity of Holy Hill and delete whatever might involve me, Tim or Bobbie," Spider said.

By now, I was used to Spider's superhero computer skills. His statement didn't faze me.

***

Bram used his special ops skills to unlock my office door. Inside, I flung my jacket on the coat tree, told Bram, "Back in a minute," and rushed down the hallway to the bathroom. I caught sight of myself in the mirror over the sink and grimaced. It wouldn't do to fix myself up, though. The police would expect a woman in a state of disrepair, given the circumstances. I wet my fingers and ran them through my hair to reinstate the spikes a bit, and went back to the office.

Bram had picked the locks on my credenza and desk, and was perusing the papers in the file marked 'Wagner, Marcy.' "I figured your inside keys were still in the trunk of the car, too," he said.

"Right. Uh, thanks?"

He gave a slight grin. "Not much in here that's current. Nothing at all on the nursing home raid. I think it's okay to make the call. But first, how much do you want to tell the police?"

That gave me pause. "They'll make the connection to Severson through fingerprints, same as Spider, right?"

"No doubt. But they won't connect to the Stevens Point identities unless you provide them. Is that what you want?"

"It seems … unnecessary, somehow. None of that matters. It was just Hank's way of hiding out. I'm the one who put him into the path of danger. Before that, he was safe."

"You're probably right. But I learned the hard way that dwelling on what you did in good conscience is counterproductive. For now, you need to decide what to say about your involvement."

"Okay," I said, "here's what I'm thinking. I'll tell them about my search for Hank, and how I found the obit online. I'll explain that I talked to the lawyer who drafted the will and paid for the obituary and say that he had Hank's email address." I pictured Jamieson. "If they contact the lawyer in the Point, he'll probably tell them about the shelter. But I'll make no mention of it. I'll simply tell them that I emailed Hank and he responded. We agreed to meet at Holy Hill, where he told me about his connections to the Philly Mob and asked me to keep a lid on his whereabouts and protect Marcy and his kids. Before I could object, he was dead." I looked at Spider. "What do you think?"

"It works, but just barely. Let's hope they don't decide to get a warrant for your computer, or talk to the attorney, since he'd have to divulge that you knew about Hank's Beltran identity. No reason why they should, though, once they learn about his life in the Mafia."

"I need to ask Marcy if she'll pretend ignorance." I sighed. "Which means I have to tell her that Hank is dead and the police will be there to talk to her. Damn, I hate to do this on the phone." The image of Hank lying on the path, with blood on his robe, sprang up.

Bram said, "Use this phone. It won't trace back to you or me."

Marcy answered quickly. "Yes?"

"It's Angie, Marcy. I have some terrible news to share. I wouldn't do it this way, but the police will be at my office soon and then they'll come to see you." I took a deep breath. "I met with Hank this morning. There's a lot I need to tell you personally, but the reason I'm calling now is that … God, I don't know how to say this except to just do it. Marcy, Hank was shot and killed while we were talking."

She keened a low "Nooo."

"I'm pretty sure it was his friends in Philly, the ones we talked about yesterday."

"Omigod. I'm getting the kids and leaving now."

"No need to panic. I don't think you're in any danger. They eliminated the threat and they may not even know you exist."

Bram broke in. "I'll call Tiny Tim for protection detail."

"Marcy," I said, "Spider's associate Bram is sending an operative over to watch your house. You probably won't know he's there. Do you feel okay sitting tight until you talk to the police?"

"Are you really sure it's okay."

"I wouldn't leave you in a dangerous situation," I assured her. "There's something else I need you to do. When the cops show up, can you play dumb about Hank's past connection? They'll discover it like we did, based on his fingerprints, but I'd rather they didn't realize right away."

With a little gulp, she said, "I see. So when they get here, I'll let them tell me he's dead and pretend I have no idea why." She paused. "If it will protect my kids and me, I can do it."

"As soon as the police take my statement and leave, I'll drive over to your house. And Marcy, thanks. This will keep me out of hot water, too, although that's not why I'm asking."

"Come as soon as you can," she said.

I ended the call and handed Bram what I assumed was his burner phone. "I'll call 9-1-1 from my office line," I said.

He nodded. "Men's room down the hall?"

"To the right," I told him. "But before you take the walk, are you sure you want me to involve you in this?"

He shrugged. "Your car's at Holy Hill and you're here. Somebody picked you up. Might as well be me." With that, he left.

Fingers a little shaky, I lifted the handset and dialed.

"Nine-one-one, what is your emergency?"

"I just left Holy Hill. There's a dead body on the path of the Stations of the Cross, below the church. Behind the grotto for the first station. A man. He was shot."

"Are you in danger?"

"No, I left the area with a friend. We're at my office in Milwaukee." I gave her the address as Bram returned and settled into my client chair.

"Your name?" the woman's voice asked.

"Angelina Bonaparte." I spelled it and confirmed my phone number.

"Are you certain the man is dead?"

"Yes."

"I'm notifying the Lisbon police. They're closest to the scene. Please stay at your location. Someone will be there shortly."

I disconnected and turned to Bram. "I should probably call Wukowski."

"Did you tell him about Hank? About the case, that is?"

"No. It wasn't police business then."

I quickly placed my 9MM in the desk drawer. Although it hadn't been fired, I didn't want to explain why I had it with me when I went to meet Hank.

Bram took what looked like a folding knife from his pants pocket. Rather than a blade, it opened to reveal a set of picklocks, which he used to re-lock the desk and credenza. "No reason for the cops to think you secreted anything, right?"

I nodded, and we waited for the MPD.

Chapter 25

If intimidation is your game plan, I hope you have a better one.
— Colin Kaepernick

In under five minutes, a siren sounded in the street below, followed by heavy footsteps in the hallway. The office door burst open and Wukowski rushed inside and stopped. "Jesus, Angie, you okay?"

"Other than being a bit shaken, yes." I gestured to my visitor chair. "You remember Bram York, from the Johnson case. I called him after the shooting and he, uh, exfiltrated me."

"Thanks for that," Wukowski said to Bram. Then he huffed out a breath. "Look, I was the only guy in the bullpen when the call came in. The captain sent me with very specific orders. I'll escort you downtown to make a statement. No discussion about the case before you get there." His hands clenched. "I get the feeling they don't trust me to be impartial. It burns me." With a look to Bram, he said, "I'd appreciate you coming along, too. It'll save time if we get your statement right away."

"I can do that," Bram said.

I reset the alarm panel and used the keypad to lock up. We all trooped downstairs and Bram and I followed Wukowski to police headquarters and homicide, where the captain dismissed Wukowski and put me and Bram in separate interrogation rooms.

It was forty-five minutes before the door opened, admitting a medium height overweight man, who wore a genial smile. "So, I finally get ta meet ya." The south side speech pattern came through as he stuck out a beefy hand. "Art Penske. We spoke last year on tha phone."

"I remember," I said as my hand disappeared into his. "You were very kind about keeping me updated on the Johnson case when Wukowski brought in the perp and wasn't able to break away and call me."

"Yeah. About that ..." With a grunt, he dropped into a chair on the opposite side of the table. "It wasn't exackly like that. See, the brass din't want Ted talkin' to ya, 'cause of your dad's situation." He looked me in the eyes. "I gotta be honest, it's the same thing now, only worse, what with ya bein' a couple an' all. Captain's 'bout to blow up, he's so red in the face. Seems the dead guy had the same connections as your old man. You know about that?"

"He told me when we met this morning." Before Penske could continue, I raised a palm. "Are you saying that Wukowski is in hot water because of me?"

"Angie, ya gotta understand, a cop with connections to the mob, well, he's under a lot of scrutiny. Internal Affairs, extra supervision, stuff like that."

Well, hell. "I didn't know," I told Penske. "Wukowski never mentioned it." *And he damned well should have.*

"Don't surprise me none. Everybody knows he's sweet on ya. Never saw him like that, even when he was married." He placed a small device on the table. "Okay if I tape this?"

"Yes, but I reserve the right to have it turned off."

"Gotcha." After the usual statement of date, time, location and persons, Art said, "Ms. Bonaparte, please tell me what happened this morning at Holy Hill, to the best of your recollection. Don't leave out any details, even if they seem irrelevant."

I raised a brow at his unexpectedly formal speech.

He gave me a go ahead motion of his hand.

"The deceased was a man I'd been trying to locate for almost six years, after he disappeared from work one day. His wife hired me when the Greenfield police gave up on the search. It wasn't an active locate at this point, but I thought it would be good training for my intern, Bobbie Russell. In January, we were pretty shocked when Bobbie found an online obituary for Henry James Wagner in the *Stevens Point Journal.*"

"Mr. Wagner's obituary was posted before his death?"

"That's right." I paused. "Detective Penske, this may be irregular, but why don't I tell you what I know and you can take it from there?"

"Yeah. I mean, right. That's sounds like a good way to proceed."

I laid out the events prior to today, omitting any mention of the shelter or the nursing home. "So I drove to Holy Hill to meet with Hank and get a decision from him about whether he wanted to reconcile with his wife and kids or have her file for divorce. That's when he told me about his connections to the South Philly Mob." I stopped and decided it would do no harm to get this on the record. "My father is entirely outside the scope of that organization." It came out a little strident.

Penske nodded. "I see. So when Mr. Wagner told you he was actually Tommaso Severson, a former accountant for that branch of organized crime, you were surprised." His look dared me to lie.

"I was very surprised," I said with a direct stare.

The door to the interview room banged against the back wall and

Wukowski's superior, Captain Charles-don't-call-me-Chuck Horton, stormed in. He had a reputation as a man more interested in making assistant chief than in supporting his officers and detectives. "That's bull and you know it," he shouted at me. "You've been withholding information about a wanted criminal, Ms. Bonaparte." He deliberately slurred my surname.

So the good captain had been supervising the interview through the one-way glass that dominated the end wall of the room. "Was Mr. Severson wanted, Captain Horton?" I asked with a deliberate look of wide-eyed innocence.

"Turn off the recorder, Penske," he said.

"Yes, that's a good idea," I said. "I'm willing to give you a statement, but I'm not a criminal and I won't allow you to subject me to intimidation tactics." I rose. "My attorney will contact you, Detective Penske, and let you know when he and I are available to finish this."

"You're not leaving," Horton growled.

"I believe that as a witness to a crime, I am entitled to certain rights under Wisconsin chapter 950. Are you arresting me?" When he didn't answer, I said, "My attorney will be in touch," and walked out. Wukowski sat at his desk, within earshot of the interrogation room and Horton's antics. He raised a brow as I passed by. I surreptitiously waggled the fingers of my left hand at him and exited.

Bram waited on a bench in the outer hallway. "Let's go," he said, and put his hand under my elbow to guide me to the elevator.

"I'm okay, Bram," I told him. "Not shaken, barely stirred."

He smiled. "I heard most of it. That little prick needed to be taken down a notch or eight. Good for you, Angie." The elevator arrived and we stepped in. "The desk sergeant says your vehicle will be in the police garage for a couple of days, so you'll need a rental. Don't even think about driving the Miata in this weather." His tone was quiet, but firm.

Alpha men can be such a pain, I thought. "I'll call a rental agency. But I need my purse. It's got my keys, the card for the condo garage, my ID and credit cards, and my favorite lipstick." I saw his lips tighten as he suppressed a smile. "Laugh if you want, but I don't know the code on the tube, so I can't even be sure I'm getting the same color at the store."

"I wouldn't dream of laughing," he said. "Even an inveterate bachelor like me knows better." With a ding, the elevator doors slid open and we exited. "Let's check at the desk."

I asked to see the police record of my impounded property from the murder site. "I understand it's a matter of public record," I added when the sergeant hesitated.

Bram and I retreated to a corner and looked over the items on the list. It all seemed innocuous. "I'm going to call Penske and see if he can get some of this released to me now." Bram raised a brow. "Yes," I said, "including my lipstick."

In ten minutes, Penske met us in the lobby of police headquarters, a plastic bag and papers in hand. "Hey, Angie, sorry about the ruckus upstairs. Horton can be a real a-hole." He extended the bag to me. "We can release the keys, 'cept for the car keys. The credit cards an' your ID are in the bag, too. No lipstick. The techs say it could be concealing somethin'. But I copied the number on the bottom of the tube for ya, like ya asked. An' I brought your sunglasses. If you'll just sign for the stuff, it's all yours."

I checked the bag against the list and signed. "Art, is Wukowski in hot water over this?"

"Nah, no more than usual. Horton's been ridin' him for results on the bike trail murders, which got nothin' to do with ya. Not to worry.

Ted's the best an' Horton knows it. Jerk just likes to flex his teeny muscles. Have your legal beagle call me directly." He handed me his card. "I'll fix the statement for when Horton's out on one of his long lunches with some dickhead politician."

"Thanks, Art. I won't forget it."

We all shook hands and Bram and I decamped to his car.

"Where to?" he asked.

"I want to go back to the office. I'll call for a car there, then contact Bart Matthews before I head over to Marcy's house." With a glance at my phone, I said, "Only two-thirty. What a day!"

Chapter 26

Life is like an onion. You peel it off one layer at a time, and sometimes you weep. — Carl Sandburg

Bram insisted on walking me to the office door and checking the premises before he left. I arranged for a 4-wheel drive Ford Escape to be delivered in an hour. Before calling Bart, I group-texted Bobbie and Spider. *All OK with U and Tim?*

The reply from Bobbie was instant. *All fine. What about U? Still at MPD?*

No. Capt Horton got on my case. I left. I'm calling Bart next. Meet later?

U bet

Spider's reply came after fifteen minutes. *All good here. Come to the farmhouse when you're free. Meet the twins and talk.*

The thought of holding the babies made me smile for the first time that day. *I'll bring the meal,* I texted back.

Lifesaver, was his response.

I placed the call to Bart. Bertha barely had time to start her raspy greeting before I interrupted. "I don't want to be rude, but this is Angie Bonaparte and I have an emergency that involves the police. I need to talk to Bart right away."

"What kind of emergency, Ms. Bonaparte?"

"The kind that can get my butt thrown in a cell. Get him on the line. Please."

"Hold."

A couple of beats later, I heard Bart cough. "What's up with you and the police, Angie?"

"The hypothetical man we talked about? He was shot dead at a meeting with me this morning. The cops are playing hardball." I heard a gasp and it didn't sound like Bart. "Bertha, are you still on the line?"

"My apologies," she said. "I wanted to be sure I didn't drop the call when I transferred." With a click, her end disconnected.

"She's getting weirder every time I call," I told Bart.

"Forget Bertha. What went down today?"

With Hank dead, I felt free to give Bart the details of the Severson identity. I didn't disclose the Beltran or Jorgensen links, though, since I wasn't entirely sure I wanted to hire Bart and could only count on his silence if he represented me.

As I played out the details of the Holy Hill encounter, Bart lit up and sucked in some smoke. After going over the Horton debacle, I took a breath. "So I need legal representation, in case this jerk tries to ramrod me again."

"I'll be happy to act on your behalf, Angie."

"That's the thing," I said. "You're the only defense lawyer I know, and I'd trust you in any other circumstances. Forgive me, but I have to be honest. Somebody likely followed me to Holy Hill by putting a GPS tracker on my vehicle. Only three people knew what I was working on: you, Papa and Hank's wife, Marcy. I doubt that Marcy would know how to hire an assassin." The tension of waiting for Bart's response tightened my gut and a headache started in my right temple. I kept silent, waiting for him to make the next move.

The seconds crept along in agonizing silence before he spoke. "I would ordinarily be very offended, Angie, but I see your dilemma. I can only assure you that I have said and done nothing concerning the matter. Nothing. However, if you have pen and paper, I'll give you a name. She has no Family connections, so you'll have to educate her about the situation. Still, she's very good."

I heard the sincerity in his voice and recalled the other two cases we worked together. At no time during the Belloni or Johnson cases did I doubt his abilities or his trustworthiness. Every time I peeled away a layer of the Wagner case, there'd been another layer to expose, to the point where I was doubting myself and those who'd always supported me.

My suspicions died away. The breath I'd been holding whooshed out. "Bart, don't bother. I can't believe it was you. And I'm damn sure that Papa wouldn't put me in the middle of Hank and the South Philly mob. I've been working the angles on this too long." I grabbed my coat and pulled out Penske's card. "Art Penske gave me his direct number. Call him to schedule a time for my statement and let me know. When my rental car arrives, I'm going to see Marcy. And once this case is wrapped up, I'm booking a flight to a beach somewhere and have the cabana boy bring me a drink every two hours, until this mess stops consuming me."

"Good plan," he said. "I'll get back to you."

***

After filling out the paperwork for the rental agency, I took a moment to text Wukowski. *Will I see you tonight? Need to talk.*

Sorry, not tonight. Can I come over in the morning, around 9:00?

Not tonight? After the blow-up with Horton, I expected he would be more concerned. Must be the bike trail case, I reasoned, hoping this meant there was a breakthrough. *Tomorrow*, I texted him.

It was time to face the hardest item left on my crisis list. I called Marcy.

"The kids are with my mom," she told me. "I didn't want them here when the police arrived."

"Good idea," I said. "I'll be there in twenty minutes."

***

Marcy opened the door before I could knock. Her eyes were red, but she didn't look ready to break down. "Come in and tell me about Hank," she said, pointing to a chair and settling herself on the couch. "The police left a little while ago."

Horton's image rose in my mind. "I hope they were polite."

"Oh, sure. It wasn't hard to play the part of the shocked wife. And the tears came easily. I think they believed that I had no clue about Hank's other life or that I knew he was dead before they told me." She clenched her hands and said, "They didn't know when the body"—her voice quavered a bit at that—"would be released. When it is, there will have to be some sort of funeral. I'm not going to let the county bury him. And I'll have to explain to the kids." Her hands rose. "What do I tell them? It'll hit Henry the hardest. He has the most memories of his father." With that, the tears began to roll.

"It's all too new to make decisions now. I suspect you'll have at least a week." I didn't add 'before the body is released.' "I've never had to face what you're going through, Marcy, but I've been in some pretty awful situations, both personal and in my business. Whenever I don't see a way out, I start a list. No particular order, no sense of probability. I simply write down every idea that comes. Somehow, it triggers my mind to take a deeper look at some things and discard others. Then I can prioritize." I struggled to decide what I should say next. Tea always helped me feel better. "Would you like some tea?" I asked her.

"Uh, sure."

"Good. Let's stiffen a couple cups."

She wiped her eyes and gave a tiny smile. "Sounds like a good idea."

I poured a miniscule drop of brandy into my cup, just to keep Marcy company, but fortified hers more liberally. With a mere sip, I set mine on the coffee table. "Let me tell you what Hank told me this morning, Marcy." I was glad that a box of tissues sat next to her on the sofa as she cried and rocked herself while I explained Hank's motivation for leaving. "The last thing he said was, 'Love.' He wanted me to tell you that he loved you and the kids." I teared up at the remembrance.

"I was so wrong about him," she moaned softly. "So wrong. Hank, I'm so sorry."

I moved next to her and put my arm around her shoulder. "Me, too," I said.

Chapter 27

I never met a lasagna I didn't like. — Jim Davis

By the time I left the Wagner home, I was emotionally wrung out and feeling slightly unstable from lack of food. My watch read six-ten. I texted Spider: *Ready to head your way with an Italian meal for supper. Driving a silver Ford Escape.* I didn't want to set off his mental alarms with an unknown vehicle.

His response was short and sweet: *Yum.*

Next I texted Bobbie, and asked him to contact Bram and Tiny Tim. Four men, two women—three, if the baby nurse was still on duty. I suspected that Bram, Spider and Tim were hearty eaters, so I called Mama Mia's to order two pans of lasagna, salad, garlic bread and seven cannoli.

Spider met me in the driveway and hefted the bags of food inside. Magdalena sat at the table in the large informal dining area attached to the kitchen, nursing a baby wrapped in a pink blanket. The other twin, wrapped in blue and seated in one of those bouncy contraptions, looked around with apparent curiosity. I quickly divested myself of outside clothing and boots, washed my hands at the kitchen sink, and made a beeline for little blue man, Daniel. "May I?" I asked Magda.

"But of course." She smiled. "He's been fed and burped and there are no noticeable smells."

I scooped him up and he stared into my face, his brown eyes bright. "I don't believe it when doctors say they can't see for a while," I said. "Look at him, so alert. And his eyebrows!"

Magda laughed. "Like his father, no?"

From the other room, Joey popped his head into the kitchen. "*Octonauts* is ovah." He saw me and bounded in. "Hi, Miss Angie. I love my nightlight! Now I'm nevah afwaid in my woom."

I sat down with baby Daniel and leaned over to Joey. "That's just what I thought when I saw it, Joey."

"Thanks, Miss Angie." He ran a chubby finger over Daniel's cheek. "The babies aw weally cute, wight?"

"They are." I feigned exasperation. "But babies can be noisy and smelly. I bet your mom and dad are happy you're not that little anymore, and they can have fun with you."

He considered that for a moment. "That's wight. Dad and I can do stuff in the gawage. And I help Mommy when she makes cookies. I'm the taste-ah."

A knock sounded at the door, and Spider invited Bobbie, Bram and Tiny Tim inside. "Uncah Bwam," Joey yelled as he barreled into Bram's legs. I winced, thinking of his injury, but he just laughed and lifted the boy into the air.

With a smile, Magdalena put a hand under the cotton blanket that discreetly covered her as she nursed, and placed Gabriela on her lap while she rearranged her clothing. "And here is our little girl," she said.

I gently settled Daniel back into the baby carrier on the table and lifted Gabby. She had a shock of auburn hair and cognac-colored eyes. "She's so beautiful," I breathed. Nestling her in the crook of my arm, I smiled at Magda. "You have a wonderful family."

She nodded. "We do." Her words were low, like a benediction.

"And how are you feeling?" I asked.

"After Joey, I sprang back very quickly. But these two … well, let's just say the nights are long. Len and the nurse are a huge help, but they can't feed the little ones. That's my main job, I'm finding. I'm a glorified milk supply." She chuckled and glanced at the huddle of men near the fridge, each with a bottle of Leinie's in hand. "But let's not embarrass the men."

In short order, I set the table and we sat down to eat. When Bobbie popped a bite of salad into his mouth, Joey gave a horrified look. "Mista Bobbie, we didn't say ouw blessing!"

I knew quite well that Bobbie was not a person of faith, but he didn't challenge Joey. "Sorry, buddy. I forgot."

It took less than thirty minutes to finish the meal. Seeing a single row of lasagna left in the second pan, I was glad that I'd ordered two. The men had indeed done justice to the dish.

Spider turned to Joey and said, "Time for lights out, son."

"Aww, Daddy …"

"No negotiating, young man." Then he looked to Magda and said in a tender voice, "No negotiating for you either, *mi corazón*. Let's get you and the babies bunked down for a few hours."

"Yes," she said with a yawn. "Please excuse me for leaving you so early, and thank you, Angie, for the lovely meal."

Joey made the rounds of the table, shaking hands good-night or hugging.

I felt privileged to rate a hug. "Don't forget that the Caped Crusader is there to watch over you, Joey," I whispered in his ear. "Sleep well."

While Spider attended to his family, I put the leftover lasagna into a container and slipped the two remaining garlic breads into a plastic storage bag. Bobbie cleared the table, Bram loaded the dishwasher, and Tim used the stick vacuum to clean up the detritus around Joey's chair. Then I shooed the men into the living room while I made a pot of coffee. With mugs, spoons, creamer, sugar and the carafe on a tray, I entered the room in time to hear Tim say, "I doubt they got you on camera, Bobbie."

As Spider's feet and legs came into view on the staircase, my phone played Ian Hunter's *The Truth, the Whole Truth, Nuthin but the Truth.* "Hello, Bart," I said, retreating into the kitchen.

"We need to be at homicide at nine tomorrow morning. I can pick you up at eight-thirty."

Crap. I'd have to reschedule with Wukowski. "No, I'll meet you there." I was hoping that I could get Wukowski away from his desk for a conversation afterward.

"Alright. See you then."

I poured myself a cup of java and settled in a large rocking chair near the stone fireplace.

Bram opened the conversation. "Let's debrief. We'll start with the peripheral actors and then move on to Angie." He nodded to Bobbie.

"It went pretty much as planned, until Tim rushed me out. I arrived at the church around ten to six, parked and went inside." He held up his hands. "I wore gloves the whole time I was in the car, so my prints won't be on it."

"Good thinking," said Spider. "It's a burner car. Can't be traced."

Burner car? I pictured Spider as the American version of James Bond's M, always with a new gadget or ploy.

"That place is huge," Bobbie continued, "and cold! I wasn't the only one inside wearing my coat and gloves. I felt I had to remove my hat, but I kept my head down. It didn't seem odd, what with all the praying. There were cameras up near the altar, so I can't be sure I'm not on their security tapes."

"I checked," Spider said in a flat tone. "You were only on camera when you entered. Good job keeping the Homburg in front of your face until you moved into a pew. After that, I lost you. Their surveillance is mostly for protecting the valuables on the altar from vandalism, so it's set to record the center and not the periphery."

"How'd you manage to check the recordings?" I asked.

"Need to know basis," was his quiet response. "Go on, Bobbie."

"There was a lot of up and down, a hymn or two, and a short sermon on keeping the faith in the midst of doubts. I watched the others in the church, the way you showed me, Angie, moving my eyes, but not my head." He grinned at me and I nodded approval. "When the others went up for communion, I stayed on the kneeler with my face in my hands, like I was overcome with emotion. After the Mass ended, the priest waited at the back door to greet people, but I remained seated. When I heard the priest approach me from the center aisle, I got up and went out via the side door to the hall. He didn't follow me. By then, it was six forty-five. I thought about going back to the car, but it might have looked odd, me sitting there in the cold."

His face grew a little excited. "There's a room off the hallway, they call it a chapel. All along the wall, there are crutches and walkers and even a couple folded-up wheelchairs. The sign says people leave them there after a miraculous healing." He looked around the circle. "It's hard to believe." Then his eyes rested on me. "You used to be a Catholic, Angie. Was that a scam?"

Shrugging, I said, "I don't know, Bobbie. I won't say it's impossible, but I don't have proof that it's real, either."

"Well, the chapel gave me a good excuse to linger, so I went in there and pretended to pray some more. Just as I began to think I'd better leave, Tim called my cell and told me to get the hell out." He laughed.

"Not a good turn of phrase, Tim, me being in a holy place. Anyway, I scurried out and met Tim on the steps. He hustled me down the driveway and into his truck."

"Good report," said Bram. "Spider?"

"Bram and I got to the staging site around five-thirty. We split up, me in the woods above the path, with one of the sleds, and Bram farther back, keeping surveillance on the area. I saw a monk come out of the monastery that's attached to the church and walk down the stairs to the path. Something about his stride made me think he hadn't been in the religious life very long. When he greeted you, Angie, I almost fell over in the snow. I listened to the conversation and relaxed a bit. We always assumed that any danger would come from Hank, but Hank came across like a stand-up guy when you were talking. So when the sniper fired, it took me a second to start the sled and head down the hill, with Bram yelling in my ear that it looked like a single shooter and you shouting that Hank was down. Your red hat and gloves were a beacon in all the white, black and gray. I homed in on you, picked you up and we exfiltrated."

"I'll take this part," Bram said. "After the shot, I surveilled the area and saw a guy in the woods behind the lot where Angie parked. He was breaking down a rifle and tripod and packing out. From his clothes, I'd say he was unprepared for the climate. I made my way on foot to his vantage point. One thing's for sure, he was a pro. Scuffed out any boot prints and even the tripod feet where they rested in the snow. He had a car waiting on the road you took in, Angie. I couldn't get there fast enough, but I did make the license plates with my long-range binos."

"Binos?" Bobbie asked.

"Sorry. Binoculars. So then I circled back to my snowmobile and made it to the truck minutes before you got there. We all met in

Johnson Creek. From there, it's Spider's story."

"The plates Bram got off the car were Illinois. Rental, under the name Frederick Priest. I traced it back to a hit man who works for the South Philly Mob."

"That confirms our supposition then," Bram said evenly.

Spider slammed his mug down on the table, splashing coffee on the wooden top. "We should've anticipated him." His voice was ice. "That was sloppy work."

Bram responded in a low, almost soothing tone. "No denying it, Spider. Now we put it behind us and decide how to proceed. What were his movements after he left Holy Hill?"

Spider retrieved his tablet from a small desk in the kitchen and began to tap. "He returned the rental car to the agency and booked a flight to Curaçao. Rented a luxury villa near one of the casinos. Seems he likes to gamble. Assassination must pay well." He gave me a long, even look. "In the old days, we'd go after him. Can't let the opposition prevail."

I could sense he was waiting for a decision from me. The idea of sending a team to Venezuela to take down a sniper was surreal, like something from Tom Clancy. "No," I said, keeping my voice firm. "We need to focus on the mission that's right here in front of us." I counted off the items in my to-be-uncovered list. "One, was Hank the only target? Two, will they leave his family alone? And three, how the hell did they know I was involved?" My voice rose with each question. I took a calming breath. "Until we find out, I want a twenty-four hour protection detail for Marcy and the kids."

Bram nodded. "Already done. Malone's back in town. He'll be there tonight, with Tim. She'll have two-man coverage until this is resolved. Don't worry. We won't let anything happen to them."

Like you didn't let anything happen to Hank? I thought. But that was unfair. Their mission was to protect me this morning, not Hank. I finished my coffee and headed for home and a hot steam shower. It could cleanse the physical debris of the day from my body, but I knew the image of Hank, his red blood marring the white snow, would not wash away so easily.

Chapter 28

What is the opposite of two? A lonely me, a lonely you.
— Richard Wilbur

The next morning, I kept one eye on the local TV news while I selected clothes. I wanted to look professional, but appealing, so that Wukowski would feel a sense of pride in our relationship. A charcoal grey skirted suit, with a drapey fuchsia blouse underneath, nude stockings and black peep-toed pumps fit the bill. Hoping for a rendezvous later, I sported a magenta lace demi-bra and rio-style thong with attached garters underneath.

Although the newscaster tried to amplify the events with shots of Holy Hill and references to sacrilege on sacred ground, the gist of the report simply stated that an unidentified man was shot and killed near the first Station of the Cross. There was no mention of me, which simplified my agenda for the day.

First, I would meet Bart at Homicide and make a statement. Then I would claim some time with Wukowski. He owed me an explanation for hiding the police harassment over his being with me. Lastly, I would head to Papa's, to tell him about the assassination and seek information about the shooter. My gut clenched at his anger and the thought of an argument, but I pushed it down. *One thing at a time*, I told myself.

Bart waited for me inside MPD headquarters. He suggested that if Marcy agreed to hire him, and he contracted with me, I would be covered under attorney-client privilege as his representative. A quick call to Marcy and the matter was done before Art Penske came down to sign for us and escort us upstairs to the Homicide bullpen. There, I surreptitiously glanced around, but Wukowski was nowhere in sight.

Art ushered us into a conference room, which was distinctly more comfortable than yesterday's utilitarian interview room. Apparently, having Bart along qualified for an upgrade.

A forty-something man rose as we entered. "This here's Lieutenant Reese," Art said.

"Of what department?" Bart asked.

"Organized Crime Division," Reese said, extending his hand. "The deceased had a, shall we say, notorious past. We'd appreciate whatever help you can provide."

"Of course, we're happy to cooperate with the police in this matter, but my primary concern is to protect my client, Mrs. Henry Wagner." He gestured to me. "Ms. Angelina Bonaparte has been acting under my direction to locate Mr. Wagner."

With handshakes all around and coffee from a carafe on the table, we sat and ran through the usual preliminaries for taping a statement. Then Bart placed his cellphone on the table. "I'll also be recording the proceedings, gentlemen, to be sure there are no misunderstandings."

Reese's already ramrod-straight back tightened perceptively.

We ran through the same material that was covered yesterday. Then Art asked the question that had caused Horton to explode. "You were surprised when Mr. Wagner revealed his true identity as Tommaso Severson?"

I didn't want to lie while making a sworn statement to the police.

"It was a shocking thing to learn, Detective Penske." Even if the shock came three days earlier.

"Ms. Bonaparte," said Reese, "if you were unaware of the true identity of the deceased, why were you there?"

"As I already stated, I was hired by his wife to find him. When I ran across his obituary, she wanted me to uncover more details of his life after he left her."

"For what reason?"

"Closure, Lieutenant. When their man walks out on them, women like to understand why."

"I see." Obviously, he didn't. "And after his supposed death, how did you manage to locate him?"

I raised an eyebrow at Bart, who said, "There are confidential aspects to Ms. Bonaparte's investigation, Lieutenant. Let's just say that the attorney who drafted the obituary and then had it published was an unwitting link to Mr. Severson."

"Not good enough, Attorney Matthews. Unless Ms. Bonaparte is willing to answer my questions, I can have her charged with obstruction of justice."

"On the contrary, Lieutenant Reese. Ms. Bonaparte is protected under the rules of attorney-client privilege. She acted under my instructions in this matter. Mrs. Wagner is the client of record."

"Funny that Mrs. Wagner never mentioned that last night."

"I'm sure she was too distraught at the news of her husband's death to be concerned with legalities," Bart responded.

Reese sighed in frustration. "Name and contact information for the Stevens Point lawyer."

I took one of Frank's business cards from my briefcase and passed it across the table. "He's totally unaware of the Severson connection. The

Wagner identity is how he knew the deceased."

Art jumped back in. "Please relate the details of the conversation between you and Mr. Severson, for the record."

That part was easy. "Hank went into hiding when he thought there was a possibility that someone he knew from the South Philly Mob might have spotted him. He told me nothing about his life after he ran, just that he did it to protect his family. When I asked if he wanted to consider applying to the Witness Protection Program, in order to be able to reunite with them, he demurred. He was afraid the Family would hunt him down, and that they might harm Marcy and the children. So we agreed that he'd disappear again and Marcy would file for divorce."

Reese interrupted with a snide voice. "A regular saint, wasn't he?"

I knew he hoped that, by angering me, I would reveal something unintended. I kept a cool head and responded, "No kind of saint at all. But he did love his family. Those were the last words on his lips before he died."

Reese had the grace to look down at the table for a moment. Then he said, "Ms. Bonaparte, your father is connected to another branch of organized crime in this city. Did he facilitate Mr. Severson's demise at the hands of the South Philly Mob?"

Bart slammed a meaty hand onto the table top, causing the recorder and his cellphone to shake. "Lieutenant Reese, that allegation is entirely unproven. In fact, it amounts to slander. My client has given an open and honest statement of the events at Holy Hill related to Mr. Severson's death. We have nothing further to say. This discussion is closed. I'll expect a transcript to be delivered to my office at your earliest convenience. Neither email nor other electronic delivery is acceptable. I find them too easily misplaced or altered. Ms. Bonaparte will sign the statement once she and I have reviewed the transcript to be sure it is accurate. Good day."

I scrambled to assemble my coat, briefcase and purse as Bart steamrolled out the door and into Homicide, where Wukowski now sat at his desk, Captain Horton and a woman hovering nearby. Wukowski rose, straightened his shoulders and walked over. "No shouting today?"

"No," I said with a shake of my head. "Just snide insinuation."

"I know all about that."

I recalled Art's comments about Wukowski being under the gun because of me. "Speaking of which, we need to talk."

Bart snickered. "The words every man dreads. Angie, I'd like to escort you out of the building. You and Wukowski can have your confab later."

"I'm afraid not," Wukowski said with a nod toward Horton and the woman. "My captain and Internal Affairs are here to supervise a discussion with me and Angie."

"Over my dead body!" Bart exclaimed. "My client has given her statement. Discussing the events with your superiors and allowing them to also brutalize her is not going to happen."

The words were loud enough to be heard in the room. Bart used them to establish the grounds for a hostile environment, should it come to that. Wily fox!

The woman who Wukowski indicated was from Internal Affairs marched over, Horton following behind. A look of muted despair passed over Wukowski's face as his shoulders drooped. "I understand," he told Bart. After a beat, he snapped into his normal posture and turned to me. "Can I see you tonight?"

Horton's face held a gleeful look as they approached. Anything that made that jerk happy could not be good for me, and probably not for Wukowski.

"Bart, would it hurt to listen to what they have to say?" I asked.

"Are you nuts?" he responded.

"No. I'm walking a high wire," I told him, "balancing between my best interests and Wukowski's. And I'd appreciate your standing by me."

The room fell into a heavy silence, with no attempt by those present to mask their interest. "One moment, Detective," Bart said, ignoring Horton and the woman while taking my arm and escorting me into the hallway. Once there, he spoke in an undertone, "You cannot be involved in an Internal Affairs investigation, Angelina. They turn into witch hunts, with subpoenas flying everywhere. And I need a smoke."

I snorted at that. "I appreciate your sacrifice thus far, Bart, and ask that you extend it long enough for us to find out what's happening with Wukowski. I'm worried about him." I took a step closer and looked up at him. "Please."

"Dammit, woman." He huffed and turned to lead us back into the still-quiet room. "Detective Wukowski, let us see what undoubtedly nefarious plans your superiors are hatching." With a Vanna White gesture to the conference room we just vacated, he added, "Shall we?"

Wukowski nodded to Horton and the woman, and the five of us trooped into the room, Horton shutting the door with a loud bang. "Oops," he said with an insincere smile.

Bart beat Horton to the punch, extending his hand to the unknown woman. "Attorney Bartholomew Matthews. And you are?"

"Captain Salina Cortés, Internal Affairs."

"My client, Ms. Angelina Bonaparte," Bart said.

We shook hands and sat, Horton and Cortés facing the door, and

Bart and I across from them. Wukowski hesitated, then sat at the end of the table, in neutral territory.

"Ms. Bonaparte," said Captain Cortés, "or may I call you Angie?"

"You may not," Bart interposed. "This is not a friendly discussion, Captain Cortes. Let's keep to the formalities, shall we?"

"Of course, Attorney Matthews." She smiled. "And my last name is pronounced with the accent on the final syllable."

Guess we share a surname pronunciation issue, I thought.

"I'll be transparent with you, Ms. Bonaparte. Your intimate relationship with Detective Wukowski has caused more than raised eyebrows in the department."

"How so?" I asked. "Surely he's not the only member of the MPD to have a girlfriend."

She laughed. "No, that's not it." Her face assumed a serious mom look. "There are those who believe that the detective has been compromised in his duties by an association with a woman whose father is, forgive my bluntness, reputed to be a leader in organized crime in the city. In addition to that, in the past seven months, he has been part of no fewer than three murder investigations involving yourself."

Her use of the reflexive pronoun was deliberately demeaning. "You" would have sufficed.

Bart spoke. "Captain Cortés, by my reckoning, the coincidental pairing of Detective Wukowski and Ms. Bonaparte during investigations has contributed to the apprehension of three killers, one of whom was a war criminal subsequently remanded to the International Criminal Court at Le Hague. For this, Detective Wukowski and his partner, Detective Ignowski, both received commendations from the Chief of Police. Is that not so?"

Horton jumped in, ready, as always, to make an ass of himself (*reflexive pronoun intended*). "Yeah, he got a fancy letter from the Chief. Big deal. Doesn't make up for the fact that he's boning a Mafia princess."

Wukowski jumped up and rounded the table. Captain Cortés rose and put a hand on his chest. "Back off, Detective. I'll handle this." Then she turned to Horton, her face bright red underneath her olive complexion. "Out," she growled and pointed to the door. "Now."

"Just a damned minute, lady—"

Before he could finish his sentence, she spoke in frosty fire. "Unless you want the full force of Internal Affairs on you for the next twenty years of your career, assuming you make it that long, you *will* leave now." When he hesitated, she said, "Of course, I could call for assistance in escorting you from the room. I'm sure that any of the detectives and officers in the bullpen would be happy to follow my orders."

I turned around and saw a sea of eyeballs watching us.

Horton stood and huffed out. There was no "oops" when he slammed the door this time.

Cortés turned back to me. "Ms. Bonaparte, you have my sincere apology and my assurance that Captain Horton will not escape unscathed for this." To Bart, she said, "Attorney Matthews, I hope that you and your client will allow me to continue with the explanation that Horton interrupted."

Bart nodded, his chins wiggling.

"Good," said Captain Cortés. After a deep breath, she spoke. "This is a very difficult situation for the department and for Detective Wukowski. All I can do is speak the truth and hope that you will understand." She shuffled a blank sheet of paper to the bottom of a small stack, and began to speak in a somewhat stilted voice as she read from the printed material that was now on the top. "The Milwaukee Police Department insists on the highest standards of conduct from all its employees. Even the appearance of wrongdoing can tarnish the department's reputation and erode the public's confidence in the department's commitment to justice. While Pasquale Bonaparte has never been convicted of any criminal activity, he is widely regarded as the retired *de facto* boss of the Milwaukee mob. This makes Detective Wukowski's association with you problematic, Ms. Bonaparte."

After laying the paper down, she looked up at me. "Please understand that Detective Wukowski's record remains unblemished. That said, Tommaso Severson's assassination by what we suspect are the direct orders of the South Philly Mob, and your own involvement in that event, have crossed a line that my superiors will not tolerate."

It didn't escape me that she was subtly disassociating herself from what would follow. I straightened and waited, Bart silent beside me and Wukowski staring blankly out into the bullpen.

Picking the paper back up, she proceeded. "The Department must act to distance Detective Wukowski, and thereby itself, from any entanglement with the crime families who may be involved. To that end, I have informed Detective Wukowski that he will be reassigned to a less sensitive post if he does not agree to end his personal relationship with you. I regret any pain this might cause either of you, should that be his decision."

I sat in stunned silence, considering a future without Wukowski or a future where Wukowski would be isolated from the work which gave him meaning.

Before anyone could speak, Captain Cortés reshuffled the papers and placed them in her briefcase before rising. "You are welcome to use the conference room for as long as you like. Whatever you have to say must be said here, as I've explained to Detective Wukowski. However, no one will overhear the conversation, I assure you."

"One thing, Captain," Wukowski said. "If Horton remains in charge of Homicide, my decision is already made. I won't work under him." His voice was impassive.

"Understood." She quietly exited the room.

"Angie—" Wukowski began.

Bart interrupted. "No reason I should remain while you talk, Detective, unless you're looking for legal representation. I can give you some names."

"Thanks," he said, "but I've considered and rejected that idea." He sighed. "I really don't want to be embroiled in a lawsuit with the Department."

"Very well," Bart said, heaving himself up. "Angie, shall I wait for you downstairs, or at a nearby coffee shop?" His voice sounded tender.

"No, but thanks, Bart," I told him. "I'll probably want some alone time when this"—I gestured around the room and the Homicide bullpen—"is done."

With a nod, he left me with Wukowski.

I glanced over my shoulder to the large glass window of the room. "Can we at least lower the blinds?"

"Sure." He stood and accomplished that, then sat next to me and took my hands. "I was ordered not to speak to you until this meeting," he said.

"What the hell, Wukowski!" The words exploded from my lips in a quiet growl and I pulled my hands from his. "Why was Art Pence the one to tell me about your being under constant investigation since we started seeing each other?"

"Be fair, Angie. What good would it have done for me to tell you that? It wouldn't change anything, right? And IA can investigate me until the end of time. They won't find anything actionable. So I just ... I decided to live with it. You're worth the hassle."

That stopped my rant. "But now ..."

"Yeah. But now. Look, *moja droga*, the MPD retirement plan is very generous. I can draw a full pension when I reach fifty-five, in two years, seven months and three days." He raked his hands through his hair. "Without that, well, you're looking at a man whose finances won't carry him to Social Security eligibility. So I figure, wherever they reassign me, I can hang on. I'll probably end up in a precinct house. Not so bad, being a detective in a precinct."

The words were upbeat, but his eyes and the set of his mouth belied them. I knew it would tear him up to leave Homicide, especially in the middle of the Bike Trail Murders investigation. "You'd do that?"

He didn't hesitate. "Yes."

I wanted with all my heart to let him do that, but though it would mean we could stay together, I shook my head. "I see what your work means to you, Wukowski. How you commit to it. How you agonize over it. I don't want to be the cause of your living two years, seven months and three days doing something that isn't fulfilling." I paused, remembering the years I struggled, trying to find a way to be something besides a wife and mom. "And what about after? I can't see you rocking on the front porch or playing *bocci* like the geezers at the Italian Center. You're too young for that. You're too much man for that. You love your work too much for that."

"So then I'll quit." He grinned. "I could take a page from you, set up as a private investigator. Hell, maybe even work for you."

I snorted. "That would be a recipe for relationship break-up, you taking orders from me. And it would still leave you missing the work that gives you meaning." I stood and slowly paced the room. "The other option is also available. We could stop seeing each other until you retire." *And I would miss you every minute,* I thought. I turned to face him. "I won't lie. It would be hell, not seeing you or … holding you. It's a long time. You might find someone else, someone less … problematic."

"Don't be a damned fool," he gently rebuked. "Before we met, I went a longer time than that without a woman. I'm not so needy that I can't wait. And I'd expect the same from you."

"That goes without saying, *caro*."

"It won't be easy, though," he added. "It's one thing when there's no one you're interested in. It's another when the person you love is out there, willing and waiting. I see some cold showers in my future." His lopsided smile was rueful.

"Me, too." And some lonely nights. "So what do you think? We agree to stay apart for the duration? That's what makes sense to me, for both of us."

"Angie." Wukowski rose and gathered me to him, hugging me tightly. I snuggled into the embrace and heard his heartbeat, steady and strong. "I do not deserve you, but I'm awfully glad I have you."

"Ditto," I said, thinking of the lovers in *Ghost*. At least *I* knew the precise duration of our pending separation.

I rubbed circles on his back. He bent to nibble on my ear. After a few minutes, we broke apart reluctantly. "What happens next?" I asked.

"According to Cortés, I'll need to sign a statement that I will not be in contact with you, either physically or via electronic communication, while I'm still on active duty. Iggy can come over to your condo and pick up my stuff. Keep some boxers, my toothbrush and razor, though, because I *will* be at your door in nine hundred and fifty-six days and ..." he checked his watch "... thirteen hours and twenty-eight minutes. Twenty-seven minutes. And I won't leave until the morning, unless you ask me to. Deal?"

"Deal."

He pulled me to the vacated chairs and we sat. "So, tell me about Severson and how you got involved. And by the way, since you chastised me about not divulging my work issues, I might say the same to you." His hands tightened on the arms of the chair." You were a sitting duck, Angie. The shooter could've picked you off with no problem."

I heard the darkness in his voice and decided to respond to the spirit of his words, rather than the words themselves. "He wasn't after me, Wukowski. It's pretty obvious that he was sent for Hank—uh, Severson. If it was the South Philly Mob, and if they attached a GPS device to my car to follow me to the rendezvous, then they knew who I am. I wasn't in danger."

"Assuming that's true, bullets are pretty impartial and human beings are fallible." He sighed. "Of course, I know that once you're caught up in a case, you're not going to back down. So tell me about it."

No more secrets, I decided. I laid out the entire story, even including my nighttime foray into breaking and entering at Padua Manor, but I was careful to keep Spider's and Bobbie's participation to myself.

"Jeez, woman, you're a female Jason Bourne. I'll have gray hair the next time we meet, imagining all the stuff you've been up to. But I admit, sometimes I wish I could bend the rules like that. Thank God this is over."

Should I tell him the rest of it, knowing it would cause him nothing but anxiety?

I put myself in his place and knew that his code of justice and my code of truth demanded it. "Not entirely," I admitted. "The South

Philly Mob had no reason to believe I was involved with Severson. Only a handful of people knew. One of them betrayed me and I have to find out who it was."

"That's a dangerous path, Angie. There are sure to be connections to organized crime."

"I'm counting on it," I told him. "And I'm counting on Papa to be a buffer for me."

He thought a moment. "Your father is a fairly minor figure in the larger picture. The Chicago Outfit took over control in Milwaukee when Balistreri died. They wanted a titular presence here, and that's the role he played." His chagrin was evident when he added, "I wouldn't have become involved with you, if that weren't so. IA is right to be leery. If Pasquale were active, I would've walked away, despite my attraction. That said, I'm not sure he can protect you from the South Philly Mob."

"You may be right, but Chicago will not take an intrusion into their territory lightly. I'll talk to Papa after I leave here and ask him to make clear to them the scope of what happened, and to insist on finding out their involvement with me." I smiled. "Horton's wrong about me being a Mafia princess, but I am my papa's princess. He won't let this go."

With a short knock, the conference room door opened a crack. Joe Ignowski, Wukowski's partner, peeked in. "Hey, I'm sorry to be the one to interrupt, but Cortés just called me to tell you that time's up. She asked me to escort you out, Angie." Then he stepped inside the room. "Oh, yeah, and Horton's cleaning out his office. I hear he's on special assignment. Looks like the big brass needs some help compiling traffic stop statistics." His throaty chuckle made me smile. "Matthews made a call to the chief."

"That's good to know, Iggy," Wukowski said. "Shut the door and come in." He explained our plan to Iggy. "So Angie will hand over the stuff I've accumulated at her place, and you can pick up her stuff from my place. I wouldn't put it past IA to search my house for evidence that we haven't really separated."

"A-holes," Iggy muttered. "But I'll be glad to take care of that for both of you. Let me know when you have Ted's belongings assembled, Angie." He looked from Wukowski to me. "I'm seriously sorry about how this rolled out. For you guys, but also for me." His gaze swung to me. "He was so easy-going after he spent some time with you." Raising his hand, he said, "I'll be back in five."

We spent the final minutes cuddling, kissing and reassuring one another that the time would go quickly. Wukowski suggested that if I really needed him, I could get a message to him via Aunt Terry to Iggy's wife, Marianne. I stood back and took a long, long look at the man I loved, burning his image into my mind. Then he raised the blinds and we exited the room, he to his desk and me, head held high, downstairs, with Iggy as an escort.

The day was sunny, if cold, and I still had business to accomplish. Marcus Aurelius' advice sprang to mind: "Concentrate every minute like a Roman—like a man—on doing what's in front of you with precise and genuine seriousness, tenderly, willingly, with justice." I would do that.

Chapter 29

Whoever does not have a good father should procure one.

— Friedrich Nietzsche

Bobbie needed to know what my statement to the police contained, in case he was also questioned. We met at the office and agreed that he would say that he was only tangentially aware of the case when I needed to leave town and he filled in. He was highly indignant about the department's insistence that Wukowski and I remain apart. "Who are they," he stormed, pacing, "to stop someone from loving someone else?"

I knew that part of his anger was directed at society's response to his gay relationship with Steve. "That's the one thing they can't do, Bobbie. They can't stop us from loving one another. And the time will pass. Somehow."

He pulled me up and hugged me. "Anytime you need to talk, whether it's early or late, call me."

Tears welled in my eyes, but I held them back, fearful of releasing the built-up anger, frustration and sadness of the morning. "You're a good friend and a good man," I said. "I'll take you up on that offer."

It was almost noon. The talk with Papa loomed. Time to do what was in front of me.

He answered on the fifth ring.

"Are you busy, Papa?

"Preparing antipasto salad for lunch. There's plenty for two, with leftovers for Terry whenever she finishes her parish visits."

Papa's antipasto was a structure of delight, the crisp romaine covered with genuine Genoa salami, Giardiniera, green and black olives, roasted peppers, marinated artichokes, all covered with his own blend of balsamic vinegar and Lucini Italia extra virgin olive oil. Despite my trepidation, my mouth watered. "I'll be there in twenty minutes," I told him.

When I entered the back door, which led into the kitchen, a sliced loaf of Sciortino's Italian bread rested on the counter, with a nearby dish of seasoned melted butter and olive oil. I divested myself of cold weather gear, gave Papa a kiss on the cheek, and washed my hands at the kitchen sink. The salad bowl beckoned from the kitchen table. Papa reserved the dining room for Sunday meals and special occasions.

"Shall I prepare the bread?" I asked.

"Not yet. *Mia cara figlia*, what have you been up to now?" His voice was stern, but soft.

When I was fifteen, Papa caught me and Sam Whittier making out in Sam's car after a movie. Papa didn't yell or berate. Instead, he sent Sam home with a warning that he and Sam's father would soon have a talk, and he sat me down at the kitchen table. I felt like the Angie of so long ago, who had caused her papa worry and concern, and who was facing a parental rebuke.

"Papa," I said, "I'm here to talk about a difficult matter. It seems, though, that you already have an inkling of what has happened. Is that so?"

He inclined his head and gestured to the gleaming new espresso maker on the counter, a Christmas gift from me. "Before we sit, *un caffè?*"

"Yes, please," I said.

While the machine buzzed, I waited, wondering what Papa already knew. There was no reason to hide the facts from him, I decided. I would be forthright about Hank and the Severson connection.

Papa carefully placed the cups on the table and sat. "This morning, I received a call from the Chicago *consigliere*, who had been called earlier by a contact in the South Philly Mob. Marco would not give me the name. He told me of your involvement with Tommaso Severson." Papa took a sip of the strong, hot brew. "He also advised me that beatings at an earlier age might have curbed my headstrong daughter." He sighed. "But I knew that such actions would only drive her farther toward whatever it was she sought."

I gave silent thanks that Papa's call was from the trusted counselor of the Chicago head, and not the boss himself. As for beatings … well, Papa never touched me in anger. His reprimands were bad enough.

"I came here to explain, Papa."

"And you could not come here yesterday to tell me, so that I would not be caught unawares this morning?"

I spread my hands. "The events and their aftermath were, well, time-consuming, and they involved others, whose welfare I had to consider. That, and meeting with the police, took up my afternoon and the morning. I'm so sorry if that put you in a difficult place."

He shrugged. "I am in no trouble. Which is more than I can say for you. This involves the anonymous man we spoke of?"

I nodded.

"Since he is now dead, perhaps you can tell me the whole story."

I gave him the facts, without mentioning Spider or Bram. Since Papa knew and accepted Bobbie as my intern, I didn't edit that part.

"You were in grave danger, there in the open with *un assassino* shooting at Severson, who stood mere feet from you. My father's heart sinks at the thought. I could not stand to bury you, Angelina. It would kill me."

The undercurrent of anguish came through from his calm statement. I thought of my own beloved children and grandchildren. It would kill me to bury any of them. "Papa," I said, reaching for his hands, "I can only say that I had no notion there would be a threat from … outside. I thought any threat would come from Severson, though he didn't strike me as a violent man. Still, I was armed and prepared for that. I'm so sorry to cause you such concern."

"*Bene*," he said, ending the conversation. "I will prepare the bread for the oven. Let us eat." He started to rise.

The easy part of the conversation was over. Now came the hard part. "Papa, before that, I have to ask you something that is difficult."

He sat again. "Go on," he said.

"You see, Henry Wagner went into hiding, all those years ago, because he saw a face in a deli in Milwaukee, a man who knew him as Severson. He was never sure if the man spotted him, but he wouldn't take the chance, both for his own sake and for his family's. Was he right to run? Did they see him?"

"They did not tell me that, but I doubt it. They would have applied to Chicago for permission to enter Wisconsin and hunt him down, if they had known. It would not be a problem. The Chicago Outfit would have contacted me and I would have agreed."

I gave a little start.

"I told you before, Angelina, that a man cannot leave the organization he has vowed to."

Even priests and nuns can gain a dispensation from their vows to God, I thought. However, Papa's mindset could not be disputed.

"That brings me to the tough question. How did they know to hire a contracted hit man and how did that man know to follow me? The only ones aware of Severson's other identities were me, Bobbie, an associate who helped me with internet searches and whom I trust with my life, and Marcy Wagner. I cannot believe that any of us would betray Severson to the South Philly Mob."

"That is a puzzle," Papa said. Then he gave me a sharp look. "You also spoke with me, in vague terms. If I had wanted to search out possibilities, I would likely have uncovered Severson." His hand went to his heart. "But I assure you, I did not."

I gave a silent thanks. "I believe you, Papa. But I'm still stuck with the question, so I come to you for help. Can you uncover the person, through your Family connections? I cannot rest, thinking that someone close to me has done this. After all, he or she might divulge my business again, in the future." I played the ace. "It could place me in danger again."

"That is so," he said. "But this could all be avoided if you ceased engaging in the detective business. You know how I feel about my daughter being entangled in such unsavory things. Not to mention the possibility of harm." Before I could speak, he sighed and said, "But I know that is not an action you would consider. So I will do some investigation of my own."

"My heartfelt thanks," I said.

"So, now shall we eat?"

I dug in, happy that my stomach could handle food, now that Papa and I were back in sympathy with one another.

Chapter 30

Be still my heart; thou hast known worse than this. — Homer

The condo smelled stale and lifeless as I entered and put my stuff in the front closet. *Too bad I already cleaned*, I thought. A good bout of housework could help take the edge off my anxiety. I resolutely marched barefoot into the kitchen, grabbed a paper bag, and headed for the bedroom.

Wukowski's things occupied a drawer in my dresser, a corner in the big walk-in closet, and a shelf in the bathroom. He wasn't one to make himself thoroughly at home, any more than I did at his house. We both needed our space.

Space. I'd have plenty of it for the next two years, seven months and three days. And time. Lots of time. Alone time.

Damn it! Damn him for breaking through my wall. Damn me for letting him. Damn the MPD for forcing us into this damn separation.

I crumpled the bag and drop-kicked it into the hallway. Then I burst into tears, not sure if they emanated more from rage or heartbreak, and sat down hard on the carpeted floor, resting against the side of the big, solitary, king size bed.

I might have sat there for a long time, letting the tears run down my cheeks and the snot drip from my nose, too miserable to get the box of tissue from my nightstand, but the landline rang. I wiped my eyes, blew my nose and headed for the kitchen.

An 800 number appeared on the display. I ignored it and let it go to voicemail. Almost immediately, a 414 number with a downtown prefix buzzed the phone. I answered with a cautious, "Yes?"

"Ms. Bonaparte, this is Amy Gleason from WITI-TV. I'd like to interview you concerning the death of Tommaso Severson."

Crap! The newshounds are on the story and they know I'm involved. "I have nothing to say, Ms. Gleason," I told her, remembering her snide on-air comments about a "personal relationship" between me and Wukowski after the Johnson case broke.

"If you give me an exclusive, I assure you that I will handle it with the utmost respect, Ms.—"

I hung up and disconnected the phone, knowing from experience that the calls would not cease until the story died. They'd be dogging Wukowski, too. At least last time, we had each other to turn to. Blasted reporters!

The cellphone ringtone signifying an unknown caller startled me. Surely reporters didn't have that number. I answered with silence.

"Angie? You there? It's Iggy."

"Hi, Iggy. Sorry about that. The newshounds are on the story."

"Yeah, the department's PR just issued a statement. I'll have a copy for you. Which brings me to the point. Okay if I come over in an hour? I figured I'd pick up stuff at your condo and then meet Ted after work, maybe take him out for a drink. He looks like he can use one."

A selfish little corner of my heart was glad to know that Wukowski shared my misery, but I hated for him to be unhappy. "Sure. I'll be here."

I disconnected and went back to the master bath to wash my face.

To hell with makeup. Iggy won't care. Feeling a little restored, I headed for the hallway and the abused paper bag. It would do for recyclables, but not for Wukowski's personal belongings.

A freebie gym bag from Rick's lay folded flat in the corner of the closet, with Wukowski's trainers on top. I put the shoes in a plastic bag and then inside the duffle. His toiletries would stay in my bathroom, as he asked. From the drawer allocated to him, I took out a pair of gym shorts, a couple of tee shirts, jeans and socks, reserving one of each. I would keep the sleep pants, although he hadn't asked me to. Or maybe not. In two years, seven months and three days, it would be the end of August. He wouldn't need flannels then. Even if the weather was chilly, *I'd* keep him warm. Thoughts of a hot reunion, regardless of the temperature, brought a saucy smile to my lips.

I carefully folded his two dress shirts, rolled the corresponding ties, and placed them on top of the contents of the duffle. The suit would stay on its hanger, with a plastic covering for carrying. After a last check to be sure I hadn't overlooked anything, I turned to zip the bag, which lay on the bed.

A picture of Wukowski and me, captured by my BFF Judy when she and her husband met us for drinks, stood in its frame on my side of the bed. *My side? When did I concede that Wukowski had a side of his own?*

I picked up the photo. It had been one of those magical late summer nights, with the sun starting to dip lower and the breeze off Pewaukee Lake cooling the humid air. We stood on the restaurant's outdoor patio, with his arm around me as we grinned at something silly that Judy said to make us smile. *What was it? Oh, right,* "Okay, kids, pretend that you just had a make-out session."

I will not cry, I told myself. *I will not cry*. I clutched the picture and impulsively decided to hide it in the bottom of the duffle. I wanted him to remember. I wanted him to wait.

***

When the lobby intercom rang, I buzzed Iggy in and met him at my entrance door.

"Hey," he said as he hugged me. "You doing okay?"

"The patient is in critical, but stable, condition," I answered into his winter jacket. Breaking away, I said, "Come in, please. Tell me what's happening at headquarters." I stopped. "Unless you can't, I mean."

"Nah, s'okay," Iggy said, handing me his coat and toeing off his shoes. "Reporters are outside the building, along the edge of the driveway to the garage. They didn't pay any attention to me, though."

"Let's hope it stays that way."

He grimaced. "There were some questions at the press conference about your involvement with Wukowski and whether he was assigned to the case."

I was well over my quota of swearing today, so I held back. "What was the answer?"

"A simple 'no.' It'll be on the six o'clock news."

"Undoubtedly."

"So I have to tell you, Ange, I'm worried about my partner. I don't want to see him back where he was after Liz's death."

"Me, either. But I don't think this is the same thing. I'll still be here when he decides to retire." I paused. "He did tell you about that?"

"Oh, yeah. Truth be told, I'm eligible two months before Ted, but I figure I'll wait and we'll go out together. No sense in his breaking in a new partner, right?"

I could hear the undercurrent of worry and commitment in Iggy's voice. He would hang on for Wukowski's sake. "You're the best," I told him.

"He'd do the same for me, if I was a miserable single guy who just lost the best woman he ever had." He grinned and then sobered. "Not entirely kidding there, Angie. And you can expect weekly calls from Marianne, to console and strengthen you."

I could see the invisible air quotes.

"And," he continued, "if a little information passes back and forth, who's to know except the NSA?"

That lifted my spirits. "Right."

Iggy slapped his hands on his thighs. "So, on to the hard part. Where's the stuff for Ted?"

"In the bag near the hall closet."

At the door, he geared up to go outside and I handed him the duffle and suit bag. He gave me a one-arm hug and said, "Call me if you need anything, hear me? I'm serious. I wouldn't mind a little peace and quiet at a precinct."

We parted with a smile, he to take most of the belongings of my *caro* and me to keep busy and avoid maudlin thoughts.

***

The five o'clock news broadcast led with "Organized Crime Killing at Holy Hill." Pictures of the first Station, with a close-up of rusty stains on the path and footprints leading into the grotto, flashed on the screen as the announcer intoned the story of a Mafia-related murder at the shrine. I listened closely for any mention of Henry Wagner or ties to Marcy, but breathed a sigh of relief when I realized that they hadn't made the connection yet. Then came the moment of dread. My face appeared, punctuated with the pronouncement that "Private

Investigator Angelina Bonaparte, who was instrumental in uncovering the conspiracy killings of Serbian immigrants John and Yvonne Johnson last year, was on the scene when the victim, Tommaso Severson, was gunned down by a sniper." He looked up with a slight smirk. "You may recall video of Ms. Bonaparte and her associate, Bobbie Russell, escaping the Johnsons' murderer by jumping into a moving load of very large pipes at an Illinois truck stop."

We'll never live that down, I thought.

"The MPD had this to say at a press conference earlier today." He cut to film of the event, including the station's reporter shouting out a question about whether "Ms. Bonaparte's current romantic partner, Homicide Detective Ted Wukowski," was involved in the case. With a simple "No," the MPD spokeswoman turned to another reporter.

Obviously, it wasn't dropped, since the news crews camped outside, waiting for me to emerge. I called the building super and left a message that he should remind the reporters to stay off the property and on the sidewalk, and to call the local precinct it they impeded progress into the building.

Time to take care of business.

Chapter 31

Helping others is like helping yourself. — Henry Flagler

When the news crews surrounded me after the Johnson case broke, I discovered a way to sneak into my office building via the dry cleaners that backed onto it. But first, I would have to exit the condo complex. I knew from experience that all it took was nerves of steel and a determination to ignore the press. Running the gauntlet was a breeze in the Escape. With the windows up and the radio blasting, I pulled out onto Lake Drive, thankful for the one-way street and an opening in traffic.

Tony Belloni owned a small outdoor lot eight blocks from my destination. I pulled in, rolled down my window and prepared to beg and bribe. The attendant, a man in his mid-thirties, limped toward me. His nametag read "Hi, I'm Rodney." He had good cheekbones, a strong jawline and a full head of dark brown hair, but a scar that ran from his temple to his chin marred his face. A Family soldier, I surmised.

"Ma'am, we only park subscribers here."

The clear voice and educated speech surprised me. I expected something on the lines of, "Lady, ya can't park here." *That'll teach me to assume!* "I'm a personal friend of Tony Belloni," I said, "and I'm in a bind. The press is on my tail and I need to get to my office on Prospect without being followed." I held three twenties out, smiled with sincerity and batted my eyelashes a little. "Give Tony a call. Please?"

He leaned down and looked into the car. "Hold on a minute," he said, disappearing into the little shack where the lot personnel spent their time. He emerged with a folded newspaper and his head swiveled from it to me. "Ms. Bonaparte?" he asked, mispronouncing my name as he showed the cover page to me.

They'd resurrected a shot of me from last year, alongside a head shot of Tommaso Severson from his days out east. *Yep, there I was, in all my glory, ass hanging out of a giant pipe.*

He grinned. "Listen, there's a spot in the back that we keep open for Mr. Belloni's guests who don't want to be ... bothered. I'll slide your vehicle in there. The rest are all monthly self-parking spaces, so anyone who wants their car out can get it without my help. I'll give you a ride to your building, if you don't mind my Corolla." He gestured at a rusty Toyota that had to be more than ten years old.

"Perfect," I told him. I shut off the engine, took the ignition key off the ring and handed it to him as I levered myself out of the car. While he parked, I idly wondered why a lot that basically ran itself had an attendant. Maybe he was a Mafia charity case. The Family took care of its own, as evidenced by Bart's long-suffering association with Bertha Conti.

By the time he maneuvered my car into the special spot, I couldn't see it from where I stood. He slowly hobbled back to the entry and escorted me to his Corolla, where he held the door for me. The inside was fastidiously clean, even though the seats were repaired with duct tape. Rodney carefully closed the door and rounded the car to the driver's side. He eased himself in slowly, using a hand to lift his left leg in. Once settled, he asked, "Where to?"

I gave him the street address of the small dry cleaning store I patronized on Farwell. I could walk through and out to the back entry of my building.

"Sure thing, ma'am."

"Call me Angie." I set the money between us, on the bench seat. He waved it away. I let it lay there. "You're a real life-saver, Rodney."

He laughed and started the car. "I'm Julius. Rodney quit a few weeks ago and Tony hired me on as a temp. He said there was no point in making a new name tag if I didn't intend to stay."

That piqued my curiosity. "What's your next step?"

"I'm starting classes at Marquette. Pre-law."

"Impressive."

"Well, I scored some points for being a vet, but I did well on the admissions exams, too."

Were his limp and his facial injuries in the line of duty? "How long have you been out?" I asked.

"Eight months. I was at the VA hospital for a while. Afghanistan was not kind to me."

I swallowed hard. "Are you making it okay? I know a lot of people who know people. It would be an honor to help you, however I could."

"Thanks, ma'am, uh, Angie. I'm doing okay."

I took a business card out of my briefcase and put it on the seat. "If you ever need some help, call me."

"That's real nice of you." He pulled up to the curb. "I could walk you into your building, Angie. I'm not fast, but I won't let anybody get to you."

"You're a sweetheart, Julius, but this is a stealth operation."

He handed me a card with the lot rates on it. "Call me at that number. I can be here in ten minutes."

"Deal," I said, "and thanks." I exited the Corolla, glad that he hadn't refused my money and wishing that there was something more I could do for him.

The Vietnamese couple who ran the cleaners was watching a small wall-mounted TV when I entered. Apparently, the Severson story had hit the national news. Mr. Phan escorted me to the back door, where I quickly surveilled the alley leading to my building. Seeing no one, I proceeded across the slushy blacktop while he stood on the outside stoop and watched over me. I opened the service door and waved to him as I went inside. It was nice to know that he had my back.

It took me more than an hour to organize and write up my notes. Images of Hank resurfaced as I typed: the monk proceeding along the path in hooded robe and snow boots; the anguish as he explained why he had to abandon his family and why he couldn't return to them; the imploring look as he whispered his last word, *Love.* I stopped twice to wipe away tears. *If I hadn't interfered, he would still be alive*, I thought. *And there would still be a chance for the family to reconnect.* "I didn't mean to bring you harm, Hank," I whispered. Then I made a cup of tea and read the file, assessing what I could and couldn't share. There were so many secrets in this one man's life, with its layers upon layers of obfuscation. I'd welcome the familiarity of running background checks when this was closed.

Before that could happen, I needed to unmask the person who betrayed me by identifying Hank as Severson to the South Philly Mob. I printed the report and shuffled the papers into a neat stack. Reaching for the credenza, my hand stopped. Although I had the best security that Spider could install, I decided it would be wiser to store this file in the safe.

***

True to his word, Julius picked me up in front of the Phans' store within ten minutes of my call. I drove with him back to the lot and got into the Escape. "I'm serious about the offer of help," I said.

"Same goes for me, Angie. Call me if you need to escape the press again. Or anyone else, for that matter." He gave me a two-fingered salute as I pulled out of the lot.

Knowing the fridge was bare, I decided to do a little shopping. Glorioso's was sparsely populated. Keeping my head down, I selected fresh vegetables, homemade Giardinieria, sausage, cheese, prepared meatballs in marinara, and wine. I managed to get outside without being recognized. In front of the market, I called Julius and asked him, "What's your favorite cookie?"

"Glazed biscotti," he said with no hesitation.

"I'm on my way home from Sciortino's. I'll drop off a bag."

"Oh, man, that makes my night!"

I bought three loaves of Italian bread and assorted cookies, along with a dozen biscotti. At the lot, Julius opened the bag, immediately bit into one and sighed. "*Divino*," he said.

***

The press blocked the driveway to the condo's underground garage and thrust their mics at me, while their cameras and TV lights almost blinded me. I opted for a friendly smile as I rolled slowly forward, and they moved aside.

It was just after seven when I finished unloading the groceries and assembled a meatball sandwich and veggies for supper. The dining room taunted me with memories of meals shared with Wukowski, so I settled on the couch with my plate and a glass of wine, put on a Netflix episode of *Doc Martin*, and prepared to lose myself in the story.

Unfortunately, Martin's and Louisa's rocky romance did little to soothe me. I decided to switch to the Science channel's *How the Universe Works*. World-destroying comets and exploding stars matched my frame of mind much better. Four small chocolate butter star cookies from Sciortino's topped off a meal of indulgence, both gastronomic and emotional. It was time for bed.

Although sleep would probably elude me anyway, I knew it would be impossible if the clean male smell of Wukowski wafted up from the sheets. I stripped off the bed linen and tossed it into the laundry room to deal with tomorrow. Later, with the bed made and the teal and gold damask jacquard comforter back where it belonged, it struck me that the room was decidedly feminine. *Did Wukowski feel out of place here? How could I have overlooked that?* Some shopping therapy beckoned.

The weepiness of the day was gone, for the moment. Right now, self-care and business concerns were the focus. I showered and climbed into bed, a second glass of wine and a new V.I. Warshawski novel at hand. I woke up hours later, hugging Wukowski's pillow, with the book on the floor. Reaching over, I clicked off the light, snuggled into the pillow, and lay half-awake until the alarm sounded.

Chapter 32

The end is where we start from. — T.S. Eliot

A new client request awaited me in the office the next morning. It involved the bread-and-butter of the business. Someone was fudging the cash drawer at a local eatery, whose proceeds were down dramatically. I decided to turn Bobbie loose on it.

He rolled in at the usual time, around ten. After settling his things in the conference room, he strolled out and perched on a corner of my desk. "How ya doing?"

The concern in his voice almost overcame me, but I swallowed hard and said, "So-so. Last night was tough. But we have a potential new client"—I waved the printouts from the inquiries of the morning—"and I'd like you to handle it."

"On my own?" His eyes opened wide in excitement.

"Yes. I think you're ready. Get in touch with the restaurant owner and set up an interview. Then give me your written notes and we'll talk about whether it's a good fit for the agency." I handed him the paper for his case.

"I'm on it, Ange. What about the Wagner case? Are we closing it?

"Not yet. I need to find out who put Hank in the crosshairs. Papa's making some inquiries for me among his contacts, so the Wagner case is in a holding pattern right now."

He started toward the conference room, but stopped midstride. "As for the nights, you can call me any time."

"I know that, and I really appreciate it. Now scoot."

I started a to-do list: find a new cleaner for my condo, schedule a haircut and pedi, sit down with Bobbie to finalize office furniture for his work area, talk to Marcy, talk to Papa, talk to Bart, talk to Spider and Bram, redecorate bedroom. On second thought, I might save that last one until the time neared for a reunion with Wukowski.

Ten minutes later, a knock at the office entry door broke my zoned-out reverie of nights spent in that bedroom. "Come in," I called.

Two burly guys in overalls entered. "We're here to pick up Ms. Neh's office furniture."

"It's all over there." I gestured toward Susan's corner of the room, with its stacks of cardboard boxes, empty filing and shelving units, desk and a chair. The neither-here-nor-there nature of it depressed me. I hoped I'd feel better once the deed was done. "Be very careful with the shoji storage units. The sliding paper fronts are fragile … and expensive."

The older man made a note on his clipboard. "Ms. Neh here?"

Susan bustled in just as he spoke. "Here I am. Sorry to keep you waiting."

"No problem, ma'am. We'll start by loading the big pieces." His partner brought in a dolly, filled to the top with folded furniture pads. "Jeff, you take care of the desk, filing cabinets and chair. And be sure to cover the corners. That's where the damage always happens. I'll do the screened shelving units." They set to work, wrapping everything in pads and taping them down.

After a minute of the sound of ripping tape, Susan and I repaired to the conference room. "Okay if we invade your territory, Bobbie?" I asked.

"Of course," he said. "So, it's the big day, Susan. Excited?"

"Oh, yes. And scared. And sad." She gave me a mock glare. "I want your promise to call me every week and meet me for lunch at least once a month. No, twice. Once is too infrequent."

"I promise," I assured her.

"And you." She pointed at Bobbie. "I expect you to keep Angie away from all these dangerous cases."

"I promise to do my best," he echoed me.

Susan broke the melancholy of the moment with a sudden twist toward me. "What's all this on the news about you getting shot at and the press going after you and Wukowski again?"

When I told her the story of Holy Hill and my forced estrangement from Wukowski, she blanched. "No way! No darned way!" A 'darn' was as close as Susan generally came to cursing. "They can't do that! Keep two people in love apart for …"

"Two years, seven months and two days," I intoned. "I'm afraid they can, since he needs to get to retirement eligibility."

"Well, that just stinks."

"It sure does." I sighed. "But I'll get through it. It's not forever." *Seems like forever*, my brain insisted.

The movers took a little over an hour to load the truck. With hugs and a few tears, Susan headed out to a new chapter in her work life. Our office cleaner would be in tonight, but I went down to the super's office to retrieve a broom and dustpan, and swept up the dustballs, paper detritus and assorted other debris left behind. "Bobbie," I called, "come give me your considered opinion."

"What's up?" he asked, stepping out of the conference room.

"It looks dreary in here, but I'm not sure if that's my mood or reality."

Standing in the middle of the office, he slowly spun around and came to rest facing me. "Could use a little freshening up. Paint. Some splashes of color."

"What palette are you imagining?"

We spent the next hour online, happily considering color schemes that would project soothing professionalism, since the nature of my clients' concerns naturally raised their anxiety levels. People only hire a PI when they have a problem they can't solve themselves and they're willing to pay for the solution.

We decided that Bobbie would pick up paint samples for a grayish-green wall, with pops of brick red in accents around the room. I gave him a budget for furniture and we agreed that he would select something harmonious with mine, but not necessarily identical.

Next, I rang Bart's office. When I asked Bertha for ten minutes of Bart's time, to update him on a Family matter that he and I already discussed, she shocked me by categorically refusing to put me through to him. "He is far too busy at the present time, Ms. Bonaparte, and will be for the foreseeable future."

I knew Bertha didn't like me, but for her to act so unprofessionally was very far out of character. "Perhaps you could simply slip him a note with my name on it? I know he'll want to hear what I have to tell him."

"No." After a few beats, she unbent enough to add, "I'm afraid that's not possible." Then she hung up on me.

I sat in stunned silence, office phone dangling from my hand. What the hell! Gathering my winter paraphernalia, I called out to Bobbie. "I'm heading over to Bart's office."

"Sounds good. I'll call the restaurant after the lunch hour winds down and see if the owner can meet me off premises. Don't want to raise suspicions among the staff."

"That's why you're a natural at this, Bobbie. You think several steps ahead." With that, I headed for the Third Ward and Bart's office.

***

A rent-a-cop whom I'd never met manned the lobby security desk. "Who are you here to see?" he asked.

"Bart Matthews."

"And you are?"

"Angelina Bonaparte."

He picked up the phone and called upstairs. No eye contact, no small talk. After announcing me, he listened for a moment and then replaced the handset in the cradle. "Mr. Matthews is unavailable. You'll need to call for an appointment."

Glancing at his name tag, I said, "I already did that, Mr. Carlson."

He shrugged. "Can't help you."

"Then I'll help myself," I said, and bustled past him for the stairs.

"Hold on," he yelled. "You can't go up."

"Call Bertha. Tell her I'm on the way and if she wants you to call the cops, fine with me. That will at least get Bart's attention." I paused outside the office door to fold my coat and lay it on the floor before turning the doorknob.

Bertha rose from behind her desk as I entered and moved to stand in front of the door to the inner office. "You think Bart must drop whatever he's working on to see you?" She pointed her finger at me in accusation. "Spoiled, that's what you are," she hissed.

"I think no such thing, Mrs. Conti." I let my voice rise. "But I'm damned sure that Bart will not appreciate knowing that you refused to even book a future appointment for me. Perhaps if my papa were to call …"

"That's what I mean." By now, she was shouting. "You use the very organization that put bread on your table and clothes on your back, that paid for your education, that sends you clients, that arranges perks for you, that protects you." She heaved in a deep breath and then fairly spat the next words at me. "But do you support that organization? No, you revile it, you turn your back on it, you—"

Bart's door flung open. "What in God's name is going on out here?" He peered from me to Bertha, frowning.

Before Bertha could continue her tirade, I spoke. "Mrs. Conti refused to allow me to speak with you earlier, nor would she book an appointment for me. And she told the lobby guard to deny me admittance."

With a dazed expression, he turned to her. "Bertha, what's wrong?" His voice was gentle, questioning. "Come, sit down in my office, both of you, and let's talk." He placed a hand under her elbow and guided her into one of the client chairs. "Now, tell me what the problem is with getting Angie in to see me," he said.

Bertha clutched the chrome arms of the modern chair and stared down, refusing to make eye contact with either Bart or me. A pulse beat at her forehead and she breathed hard. Then she released her white-knuckled grip on the chair and hurled herself up. "I'll type up my resignation and have it on your desk in five minutes. You can supervise me as I pack up my personal effects. I quit."

"Bertha!" Bart said. "Please, sit down and tell me what's bothering you. Surely after all these years of faithful service, you don't want to leave in such a way." He tossed me the pleading look of a man out of his depth in the roiling waters of a woman's emotions.

"Mrs. Conti," I said, "I apologize sincerely for causing you distress. I'm going to leave now and let you and Bart work this out." I turned to the door.

Bart heaved himself up—twice in under ten minutes surely constituted his aerobic workout for the week—and approached Bertha. "I'll get back to you, Angie" he said. As I closed the door behind me, I heard him say, "We have too many years together to end like this, Bertha."

What in the world set her off like that? I wondered. We had our differences, but this was way beyond normal.

Chapter 33

Forgive your enemies, but never forget their names. — John F. Kennedy

The security guy glared at me as I walked past his desk. "I could lose my job over that," he said.

With a sigh, I stopped. He was right and I owed him, if not an explanation, at least reassurance. "Mr. Matthews and Mrs. Conti are in conference right now. Mr. Matthews will call me later, and I'll swear that you did nothing wrong and do not deserve any censure for what happened." I pulled a business card from my purse. "In case you need help, call me."

"Uh, well, thanks."

I nodded and headed back to the car, where I sat for several minutes, regaining my equilibrium. Had Bertha always felt that way about me? Was that the source of her antipathy? And was there a germ of truth in what she said?

Papa hadn't spoiled me, but he certainly had protected me and still did, to the degree I allowed it. I refused to consider that wrong, or worthy of Bertha's scorn. But the other accusation, that I accepted the Family connection and used it to my advantage, even as I scorned it–she wasn't entirely wrong. Thinking back to the recent past, I recalled the times I asked Tony Belloni for assistance, even to using his parking facility just yesterday. And last year, when Bart stepped up at my request to represent Adriana Johnson. And my turning to Papa for help with the South Philly Mob.

My insistence that I made my way due to my own hard work, with no Mafia help, was not factual. I didn't use the criminal aspects of the organization, but I did call on it when I could gain an advantage or help a client. So much for my vaunted denial of being a "Mafia princess." Bertha had a point.

But why the overreaction on her part? What triggered that? I hoped Bart would enlighten me when he called later. I didn't want him to lose Bertha at such short notice, with no replacement in sight. And I didn't want her to leave a job that probably constituted the center of her life.

My stomach growled, whether in reaction to the encounter with Bertha, or from a need for food, I couldn't say. A soup and roll lunch at Ma's would fill the inner me, without laying too heavily on my insides.

It felt strange to sit at a table alone. Thankfully, I didn't focus exclusively on Wukowski, since Bobbie and I often met there, too.

***

Bart didn't contact me until after seven that night. "Angie," he said with a little wheeze, "it's been a difficult day. I'm sorry it took me so long to get back to you. Are you by chance free to come to my office now?"

What did he have to say that couldn't be said on the phone? I wondered. "Of course, if you feel a face-to-face is necessary."

"I do. Park in Bertha's space. I'll tell the guard to let you in."

"Okay. I'm on my way."

It was only a ten-minute trip at that time of night. I pulled into

Bertha's spot, as directed, and rode the elevator from the small underground garage to the lobby, where Mighty Mary sat. "Hey, Mary," I called. "How are things?"

There was a grim set to her face as she shut the textbook she'd been reading. "Been better, Angie. What the hell happened today with you and Mrs. Conti? Mr. Matthews told security to deny her access to the building."

"Really? Honestly, I don't know what's going on. She suddenly decided that I'm a demon in disguise and refused to let me see or talk to Bart. I'm on my way up now to find out the story. Okay if I leave my coat and briefcase with you?"

"Sure." She moved aside to allow me access to the guard desk shelf. "You're cleared to go up," she said. "Hope it turns out okay."

"Me, too." I climbed the steps slowly, feeling a slight sense of dread. After arriving at Bart's outer office, I knocked and entered. "Bart," I called, "it's Angie."

"Come through," he told me. "Please take a seat." Bart's mouth was a thin line and his complexion had a slightly grayish-green hue.

I settled uneasily in one of the visitor chairs and waited to learn what he had to say.

"Angie, I owe you and Mrs. Wagner a huge apology and will do all that I can to make things right."

"I don't understand, Bart. Aren't we meeting to talk about Bertha?"

He exhaled and looked down, then handed me a printout. "That's a listing of my office phone records since you spoke to me about your theoretical accountant client with Mafia ties. It includes calls to the South Philly organization. I did not make those calls."

I stared at the paper in my hand. "Bertha?"

He nodded. "I confronted her about her inappropriate behavior when you left the office. She began to rant about her duty to the Family and your withholding information from them. She said that she answered to a higher authority. You'd think Mazzoni was the Pope. Then she stormed out. I contacted the phone company for a current listing of calls from the office number." He flipped the switch to activate the exhaust fan and lit a cigarette, the hand that held the butane lighter trembling slightly. "I have no idea how she knew of our conversation, Angelina. I swear that I said nothing to anyone."

Leaning back and shutting my eyes, I recalled the day that I met with Bart to ask if he would broker an agreement to let Hank—Tommaso—live the life of a free man without interference from the mob. "Bertha was angry, the day of our initial discussion. Remember how she huffed over to your desk when you asked her to leave the room, ostensibly to black out our meeting on your desk blotter? I think she used that as a cover to press the intercom button so that she could listen in on what we discussed."

He held the smoke in his lungs for a count of three, then spat it out as he cursed, "*Merda.*"

"Indeed." I steepled my hands. "It makes a weird kind of sense, Bart. The Family supported Bertha when her husband was killed. She's worked for you for decades, helping you defend those in the organization. We've even joked before that Bertha personifies the phrase, 'married to the mob.' So when I tried to protect Hank Wagner, whom she probably sees as a defector and therefore a betrayer, she acted."

After several more pulls on the unfiltered gasper, he stubbed it out and leaned toward me. "There is a certain logic to your deductions," he agreed, "but in exposing Hank as a betrayer, *she* betrayed *me*. I can neither forgive nor forget that. I do not think that Chicago will either, since Milwaukee is under their control and she essentially invited an outside Family into their territory to perform an execution. Mrs. Conti will find Milwaukee to be too hot for her, even in the dead of winter."

An image of Bertha's body unfolded in my imagination and I inwardly shuddered. I wanted no more deaths on this case, but I had to tread carefully. This was a Family matter and not one in which I had more than tangential input.

"Bart, on behalf of Marcy and on my own behalf, I ask you to hold back on informing the Chicago boss for one day. Only one. I want to take this to my papa and ask his counsel. He has already approached them to ask them to contact Philly for more information. If he believes that they should know about Bertha, then I will step aside and let him handle it. Will you agree?"

"She dishonored *me*, Angie, not Pasquale."

I nodded. "I see that. But for the sake of the many years of service she gave you, can you give me that day? I will be in your debt."

"Rot! It is I who owe you. My office broke faith with you, which led to the death of your client's husband and your own immediate danger. I let you down."

He swiveled his chair away from me and I waited in silence.

Turning back, he said, "I will speak to Pasquale tonight and explain what has occurred. He and I will reach a consensus and then I will tell you as much as I can. That is the best I can do, Angelina."

It was the best I would get, either from Bart or, I suspected, from my papa. "Very well. I will wait to hear from you." I rose and paused, looking him in the eye. "Please, Bart, no further violence. I cannot lie on your behalf if that should occur."

"I would not ask you to, but I make no promises." He rose and rounded the large desk. Placing his hands on my shoulders, he said, "I know you do not understand the code that we live under, Angie, but it is not one that I will breach. For your sake, though, and because you are also an injured party, I will extend as much leniency as I can." Then he bent down and kissed me on each cheek.

Bemused, I reached around his big body and hugged him. "Thanks, Bart." Then I turned and drifted down the stairs to the security desk.

"Here's your stuff," Mighty Mary told me. "Everything okay?

"It's a delicate situation," I responded. "I'm afraid I can't say more." I grabbed my belongings and headed for home, where I spent a restless night worrying alternately about Wukowski and Bertha Conti.

Chapter 34

The point of decorating … is to create the background for the best life you can have. — Deborah Needleman

Bobbie was already in the office when I arrived the next morning. "I'm in the conference room, Angie," he called. "Can you take a minute to look at some things?"

"Sure." I hung up my coat, grabbed my cup of Joe and headed into what appeared to be a maelstrom of brochures, swatches and paint chips.

"I've got some great options for my office space," Bobbie told me. "I'll start with my top picks and we can work downward from there. I don't want to break the budget."

"That's very thoughtful," I told him, settling in a chair while he made what amounted to a designer presentation. Two hours later, we agreed on what he called The Look. I could honestly hear the capitalization.

I sat back while Bobbie carried on a bit about a mid-century upholstered club chair that his partner, Stephano—real name Steve, but that was far too plain for a person in the high-end clothing industry—wanted to donate. As he talked, I thought that I would miss Susan and our old office. Then Lela popped into my head, followed quickly by Wukowski. So must loss in such a short space of time. I would treat myself to chocolate tonight.

Bobbie gathered the design materials into a folder, reserving the choices we made, and headed into the office area to paint the wall samples. "We'll have to wait until these dry to be sure, but I like them already," he told me.

"I agree."

After a trip to the men's room to wash up, he settled in my visitor chair with a notebook. "I met with the restaurateur, Jimmy Malone, at a coffee shop yesterday. He's a piece of work, Angie. Thinks he's Irish Mafia or something. Very abrasive and hard-nosed. I channeled my inner Angie to keep from walking out on him."

"Inner Angie?"

"You know, professional, good listener, not easy to rile. He referred to the barista as a fag. I bit my lip and added ten percent to the potential bill."

With a snicker, I said, "Works for me. So, what did he have to say?"

"We went over receipts, which are definitely down, and work schedules for all the staff. He doesn't want cameras at this stage." Bobbie leaned forward a little. "I think there may be some funny stuff happening at the place, and he doesn't want it recorded."

"Funny, how?"

"No idea yet. It's a gut feeling."

Like Wukowski, I thought, but quickly shoved it to the back of my mind. "What are the odds you can figure this out? Shall we accept the client?"

"I think so, and not because it would be the first case on my own." He removed a check and handed it to me. "Retainer," he said. "I can return it if you disagree."

Glancing down, I felt my eyes widen. "Nice," I said.

He smirked. "Told you I'd make him pay. So here's my plan." He detailed ideas to identify a pattern to the losses and the possibility of Susan reviewing the books. "If none of that pans out, it's either camera surveillance or I go undercover on the staff, which will be pretty expensive for Mr. Jimmy damn-fag Malone, I assure you. Am I missing anything?"

"I'd run background checks on his workers. Depending on how many he employs, it shouldn't be too costly. Look for anyone with a criminal background, someone living in an upscale neighborhood that a restaurant salary wouldn't support, that sort of thing. And don't forget to do the same for Malone. It wouldn't be the first time an owner robbed the till and tried to claim insurance."

Bobbie made notes as I spoke. "I'll find out who his agent is. Won't hurt to contact them regarding recent claims."

"Good work, Bobbie," I said. "Print out the client forms and email them to Mr. Malone, if you think it's secure. He can fill them out and bring them when he meets you. I always insist on a real signature. Electronic ones are too easy to deny."

Bobbie rose and headed for the conference room. "I'm meeting Steve for lunch. Want to join us?"

The idea of being with a happy couple gave me a slight bellyache. "I'll pass, but thanks. And thank Steve for his help."

"Will do."

After Bobbie left, I checked the time on my watch and then verified it on my phone. Twelve-twenty. *Had Papa and Bart reached a consensus regarding Bertha?* I wanted to call her home and tell her to get out of town, but I'd made a deal with Bart and I had to honor it. *How long would it be before I heard from them?* I decided to go back to the condo for lunch, now that the reporters weren't camping out in my driveway.

At home, I brewed a cup of tea and assembled a small plate of cheese and sausage on crackers, with a savory artisanal mustard. A side of Glorioso's Giardiniera filled out the plate. I sat at the table and pulled out my tablet to check personal email.

The landline rang mid-chew. I jumped up to answer it and saw Papa's number on the caller ID. "'Lo," I mumbled through the crackers in my mouth.

"Angie, this is Papa. You sound rushed. Should I call back?"

"No, don't hang up. I just need a swallow of water." I took a couple of gulps and picked up the handset again. "Sorry, Papa, you caught me eating lunch, but I didn't want to miss the call."

"Ah. I'm sure you've been a bit anxious."

Too right, I thought. "You might say that. Have you and Bart reached an agreement?"

"We have. Perhaps you would join us at his office."

"I'm on my way." I took a moment to dump my tea into a go-mug, then hustled out, leaving the messy table for later.

Chapter 35

No evil is without its compensation. — Seneca the Younger

Mighty Mary grabbed my coat and waved me upstairs, where Papa and Bart waited for me in Bart's office. "Lock the outer door, please," Bart called as I entered what was once Bertha's realm. A tingle of foreboding ran up my spine at Bart's words.

Papa rose to plant a kiss on my cheek. *At least this isn't all business*, I thought, remembering my meeting with Don Pasquale in the family kitchen. Bart rose slightly from his big chair and nodded. I sat next to Papa in one of the visitor chairs and waited.

"Angelina," Papa said, "Bart and I have done a great deal of what you might call leg work since yesterday." He looked at Bart, who nodded to him to proceed. "I contacted the Chicago *consigliere* after you left, to protest the danger that you were in and to ask for his help with his east coast counterpart to determine who notified them of Severson's whereabouts. Marco assured me that he would take the matter up with the acting boss. When Bart called me last night to inform me of Mrs. Conti's deceit, I notified Marco." Papa nodded to Bart.

"Louie Tomatoes, that is, Louis Marino, was in negotiation with Joe Merlino in Philadelphia this morning. There was an acknowledgement of wrong-doing on the part of our friends on the east coast in coming into our territory uninvited. We reached a deal that, while it cannot restore the life that was taken, can go a long way toward helping Mrs. Wagner raise her children.

"The Philadelphia Family," he continued, "will pay Mrs. Wagner thirty thousand dollars for funeral expenses. They will also double the face amount of the policy that Hank took out—one million dollars—in the form of a trust from which she can draw up to one hundred thousand per year, or more if necessity demands for things like medical bills or college for the children. The residual will be available when her youngest child completes college or attains the age of twenty-five. I will administer the trust."

I sucked in a big breath at that bombshell. "That's ... very generous, Bart. Of course, Marcy may refuse the settlement, given that it constitutes blood money, but I will advise her to accept, for the sake of her family."

"Very wise," Papa said. "There is also the matter of your own safety, *mia amata figlia.*"

My beloved daughter. I blinked rapidly to stop the welling tears.

He continued. "There is not enough money to compensate for your being in the path of mortal danger, even if the *stronzi* insist that their man would never miss his target. Still, they offer the sum of one hundred thousand dollars for disturbing your peace of mind."

If Hank hadn't been killed, would the MPD have continued looking the other way on my relationship with Wukowski? How could money make up for the years ahead of me without him? Like Papa, I found little solace in the offer and felt uneasy, for the same reason that Marcy might. "I'll weigh that decision once I've talked to my client," I told Papa and Bart.

"Quite right," Papa said with a nod.

Bart cleared his throat. "As for the matter of Bertha Conti, I considered your plea for her life and also her years as a dedicated assistant, as well as her obvious mental and emotional upheaval. Her friends in Philadelphia will arrange for her to relocate to an undisclosed location in their territory and will compensate me for the loss of her services. We will say no more on that." He leaned back, causing his reinforced chair to groan for mercy, and folded his hands over his belly. "It now remains for you to talk with Mrs. Wagner. Once we have her decision, the matter will be closed."

***

When I called Quad-A, Larry told me that Marcy decided to take some time off. I rang her at home. She answered in a dispirited voice. *Small wonder*, I told myself. I asked if she could arrange for her mother or sister to babysit so that we could talk privately, and she agreed to make arrangements for the children and meet me for a drink at Ed's Tap around five.

I waved from a back booth as she entered the small bar. We exchanged hugs and I asked what she'd like to drink.

"Oh, anything," she said.

"Beer, wine or something stronger?"

"Wine."

Her tone and appearance reflected a woman being sucked below the water by an undertow. Somehow, I had to toss her a life preserver. "Two glasses of the regular," I told Marlene, who poured Gewürztraminer with a flourish that made me smile. The first time I met Wukowski here, during the Morano case, she called it grab-a-geezer and he asked if she was referring to him. I asked him, "Were you more worried about her labeling you a geezer or about me grabbing you?"

Was everything going to remind me of him? No, I decided, *just the places we'd been and the things we'd done and the food he ate and the ... Stop*! I commanded. Grabbing the wine, I returned to the booth.

I lifted my glass in a toast. "To friends." We clinked and each took a small swallow. "Marcy," I began, "I have some information that you may find disturbing. I hope you'll hear me out, though."

"About Hank?" Her eyes drew tight with anxiety.

"Yes, about Hank. Before I met him at Holy Hill, I tried to feel out the east coast mob, to see if they were willing to ignore him and let him get on with his life."

She gulped and took a sip of wine. "That didn't work out very well."

"No. It went horrendously wrong. You see, I spoke with a local Mafia attorney, never mentioning Hank by name, just posing a hypothetical situation. Unknown to the lawyer or me, his office assistant listened in on our conversation and decided to search for a real-life correlate to the one I described. When she came across the article in the *Philadelphia Enquirer*, she contacted the South Philly Mob. You know the rest of that story. They sent a hit man to be sure Hank would never reveal what he knew as Tommaso Severson."

"Why would she do that?" Marcy's voice rose and Marlene glanced over, eyebrows raised.

I gave a small shake of the head to let her know I didn't need help. "This woman's husband was a soldier—a member of the local Milwaukee crime syndicate—decades ago. When he was killed, the organization took care of her, even getting her the job working for my attorney friend. Her sense of loyalty overcame her judgment."

"Even knowing about me and the kids?"

"The newspaper account was from many years ago, before Hank moved here and met you, so I doubt it."

"So she and the Mob walk away, scot-free, while my kids have no hope of knowing their father and I have no chance to see Hank again or talk to him about what happened between us. Tell me her name." Her voice sounded bitter and her hands clenched so hard on the stem of the wine glass that I feared it would snap.

"I can't do that, Marcy. But I can say that her life, such as it is, has been turned upside-down. She's lost the job that meant everything to her and must leave the area to avoid the wrath of the Chicago Outfit, whose territory was violated by her actions."

"Pardon me if I lack sympathy for the self-righteous bitch."

"Marcy." I laid my hand on hers. "I didn't tell you this to elicit sympathy. As I mentioned at our last meeting, my papa has ties to the organization. He and the attorney approached those in top positions in Chicago, once they knew how Hank's death was orchestrated. They in turn let their displeasure be known to the leaders in Philadelphia. The upshot is that Chicago brokered a deal to provide you and the kids with monetary support, as a sign of their desire to make compensation."

"They want to pay me *money* for my husband? For my children's father?"

A young couple rose and left the bar, obviously disturbed by the words that Marcy almost shouted.

"Please, take a drink of your wine and hear me out. I'm on your side. I'll do whatever you decide. Okay?"

She knocked back a good amount, exhaled a ragged breath and nodded. "Okay," she said, unblinking eyes on me.

"Because Hank set up the life insurance policy under false pretenses, it most likely will not be honored. The Philly mob is willing to establish a trust fund for you and the kids, for double the face amount of Hank's policy, two million. The trust will pay you up to one hundred thousand a year, plus any extraordinary expenses like medical bills or school tuition." I took her hand and squeezed it between my own. "I know that money is not enough to compensate for a man's life, for the future that your family will face without Hank. But it will give you financial security, both now and in the future. When the time comes, Henry Junior can pursue a science degree. The girls can go to college and get good jobs. The financial burden you've been carrying will disappear. If you want, you can ask the trust to pay off the house and quit work." I leaned in slightly. "It's pitifully inadequate for the cost you've paid, Marcy, but it can help you face the future without worry. They've also agreed to pay thirty thousand toward Hank's funeral expenses. Will you think about it?"

"Give me a minute," she said, and headed for the bathrooms at the back of the tavern. When she returned almost five minutes later, her makeup was washed off and her lips were set in a grim line. "I'd be hurting my children if I refused the money." She stood over me. "So tell them I'll take it. But also tell them I hope they rot in hell."

As she marched out of the bar, I murmured, "I have no doubt they will."

Chapter 36

The life of the dead is placed in the memory of the living.

— Marcus Tullius Cicero

While she waited for the county to release Hank's body for interment, Marcy made funeral decisions. Today, she would commit the man she hadn't seen in five years to the ground, grieving the life they might have had.

I slipped a light gray coatdress over an as-yet unworn berry-colored demi bra and hipster panties, thinking of Wukowski's hands on my skin as he undressed me. Before I could get maudlin over yet another memory, I allowed myself a moment to revel in the feelings. Then, with a sigh, I checked myself in the mirror.

I'd toned down my usual spiky hairstyle, opting instead for a side-parted, gelled look. *Maybe I'll let it grow out a bit,* I thought. *Asymmetrical bangs might be fun.* I needed a change. No, I needed distraction. After inserting small platinum and diamond earrings into my earlobes, I grabbed a pair of stacked-heel black pumps and made for the front door.

When Marcy asked me whether she had to use the Family-backed funeral home that Bart recommended, I assured her that the choice was hers. "Good," she said, "because I won't put their money back into their pockets." So the service was at a mid-sized, well-respected establishment near her home.

Local news teams were set up along the perimeter of the parking lot, trying to get sound bites from mourners as they passed by. I even spotted a Fox 29 Philadelphia logo on a shoulder-hoisted camera. For once, I appreciated the bitterly cold wind. *Let them freeze*, I thought, ignoring mics thrust in my face.

Inside, the funeral home staff was in the process of opening sliding dividers to create more space for the overflow crowd in the hallway leading into the parlor where Hank's coffin rested. A multitude of young men and women, Hank's students from six years ago and earlier, gathered in small groups, talking in undertones and laughing, then stopping themselves as they attempted to regain the somber expressions that the occasion seemed to demand. *How lovely that Marcy would have this remembrance of Hank's positive influence. He was so much more than a Mafioso.*

I hung up my coat and made my way into the room where the family stood greeting visitors. Two women flanked Marcy. From the resemblance, I decided they must be her mother and sister. A small herd of children played in a side parlor. I picked out Henry Junior, looking older than his ten years in a suit and tie; Susie, an eight-year old image of Marcy; and little Marjorie, only six, twirling around so that her pretty blue dress swirled around her. Young Henry would be the only one to hold real memories of his father, and those would fade all too quickly. That saddened me more than Hank's death.

When I got to the front of the line, I shook hands with Marcy's sister and mother, and embraced Marcy in a gentle hug. "I'm so sorry I never knew Hank," I said. "He touched a lot of lives for good." She nodded and dabbed at her eyes.

Before I could say more, Bobbie spoke from behind me. "Angie, I'm sorry I'm late. Augusta kept me waiting while she primped."

I turned abruptly, looking into the smiling eyes of my Padua Manor co-conspirator, and felt ashamed that I was so caught up in the drama surrounding Bertha that I hadn't thought to call her. Thank goodness for Bobbie!

He gently nudged her forward. "Marcy, meet Augusta Simmons, who is a resident at Padua Manor in Stevens Point, the place where Hank worked as an aide for a time."

Decked out in a cobalt blue dress, Augusta was a pop of color in a sea of somber tones. "My dear," she said, reaching for Marcy's hands, "your husband was a kind soul—and helpful, too. I still miss him when I try to balance my checkbook. I refuse to wear black for Jim. That's how I knew him, as Jim. I celebrate his life in joy."

The two women hugged, and I saw Marcy's mother raise an eyebrow.

Bobbie, Augusta and I settled on padded chairs as the background music ended and the funeral home director announced that the service would be starting. To my surprise, Bart Matthews approached us from a side aisle and we moved to give him two seats at the end of the row.

The priest stammered a bit through a very short homily, obviously struggling to deliver a message of hope for a man who belonged to an organized crime syndicate, married under false pretenses, and then deserted his family. It was the young people whom Hank taught who delivered the real eulogy and whose words resounded with respect for their beloved teacher. Many broke down in tears as they told of the hours Hank spent one-on-one with them, tutoring them to pass math exams, helping them write college application essays, even finding them part-time jobs so they could stay in school.

Marcy's face went from distressed to peaceful, her posture from slumped to straightened. She whispered to Henry, Susie and Marjorie, obviously directing them to pay attention to what was being said about their father. I offered a silent thanksgiving that this moment would be the defining one for Hank's memory.

When the services ended, people mingled to talk and reminisce. Bart invited Bobbie, Augusta and me to lunch at Tre Rivali, near his office in the historic Third Ward. "Please be my guests. I would invite Marcy's family also, but she is a bit … chilly toward me, due to my connections."

"I expect that she'll want to get the children home, Bart. Or maybe her extended family will gather." I turned to Augusta. "Please say you can join us."

"It all depends on dear Bobbie," she said. "He's my driver. I'm happy to spend as much time with you, and away from you-know-where, as I can."

"Then it's settled. Shall we meet you there, Bart?" I asked, sure that he would want to smoke on the way.

The reporters didn't notice me, escorted as I was by a gorgeous young man and a sprightly older woman. We got to the car without incident and motored away.

Once seated in a small private room of the restaurant, the waiter asked for our drink orders. I decided on a brandy old-fashioned, sweet—a Milwaukee classic.

"Oh, my," Augusta warbled, "it's been years since I had a cocktail. Let me see, what was it that Myrna and I used to enjoy?" She thought for a moment and then clapped her hands together. "A pink lady! That was it." She gave a sly grin. "It's not as innocuous as it sounds. Good thing I'm not driving."

We placed our orders for drinks and perused the Mediterranean menu. The men opted for strip steak, but Augusta and I decided to split an order of mascarpone cheese ravioli. We wanted to save room for dessert.

When the drinks arrived, I lifted my glass. "To Henry Wagner, husband, father, teacher, helper. May his memory live on in those who knew and loved him."

"Hear, hear," Augusta seconded, and we clinked our glasses and drank.

"Mrs. Simmons," Bart said, "I'm fascinated to know more about how you became involved in Angie's investigation."

"Well, let me tell you, it was the most exciting and interesting thing that's happened to me in years!" With much drama and charm, she told the story of our clandestine meeting at the city park and her subsequent assistance in getting Bobbie and me into the facility for a nighttime reconnaissance.

At the end, Bart toasted her with a "Well done," and turned to me and Bobbie to say, "I'd certainly like to learn more about that foray."

"Plausible deniability," I told him, and he guffawed.

When I asked Augusta how Myrna was doing, she shook her head sadly. "She's going downhill, I'm afraid. I will be glad when her trials are over."

"I want to keep in touch," I said. "Do you think Mrs. Rogers will cause trouble for you if she sees me come to pick you up for lunch occasionally?"

When she hesitated, Bart said, "Leave it to me. I'll make sure you and your sister have no repercussions over a visit from … Ann Carson, right?"

After a delicious meal and an even more delicious dessert and coffee,

Bart excused himself to return to the office. I drove Bobbie and Augusta to the funeral home, where we hugged before he settled her carefully into the Jetta and turned to me. "I'll be in the office tomorrow."

"Thanks for thinking of Augusta," I told him.

"No prob. I knew you had too much on your mind." He backed away and peered at me. "What's the rest of the day like for you?"

"There are a few other loose ends I need to tie up on the Wagner case. After that, I see a bubble bath with a glass of B&B in my future."

"Good. You need to pamper yourself a little."

***

I returned to the office to smooth out the remaining details of the Wagner case. A lot of people helped me find Hank. They deserved to know at least part of the outcome.

"Frank Jamieson," said the voice on the phone.

"Hello, Frank. It's Angie Bonaparte. You helped me on the Hank Wagner case."

"Of course. I've been following developments in the news. You were … present when he died."

"No need to tiptoe around it. I was present when he was killed. Executed, by a branch of organized crime in Philadelphia. It was truly sad, Frank, a real waste of a good man's life. I wanted you to know that."

I heard him swallow. "That's rough," he said. "I'm glad you told me. And I'm really glad you're okay."

"Thanks. The other reason I called is to ask you about A Place To Lay Your Head. I'm wondering if there's something Doris has mentioned that they could make good use of."

"They need a new furnace, but that's not an insignificant amount of money, given the size of the building."

"How much do you estimate it will cost?"

"Nearly five thousand for a high-efficiency model."

"Get them the best. I'll cover it." *Or rather, the South Philly Mob's guilt money will.* "Another thing that's on my list. I talked with Doris about a homeless man, Willie Parsons, during the course of the investigation."

"Yep. I know Willie. He's been in court a few times on vagrancy charges. Haven't seen him around lately."

"Willie passed away at Padua Manor. It's a convoluted story, with Hank at the center. Since you represented him legally, I believe your dealings are covered by attorney-client privilege, even after death."

"True," was all he said.

"Do you want to know the whole story, or would you prefer to stay on the edges of it?"

He exhaled. "Tell me."

As I gave him the short version of the Tommaso-Hank-Jim-Karl saga, Frank made the occasional "I see" and "Jeez." When I explained about Hank working as Karl Jorgensen at Padua Manor, and that he managed to get Willie admitted under Hank's name, he stopped me. "That wasn't in the papers," he said.

"No, and I'd like to keep it that way, for the sake of one of the residents who helped me. It was a mercy, really, because Willie was in end-stage liver failure and got decent care there. His death was the reason that Hank's obituary made it into the Stevens Point newspaper and initially got my attention."

"What a tangled web we weave …"

"… when first we practice to deceive," I ended the quote. There were so many silken threads to that web, threads that led to Hank's death and my estrangement from Wukowski. It might have been better if Hank had just continued to live under the radar. But no one can undo the past. We can only live into the future. "I wanted you to know the truth, Frank. And to thank you for being a friend to Hank." I thought back to my original assessment of him. "I misjudged him. He was a good man."

Chapter 37

Promise me you'll always remember: You're braver than you believe, and stronger than you seem, and smarter than you think. — A. A. Milne

I was wrung out when I got back to the condo. Still full from my lunch at Tre Rivali, I decided to do what I told Bobbie. When I unscrewed the cap on the bubble bath, its citrusy aroma brought back the memory of Wukowski joining me in the tub barely three weeks ago. I replaced the cover and reached for an unopened bottle of homemade milk and honey bath lotion that Emma and Angela made as a Christmas gift. I needed to hold onto other memories.

With a glass of B&B resting on the low teak table next to the tub, I sank into the soothing water and closed my eyes. The next days, weeks, months and years would test my mettle, I had no doubt. I'd been alone after the divorce, but that was a time tinged with anger and resolve to find myself. I accomplished that. I created a good life outside of marriage, a life that felt fulfilled and happy, bookended by my business and my children and grandchildren.

Then came Wukowski. A difficult man, to be sure, but an honest, honorable, loving man, for all that.

I wouldn't collapse. I fought too hard for my life and I couldn't backtrack. My friends, my family, my work—those would be my consolation and my support until two years, six months and twenty-five days had passed. The day was noted in my calendar. Time to stop counting.

Seneca wrote, *Begin at once to live, and count each separate day as a separate life.* This interval would be my separate life. I took a sip of B&B. Angular bangs would look good on me, I decided. I thought Wukowski would like them, too. Someday.

THE END

"The best way to thank an author is to write a review."
— Anonymous

If you enjoyed this book, please consider posting a review on your favorite retailer's website. Reviews mean the world to an author, so I thank you in advance.

Read on for short excerpts from *Truth Kills* and *Cash Kills.*

Truth Kills

Hold faithfulness and sincerity as first principles.

—Analects of Confucius

I'm a professional snoop and I'm good at it. While on the job, I can look like the senior partner of an accountancy firm in my pinstriped navy business suit, or the neighborhood white-haired old-lady gossip. Off the job, I'm a fifty-something hottie—white hair gelled back, dramatic eye make-up, toned body encased in designer duds. Gravity has taken a small toll, but who notices in candlelight?

As I rubbed potting soil into the cooking oil that I'd already smeared on my Salvation Army second-hand clothes, I examined myself in the mirror. A short, plain woman (five foot, three inches) with choppy white hair and no make-up, wearing dirty, baggy clothes, looked back at me. A homeless person. I nodded and headed down the fire stairs to the parking garage, trying to avoid meeting any of my neighbors.

The beauty of being a woman, as the French say, "of a certain age," is that I can be invisible. Young people, both men and women, look right through me, unless I make the effort to be noticed. Older men look past me, too, to gaze upon the tight, toned, tanned bodies that they wish they could possess. Only older women seem to notice me, because they're judging me against some invisible standard and wondering how I measure up compared to them. It's not usually malicious, it's just how we were raised. Believe me, I do it myself. Is her ass tighter than mine? Are her boobs perkier? Any cellulite on those thighs? It's competition at the most primitive level, the female equivalent of two silver-backed gorillas thumping chests and roaring at each other.

Today, however, wasn't a hottie day. Elisa Morano, one of the aforementioned tight, toned and tanned, was suspected of playing house with my client's husband, Anthony Belloni, a.k.a. Tony Baloney. Tony's cellular phone bill listed lots of calls to Ms. Morano's apartment, coincidentally located in one of Tony's many real estate holdings. His credit card statement showed purchases of lingerie, perfume and a fur coat, stuff that his wife, Gracie, had yet to see. To top it off, Gracie was eight months pregnant with their fifth child and spitting mad. She hired me to find out whether Tony was indeed cheating with Elisa Morano.

Which brings me back to my bag lady persona. Dumpster diving is legal. Once the trash is on the curb, it's public property. The Supremes ruled on it, and I mean Scalia and company, not the group Diana Ross fronted. People like me make a good living, finding out stuff from the trash. The problem is getting to it. The super will stop an average Jane from digging through the garbage, but if he sees a bag lady, he'll likely turn the other way. No harm in recycling, right?

So on this hot Thursday morning in August, I parked my car a block away, shuffled up the drive to Elisa's building and jumped into the dumpster that squatted behind it. My short stature made it easy for me to hide in there as I searched for something with her name on it. These people were upper class, everything was nicely bagged and I didn't think I'd have to worry about getting crap on my car seat when I was done.

It took about twenty minutes to find the bag, full of paper that was run through a shredder. I couldn't be sure until I put it all back together, but there was a piece with an "El" still intact. Maybe it was "Elisa." It was all I found that even remotely fit, so I tossed it over the side and heaved myself out, straight into the path of a hulk in a black suit.

"Watcha doin' there, lady?" Tony Baloney's bodyguard, Jimmy the Arm, asked as he grabbed me and pinned me to the side of the dumpster. Jimmy's sleeve-defying biceps compensate for his tiny mental gifts.

I realized that Jimmy didn't recognize me, despite having seen me on numerous occasions, both social and professional. My bag lady persona was my best defense. "Nothin.' I ain't doin' nothin.' Just lookin,'" I responded.

"For what?"

"Stuff ta sell. Clothes. Shoes. Books. Cans. These rich folks toss out good stuff." I pulled a face. "But not much today, one bag. Just my luck."

"Well, leave it and get goin' and don't come back to this building. Unnerstan?" He gave a little shove for good measure, not enough to hurt. His mama must have raised him well. Of course, he'd toss a rival into a cement mixer with no qualms. But I'm not averse to using whatever advantages come my way. I earned all the white on my head, and if it gets me out of a jam, it's just one of the perks of being slightly older.

I sloped off down the driveway, looking behind me as if scared that Jimmy was following. Actually, I was checking that the bag was still lying next to the dumpster. Sure enough, Jimmy ignored it and entered the building by the super's door. Guess Jimmy's mama never taught him to pick up trash. I scuttled back, grabbed the bag, and sprinted down the street to the lot where I left my car, to drive back to the office.

I share office space on Prospect Avenue, on Milwaukee's east side, with the firm of Neh Accountants. The "s" on the end is misleading. It's a one-person company run by Susan Neh, a third-generation Japanese American. Susan and I met when we both worked for Jake Waterman. She conducted his financial investigations and I did his legwork—computer searches, tails, background checks. It didn't take Susan long to earn her CPA and go out on her own. I joined her when I got my P.I. license and needed a place to hang my shingle. Most of Susan's clientele are of Japanese descent, but lately, she's working with a few Hmong and Vietnamese. I was glad to find that Susan was out on a client call today. It saved me from explaining my less than glamorous appearance.

It took me six hours of tedious, neck-straining, eyeball-screaming work to piece the shredded paper from the bag back together. Luckily, Elisa didn't have a cross-cut shredder, just the kind that produces long strips of paper. I can reassemble cross-cut, too, given enough time and motivation. The only way to be absolutely sure that no one can read your letters is to burn them and pulverize the ashes, or soak the paper in a pail of water mixed with a half-cup of bleach to destroy the ink. Then you can toss the blank paper with no worries.

Like most people, Elisa simply put a plastic bag into the can and shredded it into the bag. When she lifted it out and discarded it, the remains were in distinct layers, making it easier to separate and reassemble. It helped that the paper had different colors and textures. It's like working a jigsaw puzzle, without the picture on the box for a guide.

Six hours later, I had a pretty fair understanding of the woman—vain (online article about Botox, with list of local practitioners), fertile (Ortho-Provera drug interaction statement from a mail-order prescription company), savvy (year-old Vanguard mutual fund statement showing a 70K balance), cautious (no intact papers with her name in the dumpster, she apparently shredded everything).

I wasn't any closer, though, to discovering if Tony was indeed making it with the beauteous Ms. Morano, and my back was screaming from hours of bending over the office work table. My skin itched, even though I'd changed out of my clean dirty clothes, and it was already six o'clock. I made copies of the pieced-together papers, tossed them in my briefcase, and headed for home in my Black Cherry Miata convertible. There aren't enough top-down days in southeast Wisconsin, but this was one and I felt good, tooling down Lincoln Memorial Drive with the cool air of Lake Michigan on my skin. Heaven.

The Miata, like my condo, was a gift to myself following my divorce. The decree restored both my self-respect and my maiden name—Angelina Bonaparte, pronounced Boe-nah-par-tay, not Bo-nah-part. Napoleon was a Corsican-*cum*-French wannabe, so he left the last syllable off, but I'm one hundred percent Sicilian and I pronounce it the way it was meant to be pronounced.

I love my car. It symbolizes my post-marriage financial and emotional independence, and the sense of personal daring that I kept under tight wraps while I was Mrs. Bozo (I call him "your dad" when the kids are around, even though they're grown and have their own kids). I still shudder to think of twenty-five prime years spent trying to fit the pattern of wife, lover, mother, housekeeper. Picture June Cleaver wearing a sassy red thong under her demure shirtwaist dress.

Bozo started playing around when he turned fifty. Funny, whenever

I heard about some guy running around on his wife, I always told my best friend, Judy, that the door wouldn't hit my butt on the way out. When it happened to me, though, I decided that I owed a twenty-five year marriage at least one chance. Or two. Three was when I changed the locks, packed his clothes and put the suitcases on the front lawn. I reminded him of Papa's toast at our wedding – "There are no divorces in our family. There are widows, but no divorces." It scared him purple.

Of course, we did divorce and I did manage to dissuade Papa from having Bozo fitted for lead sneakers, or seeing to it that his body was made unfit for further nookie. The Miata was my first indulgence after the proceedings. I went down to the dealer with a check in hand that very day. Then I put the house on the market and signed the papers for my East side high-rise condo. I heard the whispers about "middle-aged crazy" and "trying to prove something," but I ignored them. This was me, the real me, not that convention that I'd tried to squeeze myself into all those years.

I stepped into my foyer and locked the door behind me. Shedding clothes as I walked, I tossed the dirty duds into my bedroom closet's built-in hamper and walked naked into the bathroom. If driving the Miata is car heaven, standing under a steam shower with five heads massaging from toes to crown is surely water heaven.

Thirty minutes later, moisturized, gelled, dressed in yoga pants and a tee shirt, I sipped a glass of Chardonnay and stared into the fridge. Then I glared at the goods in the freezer. Why is it that there's never anything to eat when you just want to stay in? It would have to be another deep dish Milwaukee special night—cheese, sausage, mushrooms, onions, the famous "SMO." I was either going to have to step up my exercise program and cut back on the fat, or buy a bigger wardrobe. While I love shopping for clothes, the second option didn't appeal. Bozo used to pinch my waist and smirk when he could get an inch between his fingers. I love to see him assess my figure now, when we attend family functions like birthdays and baptisms. There's no way I'm gaining back that inch, so I resolved to do some grocery shopping soon. Just for good measure, I did twenty minutes of yoga/Pilates while waiting for the pizza. A couple chapters of the latest Sue Grafton (I love that Kinsey, but, jeez, one black dress for her whole adult life?) and I was ready to pound the pillow. Solo.

It's been months since my last serious involvement. He thought I wouldn't find out about the bar-time pickups. "Honest, Angie, it doesn't mean a thing. I just like a little variety." Sometimes I wish I was a lesbian, it would make life so much easier. I hear they're more than ninety-percent faithful. What a concept!

I met Kevin, my current guy, four weeks ago. My neighbor Sally and her son, Joseph, introduced us. Joseph was diagnosed with Muscular Dystrophy at age six. Kevin is his physical therapist. Picture Harrison Ford as Han Solo in the first *Star Wars* movie—a little rough, killer body, redeeming lop-sided smile that gets him out of all sorts of trouble. He's thirty-eight, so, yes, he's a few years younger than I am. Given the actuarial tables and my energy level, that's good.

We've been doing that painful boy-girl dance ever since, the one we all first learned in adolescence. Is he available? Cute enough? Is she needy? Pretty enough? Will he want to go to bed right away? Do I want to? Should I? Add today's refinements—STDs? Last HIV test? Last lover? *Ad infinitum. Ad nauseum.* Even my best friend Judy is getting sick of me. "Just DO IT," she yelled at me last week.

"Can't," I responded. "You know me." She groaned. We've been through this a lot in the course of the five years since my divorce. I have this little hang-up. I won't deal with dishonesty on a personal basis. Go figure, someone in my line of work! So I operate on the assumption that everyone is hiding something. I run credit checks and criminal and civil court searches on the men who ask me out. I watch them for signs of fooling around—scents they don't normally wear, clothes changed in the middle of the day, long lunches when they can't be called, lots of little clues that mean nothing and everything. I'm not proud of it, but I won't be a fool again. I haven't figured a way out of the morass that women and men seem to sink into. Most nights, like tonight, I sleep alone.

EMAIL ME TO GET UPDATES ON RELEASES:

contact@nancirathbun.com

(You can always unsubscribe)

Cash Kills

Don't put your trust in money, but put your money in trust.

—Oliver Wendell Holmes

My office partner, Susan Neh, walked into our shared conference room, slowly pulled out a chair and, brows furrowed, sat facing me. "Angie, there's a woman here complaining that her parents had bank accounts worth millions and she doesn't want the money." Susan leaned across the table. "Can you imagine?"

"Maybe." I thought about the illegal ways that my papa probably accumulated wealth and how I would feel if I knew the details of my eventual inheritance. "What's her story?"

Susan opened her mouth, but abruptly shut it. "I think you should hear it from her directly. She's agreed to talk to you."

"I'm not sure that's legitimate, Susan, unless she wants to retain me."

"She might. I'm trying to convince her that she shouldn't ditch the money until she knows more. Come on, Angie, at least listen to her."

I pulled my five-foot-three frame up and checked myself in the small mirror that hung on the back of the door. A private investigator has to present a professional appearance in order to be hired. The days of tough guy Sam Spade have been replaced by the era of techno-geeks and corporate types. It's hard for a woman to be taken seriously. Clients expect a man. And for a fifty-something woman like me, it's twice as hard. So I ran my hands through my short spiky white hair, checked my teeth for lipstick and straightened my Donna Karan business suit. When we entered our common office, I grabbed a legal pad and pen from my desk and waited.

Susan and I share office space on Prospect Avenue, on Milwaukee's east side. I'm AB Investigations, she's Neh Accountants. The "s" on the end of both our firms can be misconstrued. We each run one-person companies.

Susan made the introductions. "Adriana Johnson, this is Angie Bonaparte." I smiled at the Sicilian pronunciation coming from my Japanese-American friend's mouth: Boe-nah-par-tay. I'd taught her well. Don't get me started on Napoleon. The little general was a French wannabe from Corsica, who ruined the name with his attempt to Gallicize it.

"Adriana, it's nice to meet you," I said. "Susan filled me in a little. Before we talk, I need to explain what a private investigator does and how it might affect this conversation. Then if you decide that you'd rather I wasn't privy to your information, I'll bow out with no hard feelings."

I assessed her as she nodded in response. She sat scrunched tight against one side of the client chair, taking up as little space as possible. The only way to describe her was nondescript: brown hair, light brown eyes, slightly olive complexion, slender, dressed head to foot in discount store beige. Bland and quiet. She hadn't moved or spoken since I entered the room.

I gave her a brief rundown on my services: tracking information and people. I explained that, under Wisconsin law, nothing she told me was private unless I was working for her attorney. In that case, whatever she shared with me would come under attorney-client privilege.

"May I please use your phone?" she said in a surprisingly sultry voice that contrasted sharply with her image. I handed her my cell phone and she placed a call. "Uncle Herman, this is Adriana." She pronounced it Ah-dreh-yah-nah. "I'm with the accountant you recommended. Yes, Susan Neh. She introduced me to a private investigator, whom I wish you to hire on my behalf. I understand that the investigator would then be covered by attorney-client privilege." She paused and listened, her face not showing any expression. Then she spoke again. "I mean no disrespect, Uncle Herman, but if you cannot accommodate me in this way, I will find someone who will."

Hmm, the mouse has teeth, I thought.

EMAIL ME TO GET UPDATES ON RELEASES:

contact@nancirathbun.com

(You can always unsubscribe)

ABOUT THE AUTHOR

Nanci Rathbun is a lifelong reader of mysteries–historical, contemporary, futuristic, paranormal, hard-boiled, cozy ... you can find them all on her bookshelves and in her ereaders. She brings logic and planning to her writing from a background as an IT project manager, and attention to characters and dialog from her second career as a Congregationalist minister. (Her books are not Christian fiction, but they contain no explicit sexual or violent scenes, and only the occasional mild curse word.)

Her first novel, *Truth Kills*, was published in 2013. *Cash Kills*, the second book in the series, was published in November of 2014. The third Angie novel has a working title of *Deception Kills*, with plans to publish in 2017.

A longtime Wisconsin resident, Nanci now makes her home in Colorado. No matter where she lives, she will always be a Packers fan.

Let's Connect!

My website, where you can find my blog:
https://nancirathbun.com/

Like and Follow me on Facebook:
www.facebook.com/Author-Nanci-Rathbun-162077650631803

Follow me on Twitter:
https://twitter.com/NanciRathbun

Friend or Follow me on Goodreads:
https://www.goodreads.com/author/show/7199317.Nanci_Rathbun

Check out my Pinterest boards:
https://www.pinterest.com/nancir50/